DEAD RECKONING

ROB SINCLAIR

B
Boldwood

First published in Great Britain in 2025 by Boldwood Books Ltd.

Copyright © Rob Sinclair, 2025

Cover Design by Head Design Ltd

Cover Images: FigureStock and iStock

The moral right of Rob Sinclair to be identified as the author of this work has been asserted in accordance with the Copyright, Designs and Patents Act 1988.

All rights reserved. No part of this book may be reproduced in any form or by any electronic or mechanical means, including information storage and retrieval systems, without written permission from the author, except for the use of brief quotations in a book review. This book is a work of fiction and, except in the case of historical fact, any resemblance to actual persons, living or dead, is purely coincidental.

Every effort has been made to obtain the necessary permissions with reference to copyright material, both illustrative and quoted. We apologise for any omissions in this respect and will be pleased to make the appropriate acknowledgements in any future edition.

A CIP catalogue record for this book is available from the British Library.

Paperback ISBN 978-1-83561-844-8

Large Print ISBN 978-1-83561-843-1

Hardback ISBN 978-1-83561-842-4

Ebook ISBN 978-1-83561-845-5

Kindle ISBN 978-1-83561-846-2

Audio CD ISBN 978-1-83561-837-0

MP3 CD ISBN 978-1-83561-838-7

Digital audio download ISBN 978-1-83561-840-0

This book is printed on certified sustainable paper. Boldwood Books is dedicated to putting sustainability at the heart of our business. For more information please visit https://www.boldwoodbooks.com/about-us/sustainability/

Boldwood Books Ltd, 23 Bowerdean Street, London, SW6 3TN

www.boldwoodbooks.com

PROLOGUE

The smell of charred wood and cordite and ferrous blood filled his nose. He inhaled deeply, his heart pounding against his ribs. The beats came so fast now, as though time itself had sped up, careening him, and so many others, toward an inevitable and destructive outcome.

'Tell me!' he screamed, so hard that the last word sounded choked, and he was sure he tasted his own blood at the back of his throat, the lining scratched raw from the force of the demand.

His finger twitched on the trigger, but the small gesture of pulling, firing, would come with not-so-small repercussions.

A line crossed. Mental turmoil.

Again.

'Tell me, or you know what happens!'

But the man in front of him, crumpled on the floor in his dirty and torn clothes, blood streaming through his wavy, long black hair, said nothing.

'Come on, do it,' came the voice in Peake's ear. 'We don't have time. Do it now.'

'Tell me or she's dead,' Peake said to the man on the floor, not sounding as angry or even as urgent now. More... pleading. 'Just tell me.'

'You have no choice! You have to do it.'

He pushed the barrel of the gun more firmly against the woman's skull.

'Please!' screeched the bleeding man.

But it was too little, too late.

Peake pulled the trigger.

1

A feisty wind blasted down Essex Street, straight into Simon Peake's face as he strode along, looking for the bar. On a warm November day, relatively speaking, he'd left his apartment on the Upper West Side with only a thin jacket, in bright sunshine. This far down Manhattan he felt as though he'd entered another climate altogether and he shivered as he walked.

He'd not been to these streets before. Hadn't been to the bar – O'Hare's. An Irish joint. Like pretty much every other bar in New York City. Except this one really did belong to an Irish family. People who'd actually been born on the Emerald Isle, rather than those who had a great-great-grandparent who had a distant relative who may or may not have been to Limerick once.

He spotted the paint-peeling sign for the bar over the other side of the road and made a beeline for the entrance. He opened the door and stepped inside and saw everything he expected. Clovers. Irish tricolors. Dark wood fittings. Guinness on tap. A bearded and tattooed barman. A few drinkers dotted about, but the place was far from teeming on a Wednesday night.

He settled on a stool at the bar.

'Can I help you?' the barman said in a gruff voice – Irish accent – that matched his appearance. One of the family? No.

Peake ordered a beer and a whiskey chaser. He left cash on the bar and downed the whiskey before looking around the room. He'd never spoken to Sean Lafferty before, but he'd recognize him from the pictures he'd seen online.

No sign of him.

'You looking for someone?' the barman asked, one eyebrow raised as he wiped clean a glass that looked pretty damn dry already.

'Sean. Is he coming tonight?'

'Sean? Sean who?'

The guy glared and Peake found himself caught in two minds.

Then the barman laughed – overly heartily – and a couple of other patrons looked over.

'Not seen him tonight. Or any of the boys.'

And with that the guy moved off to serve someone else. Peake worked through his beer and ordered another, then another, then another as he waited, watching with keen interest anyone who came in from the street.

'You drinking alone?' the woman who'd walked up to the spot next to him asked.

He'd seen her come over, watched her in the mirror behind the bottles of spirits. Tight jeans, heels, a thin sweatshirt that showed off her figure. Curly dark brown hair. A dusting of freckles on her nose. She'd come into the bar alone half an hour before. Had sat alone with a glass of wine as she played on her phone.

'Yeah,' Peake said, turning to the woman with a half-smile before looking around the room. 'You?'

'Needed to relax. Let me guess. Date, but she didn't show.'

Dead Reckoning

'No, not a date. Work.'

She glanced at the bar-top where his empty shot glass sat next to the half-finished beer in his hand. At least the barman had cleared away his several empties.

'Long day, huh?' she said.

'Something like that.'

'So do you want some company?'

He looked across the space again. Checked his watch. Gone 10 p.m. now. Sean should have been here at 8. Peake had sat on his own, drinking on his own, for more than two hours. If the guy walked through the doors now, he'd probably be too drunk anyway.

Peake would come back another night to find him.

'Why not,' he said.

She beamed him a smile before brushing the loose hair from her face with a deft swish. She sat down on the stool next to him and the barman spotted her waiting and came over to her. He knew her. Peake could tell by the relaxed, eager-to-please look in his eyes.

'What are you drinking?' the woman asked Peake.

'Same again,' Peake said to the barman before downing what was left of the beer in front of him. She asked for a beer too but no chaser, and the barman got to work.

'I'll get these,' Peake said when she reached for her purse.

She gave him a cheeky smile but said nothing as she relented. A common trick of hers?

'I'm Katie,' she said, holding out her hand.

'Simon.'

'I've not seen you in here before,' she said, holding his eye as she took a sip from her drink.

Peake downed his whiskey then sank a third of his beer.

'No,' he said.

'You're new to the area?'

'Kind of.'

'Kind of?'

'I don't live on the Lower East.'

'I do.'

She said that with a certain directness.

'Not far from here, actually.'

'So you're a regular then?' he asked.

'Regular enough. It's not like I'm an alcoholic.' She laughed awkwardly at that.

'No. But you do come to the bar on a Wednesday night, on your own, to drink.'

'Long day. Right?'

'Right.'

They both chuckled at that, though he didn't really know why.

The opening door caught his attention, and Peake turned his head to look at the three young men walking in. Confident. Arrogant. One hit another on the shoulder – camaraderie, or machismo or bonding or something – and the two of them guffawed like juveniles but the guy at the front had a sterner look as he eyeballed the other customers.

Was that...

No. Not Sean.

'You know them?' Katie asked.

'No,' Peake said, turning back to the bar a little disappointed. He downed the rest of his beer. 'You want another?'

'Sure.'

Another chaser down the hatch and Peake's head started to spin. He didn't really care.

He stood up, grabbing for his pocket, and somehow made a

hash of it. He knocked the stool over and then stumbled as he picked it back up. He pulled out his cigarettes and a lighter.

'Not in here, buddy,' the barman said with a glower.

'I know that,' Peake said. He turned to Katie. 'You want one?'

'I don't smoke.'

'I'll be back in five.'

'I'll keep you company. Al, watch our things.'

The barman nodded and Katie followed Peake to the street. She took her beer with her. Peake hadn't bothered. He lit up and took a long drag as he rested his head against the outside wall.

'I can't remember the last time I met anyone who smokes,' she said, with a curious look on her face.

He didn't say anything as he sucked in again, the deep inhale clearing some of the alcohol fog away.

'But why do you?' she asked.

He looked down at her.

'Smoke?' He shrugged. 'Habit.'

'You always have?'

'For long enough.'

'You know it'll kill you.'

'Maybe that's the idea.'

She held his eye, and he could tell by the confusion on her face that she didn't know how to take the comment.

'So you don't care if you die?'

He didn't say anything.

'There're better ways to kill yourself,' she said.

'Are we really talking about suicide?'

She smiled, though the look carried a strangely sinister edge.

'Not first date material?' she asked.

'So this is a date now?'

'Why not?' she said, putting her hand onto his and gently stroking his fingers.

'So how would you do it?' he asked.

'What?'

'Kill yourself.'

The smile faded. But he didn't sense any offense, or disgust or discomfort – only deep thought.

'Something quick. Maybe jump in front of a train.'

'What about the driver? The poor people who have to clean up the mess?'

'Bullet to the brain then,' she suggested.

'You have a gun?'

'Do you?'

'Anyway, again, it's messy.'

'Pills and alcohol.'

Peake paused. 'Too... absolute.'

'Absolute?'

He couldn't explain it. Was this even a serious conversation? Had he considered suicide? Yes. Multiple times. Perhaps he simply didn't have the guts to do it. Or perhaps he was holding out for something.

No. More that suicide felt like cheating. The easy way out.

Smoking?

'Maybe the cigarettes will kill me,' he said. 'But I don't know when. It's not in my control. I'm happy to leave my fate to fate. If I die... when I die... it'll be because I deserve it.'

She didn't say anything to that. Just stared at him with intrigue. Like a therapist would with an eccentric patient. He couldn't believe she hadn't run a mile away from him already.

'It'd be a waste,' she said.

'What?'

'You. Killing yourself. It'd be a waste. You're...'

'What?'

'Interesting.'

He waited for more. None came.

'That's it?' he said.

'That's it.'

'Christ. I may as well have another smoke now.'

* * *

Other than the group of three men, who'd remained in the booth in the far corner at closing time, Peake and Katie were the final customers to leave. By that point Peake had had several too many and Katie held on to his arm as they stepped out into the blustery and chilly night, and Peake wasn't sure if it was her helping to keep him walking steady or the other way around.

'Can you walk me home?' Katie asked, craning her neck to peer up at him. Hunger in her eyes?

'You live nearby?'

She'd said so earlier, hadn't she? Peake couldn't really remember with the alcohol swimming in his brain.

'Not far enough for the subway. Not close enough that I feel safe to walk alone.'

He looked along the street. Quiet. Wednesday night. Like many parts of Manhattan, the area was a mix of clashing cultures and demographics. O'Hare's bar sat on a wide avenue with endless rows of cafes, restaurants, bars, independent shops, all now closed up for the night. Within a street or two there were traditional brownstones rented by young professionals and families, but also more modern high-rise condos slowly, slowly squeezing out the older projects, one gentrified building at a time. But take a wrong turn and...

'Yeah, I'll walk you.'

They set off arm in arm. Not far at all. Not even half a mile until they stopped by the stoop to a brownstone on a tree-lined street that had cars crammed either side of cracked tarmac.

'This is me,' she said, unlinking her arm and standing in front of him.

He looked beyond her to the building. A nice-looking place, really. Certainly expensive-looking.

'You want to... have a coffee?'

Peake couldn't help himself. He burst out laughing and after a moment with a doubtful look on her face, Katie did too.

'Sorry,' she said, 'it's not... I don't normally...'

'Then why me?' Peake said.

'Why not?'

He checked his watch again. Gone midnight. A waste of a night, in one sense. In another...

'You have coffee?' he asked.

'Actually, no,' she said. 'But I have vodka.'

'Then let's go,' he said with a smile.

2

Katie did have a bottle of vodka. Grey Goose, to be precise. Relatively expensive, though in truth Peake wasn't sure he could tell the difference between that and cheaper brands. Not that they drank much before they ended up in the king-sized bed in a room that, much like the rest of her apartment, was spacious and tastefully decorated.

They didn't sleep much. Peake awoke from a semi-slumber as the early morning rays poked through the gap between the hastily closed curtains. Katie had nestled up to him at some point in the night, her hand on his chest. He watched her for a few moments. She looked so... peaceful. Content. His eyes rested on her hand.

He shuffled up a bit in the bed. Slowly reached out and took her wrist gently in his fingers and turned her arm over.

He huffed quietly. He'd not noticed before. The scars. He'd been too focused on... other parts of her. But her wrist was heavily marked. Several lines of raised, lumpy flesh. Not recent. He sighed and held her a little more closely. They'd not talked much about her last night. He wanted to know more, but...

He carefully slipped from underneath her and rolled away and grabbed his boxers from the floor before he stepped quietly to the en suite. He gazed at himself in the mirror for a moment before he went to the toilet. As he washed his hands he stared at his reflection again, focusing on his eyes, a challenge of some sort. Why did he look so... disappointed?

'Proud of yourself?' he asked.

He got no answer.

He moved back out into the bedroom. Katie was awake, the covers pulled up to her neck.

'Do you always talk to yourself in the bathroom?' she asked with a cheeky look on her face.

'Not always.'

He sat down on the edge of the bed. He'd expected a hangover, but he felt fine. Actually, despite the sullen look on his face, he felt more than fine, especially with the thoughts, and the smells and the taste of last night still so fresh.

He reached for his jeans and took out his cigarettes and a lighter.

'Do it in here if you want,' Katie said as Peake stood, intending on moving to the balcony.

'You don't mind? In your bedroom?'

She shrugged. 'Normally... I don't know, it seems... very you.'

What did that mean?

Sitting back on the bed, he lit up and took a long inhale which sent a hit of calmness up into his head.

She didn't say anything, just watched him with fascination until Peake finished the smoke and grabbed his jeans and his shirt.

'I'd like to see you again,' Katie said before throwing her hand to her forehead and pushing her head down onto the pillow. 'God, that sounded so desperate.'

Peake smiled at her, said nothing.

'You know, I don't normally bring men back here, after I just met them. I don't normally—'

'Why did you?'

'What?'

'Why did you ask me back?'

He held her eye. He couldn't read the look.

'Sometimes it just feels... right. Right?'

He leaned over and kissed her forehead.

'So?' she said when he straightened up.

He didn't say anything. She sighed.

'Simon Peake. Is that even your real name?'

'Yes.'

'A man of few words. What if I googled you? Would I find out more about you then?'

Did that mean she was going to?

'If you looked hard enough.'

She frowned. 'Now I'm really not sure that I want to.'

'Don't worry, I'm not a serial killer.'

'That's a relief at least.'

He walked around to the door and paused a moment to look back to her. He wanted to stay...

'See you, Katie.'

'Goodbye, Simon Peake.'

She slumped and sighed and he turned and walked away.

* * *

He didn't take the direct route for the subway, and home. Instead he retraced his steps from the previous night, moving back toward O'Hare's. Closed, of course. But he stopped at the windows and put his face to the glass to look into the dark space beyond. No sign of anyone at all. Empty glasses remained on the table in the corner where the three men had stayed for the lock-in. What time had they left? Where had they gone?

Peake turned around and looked along the street. Movement caught his attention, up in the top windows of the building opposite. He stared but couldn't figure out what he'd seen. A flapping curtain? A bird flying by? Someone at the window?

No one in sight now.

He set off for home. He'd be back to the Lower East Side soon enough, and not just on the off chance that he'd see Katie again.

The subway was quick and incident-free and Peake walked out of the station at 86th and along to West End Ave to his apartment building. A big building, with over a hundred homes, though they were far from the most luxurious in the area. No concierge here – just one example of the relative quality and expense of the dwellings beyond the lofty but plain atrium.

Peake took the stairs, listening to the familiar sounds from the apartments beyond. TVs. Music. Shouting. English, but other languages too. Babies crying. Kids screeching – in happiness?

He reached the sixth floor then paused a beat when he saw his neighbor's door – directly adjacent to his – was open. Jelena stood beyond the threshold wearing a silk robe, her arms folded in defiance. Her hair was tied back, her makeup touched up even early in the morning, but not so much that it hid her swollen right eye.

The man standing in front of her – black shoes, jeans, big black overcoat – turned as Peake approached.

'Can I help you?' the young guy said with an angry snarl.

'No,' Peake said, looking away from him and to Jelena.

'You OK?'

She nodded, but he sensed she was withholding a whole host of brewing emotions.

'Mister, you need to mind your own goddamn business,' the man said.

Peake said nothing as he opened his door and stepped inside. He closed the door and stood and thought a moment then peered through the peephole. The man remained outside. Not shouting, but definitely pissed off as he talked to Jelena, who Peake now couldn't see. The guy shook his head then stepped away but as he reached the stairs he turned again and glared first at Jelena's door, then at Peake's. He paused there before he started down.

Peake opened the door and moved over to Jelena's. He knocked lightly.

She opened up a few inches.

'It's OK, Simon.'

'You don't look OK.'

'I'm fine. You have a good night?'

'Better than you, I think.'

She shook her head. The look of sadness in her eyes pulled at his heart.

'You shouldn't—'

'Please don't say it. Don't say anything. What am I supposed to do?'

Peake had no answer to that. The number of times he'd seen her with marks, bruises. Guys who hit her. Choked her. She took it all. How long before one of them took it too far? No. They already had. Too many times. They thought paying her meant she owed them. Anything they wanted. No boundaries.

'You want some company?' he asked.

'Not really.'

They stood there in silence for a few moments. Peake felt so useless.

'You have a good one,' Jelena said before she pushed the door closed.

Peake moved back to the stairs and stared down. No sign of that scumbag now. Peake had seen him before, like he had many of her 'clients'. He made a mental note of their faces. Particularly the ones who left her with cuts and bruises.

Maybe he'd 'accidentally' run into that guy at some point.

His phone buzzed in his pocket and he answered the call as he walked back inside.

'Jay.'

'Peake, you fucking idiot. You didn't meet him?'

'I was there. He didn't show.'

'What? Sean called me this morning. Said you were at the bar all night. Getting pretty cozy with a brunette.'

'What? Sean wasn't there.'

Or had Peake made a mistake? Too drunk, or too into Katie that he hadn't paid proper attention.

'He saw you. And he saw you leave with Katie too.'

'Katie? He knows her?'

'Yeah, you fucking moron. Have you any idea who she is?'

No, he didn't.

'Katie Springer.'

'Springer?'

'Her mother's name. But she's Harry's niece. Are you insane?'

'I swear, I didn't know—'

'Maybe not, but—'

A knock on the door. A meaty thud, more like. Peake pulled the phone from his ear. Could still hear his 'friend' blathering as he looked through the spyhole. Not the guy who'd left the bruise on Jelena's face, even if Peake had really wanted it to be.

Instead? Three men. Three angry faces that he recognized from O'Hare's.

'I've got to go,' he said before ending the call.
He thought for a moment... then opened the door.

3

'You Peake?' the guy standing at the front of the three asked – the shortest, youngest, but edgiest looking of them.

'Yeah.'

Then the three peeled aside and a fourth man stepped up onto the sixth floor. An older man. Sixties. Thinning gray hair. A lined face. A slightly overweight figure, but not so much that Peake would expect him to be so out of breath and red-cheeked from the hike up the stairs.

'This him?' the old man said after dabbing his brow with a hanky.

'This is him,' his younger minion answered.

'Do you know who I am?'

'Harry Lafferty,' Peake said.

'Good. That saves explaining then. Let's go inside.'

Peake didn't move for a moment. Not until young man stepped right up into his face. Well, more into his chest really, as Peake stood a good five inches taller.

'Come on in,' Peake said, finally stepping aside.

* * *

Harry Lafferty. Not so much a kingpin. Not really. Just a guy who knew how to make money. Cash. The old-fashioned way, some would say. As for the other men? The snarly younger one with the chains around his neck was Joey. The tallest and brutish of them with a clean-shaven head and a fighter's face – squashed nose, turned-out ear – was Dolan. Boxer, MMA perhaps, Peake thought. Or maybe he just found entertainment – or money – in brawling.

The last man was called Chops – a nickname, Peake assumed. Chops was the one who Peake found the most curious – in looks at least. At six foot two he matched Peake in height but had a rake-thin frame, wore sensible clothes and had a sensible hairstyle and wore thin-rimmed round glasses that were perched on the end of his nose as he reached up on tip toes to run his hand along the top of the kitchen cabinets.

Looking for what?

'Don't worry about him,' Harry said. Or more like croaked. His voice was dry and cracked.

Peake turned back to face the boss man, sitting on a chair across the small round dining table from him. Dolan stood behind the old man, glaring. Joey had propped himself on the back of the sofa, twisting a knife in his hands, spinning the tip around his palm.

'You came to my bar last night,' Harry said.

'Yeah.'

'You were looking for my son.'

'I was.'

'Why?'

'Work.'

'Work?'

'Jay said Sean could help me find work.'

'You know my son?'

'No.'

'You know me?'

'No.'

'So why would he give you work?'

Peake stared at Harry. What kind of a question was that?

Chops opened up the end kitchen cabinet and started rooting through. Peake glanced over again.

'Hey, dickhead,' Dolan shouted, smacking his foot onto the wooden floor for further effect. 'Pay attention when Harry's talking to you.'

'Tell me about yourself,' Harry said.

'Not much to tell.'

Harry sighed and sat back in his chair and messed with his shirt collar a little, as if trying to release pressure. 'Pretend this is your job interview.'

'I just need work. Cash. So I can pay my rent. So I can live.'

Chops had finished searching. For now. He flicked through the mail on the worktop then frowned before he took out his phone and stared at the screen.

'How do you know Jay?' Harry asked.

Was there any point in lying? 'We met... inside.'

A slight pinch to Harry's eyes. 'So that's it. You're an ex-con.'

'Have you any idea how hard it is for guys like me to get decent work in this city?'

'There are programs—'

'Been there, done that. Here I am, unemployed and broke and wondering what's the point of anything.'

'Plenty of janitorial jobs,' Dolan said. 'You too good to clean shit, pretty boy?'

Pretty boy? Peake knew his relatively soft features had often been mistaken for a soft personality, but most people would look pretty put next to that guy's gnarled face.

'How long did you do?' Harry asked.

Peake sucked in a lungful of air before he answered, reliving the lost time in that moment. 'Five years.'

Harry whistled. 'Prison change you?'

'Not really.'

'That's a long stretch.'

'Life's long.'

Joey frowned. 'You mean, life, as in, being alive is long. Or a life sentence is long?'

'What?' Peake said, confused.

'Joey, shut up,' Harry said.

'I thought I recognized your name,' Chops said, tapping his phone screen before he turned it for everyone else to see, even though the screen was too far away.

'Simon Peake. Eight years for felony assault.'

'Ah, what d'you do? Beat up your woman?' Dolan asked.

'No,' Peake answered.

'No,' Chops said, putting his phone away again. 'He beat up two boys. Riverside Park.'

Harry's face contorted into a snarl. Dolan shook his head as if in disappointment.

'You like messing with kids?' Dolan asked. 'Fuck this, I'm not working with a pedo.'

'Those boys were sixteen and seventeen,' Peake said, not that that was an explanation for anything. 'One had a gun. One had a knife. And I caught them raping a fifteen-year-old girl.'

'And I'm sure she was very thankful,' Chops said. 'But the police, the judge and the jury didn't think it necessary for you to break the arm and femur of the younger kid, or to stomp on the head of the other one, leaving him with a broken eye socket, a detached retina and a jaw shattered into so many pieces that he'll never speak or eat properly again.'

Peake said nothing.

'Is that true?' Harry asked.

'What? The injuries? I don't know. I haven't checked up on those two recently.'

'Funny guy,' Dolan said.

'I meant, is it true they were raping a girl?' Harry said.

'Yes.'

'So he's a moral crusader,' Dolan said. 'A vigilante.'

'Is that what you are?' Harry asked.

Chops had moved back to searching the kitchen. Only two more doors along until he reached it...

'I saved her,' Peake said.

'You nearly killed two kids,' Harry said. 'Permanently disfigured one of them.'

Peake shrugged. 'Maybe I... overreacted.'

Silence. And then Harry laughed and Chops and Joey did too, and Dolan looked at his boss like he didn't know what was going on.

'I like that,' Harry said. 'Dry, but funny.'

Peake hadn't intended to be funny.

'So now you're an ex-con in Manhattan, struggling for work.'

'Something like that.'

'And your friend, Jay, a distant relation of mine, told you to ask my son.'

'Yes.'

'Except Jay is a fucking disease. A drug addict who wades into deeper shit with every step he takes in life.'

Peake said nothing, but apparently Dolan found that description amusing judging by the smirk on his face. And it was pretty much true. Jay wasn't a bad guy, but he was a down and out.

Inside, he and Peake had become close, had looked out for each other, but in the real world... Jay just didn't really fit. Perhaps Peake didn't either.

'I've known his old man since I was a kid myself,' Harry said, 'but I would never give work to that moron. Neither would my son.'

'I'm not Jay,' Peake said.

'No, you're just a loser who beats up kids,' Dolan said.

Chops went to open the cupboard door. Peake leaped up from his chair, Chops spun around while Dolan unfolded his arms, at the ready, and Joey jumped from the sofa, knife in hand.

'Just... You don't need to be searching my things,' Peake said to Chops.

'Why not?'

Peake didn't answer.

'He asked you a question,' Harry said, the only man still sitting down.

'You want me to go to your house and start rifling through your shit?' Peake asked.

'No,' Harry said. 'But I'm not you. And you're not me. And you're the one who wants work. From my family. Aren't you?'

Chops turned and opened the cupboard.

He pulled out the Glock first. Looked impressed as he clanked it down on the worktop. Then he went for the little red cashbox.

'Where's the key?' Chops asked.

Peake didn't answer.

'Tell him,' Dolan said.

'Top drawer.'

Chops took the key and unlocked the box and fingered the contents before whistling.

'Cash?' Dolan asked.

'No,' Chops said, tilting the box slightly to show the four passports.

'All yours?' Harry asked Peake.

'Yes.'

'Legit?'

'Some.'

'Who the fuck are you?' Dolan asked.

'I'm no one.'

Chops took the passports in turn. 'Simon Peake, British. Simon Peake, American. Andrew Chester, Canadian. Ahmed Ali, Saudi Arabian.'

'Ahmed Ali?' Dolan said. 'You taking the piss?'

'Doesn't much look like an Ahmed to me,' Joey said.

'Amazing what a beard can do,' Chops added, showing everyone the picture.

'So?' Harry prompted.

'What?'

'Are you going to explain?'

'I reckon he's pulling some undercover shit,' Dolan said. 'FBI or something.'

'Is that true?'

'No.' Silence. No one looked convinced. 'If I was, I haven't done a very good job of covering it, have I?'

Still no one said anything.

'And why would the FBI be looking into you?' Peake said to Harry.

'FBI, DEA, whatever, I don't trust him.' Dolan spat on the floor.

'Do you mind?' Peake said.

Dolan glared but didn't rise to the challenge.

'You can see how this raises a lot of questions,' Harry said.

'Yeah,' Peake said. 'But where those came from, what I did in my past is irrelevant here. Do what you want. Search my history to your heart's content—'

'Or you could just explain here and now,' Chops said.

'He's got a point,' Harry added.

'I was born in England,' Peake said.

'Yeah, I kinda figured that from the screwy accent.'

Which Peake knew was off to most people, really. In America everyone figured he was English or even Australian, but in England people thought he sounded American. The truth was his accent didn't really belong to any one place. Just like him.

'My mother's English. Father's American.'

'So that explains two of the passports,' Harry said.

'I was in the British army and...'

'And what? They give out fake passports to all their soldiers now?'

'No.'

'So?'

'They were... necessary.'

'Shit. SAS?' Joey asked, looking almost impressed by the prospect.

'No,' Peake said. 'Not even close. And what you're looking at there is all that's left of that life. I shouldn't even still have those. Call them a souvenir or whatever.'

'You went from the British army to prison in New York for felony assault? Bit of a fall.'

'Dishonorable discharge, I reckon,' Chops said.

'That right?' Harry asked.

'Yes, actually,' Peake said, trying not to show any emotion.

'What did you do? Beat up some kids?' Joey asked before smirking at his own weak joke.

'No,' Peake said. 'You don't need to know about any of that. Believe me, I'd rather forget it too. I left the army a long time ago.

I was messed up. I came here for a new life. Then I spent five years of that new life behind bars because I snapped one time. But those five years... I've come to terms with what I am. Now I just want to get on.'

Harry nodded as if he understood.

Then he got to his feet.

'I don't like guns,' he said. 'And in this city? It's not worth the risk. Especially for an ex-con. Get rid of it.'

Peake didn't respond. Was he supposed to?

'If you're needed, we'll let you know,' Harry said.

The four of them made their way to the door. Dolan stepped out first, followed by Harry then Chops and finally Joey, who still had the knife in his hands. He held Peake's eye as he walked past, as though egging Peake on to make a move.

He didn't.

'Oh, and as for my niece, Katie?' Harry said, turning around. 'You're not the first guy, and you won't be the last. But you won't be going there again. You understand me?'

Peake nodded. Joey slapped his shoulder.

'Answer the fucking question.'

'I understand.'

'Good,' Harry said. 'Because she's messed up enough as it is. She doesn't need a miserable bastard like you around her. Five minutes talking to you and even I want to kill myself.'

Harry turned and moved for the stairs. This time it was Chops who held back. Why? The look on his face...

'See you around,' he finally said before heading off after the others.

Peake waited by the door a moment, listening to them descending, listening to their hushed conversation. What were they saying about him? But then the conversation became less muted. A brief exchange. With whom?

Peake walked to the head of the stairs and spotted the casually dressed man heading up. Forties, with wiry hair and a thick mustache like he wanted it to be the eighties still. Peake new him only as Wyatt, his surname, and he only knew that because he'd seen the name badge when he bumped into the guy in a convenience store while Wyatt was on duty. NYPD.

He never wore his uniform when he came over to screw Jelena.

'Friends of yours?' Wyatt asked as he reached the sixth floor. Did Wyatt know the Laffertys? Did they pay off the cops? It wouldn't surprise Peake in the slightest if they did, and if Wyatt was a cop on the take.

'No,' Peake said, standing his ground.

Wyatt looked unsure of himself. Like he didn't know what Peake was doing standing there, glaring at him. In the end he shuffled away to Jelena's door, looking over his shoulder a couple of times. Peake stayed there, watching, not caring about imposing. Jelena opened up. Robe gone. She was dressed up now. A tight and very short dress.

'Have fun,' Peake said to Wyatt. Jelena sent him a not very friendly look. Wyatt, sheepish now, pushed past her into the apartment. 'Be nice to her.'

She sent a silent please Peake's way before she shut the door.

4

EIGHT YEARS AGO

The Middle East. Operation Zeus – Day 1

He thought he was prepared for the heat. He'd been to the region plenty of times, including in the height of summer. Yet as he stepped off the plane onto the blistering tarmac of the runway and inhaled the superheated, dry air, it caused a stabbing in his nostrils and made his lungs ache. He was already looking forward to getting to wherever he was going so he could strip off his thick fatigues and take a long, cold shower.

'Peake?' said the man who strode toward him from the waiting car. He wore casual clothes – jeans, T-shirt – topped off with a pair of aviators, though his thick-set physique, gruff voice and generally stiff and confident manner suggested military. Well, that and the fact that he was there, at a military base, to greet Peake as he stepped off a military plane.

'Yeah.'

He looked at his watch. 'You're late.'

Was he actually suggesting Peake was at fault for the plane having left the base in England two hours behind schedule?

'Sorry,' he said regardless.

'You look like a simple army rat,' the guy said, lifting his sunglasses and running his eyes up and down Peake. 'I was expecting James Bond.'

Peake didn't say anything to that.

'You got a change of clothes in there?' he asked, indicating Peake's bulging backpack.

'A few.'

'Civvies?'

'Yeah.'

'Put them on. Leave everything else here. You won't need it.'

The guy remained staring and Peake stared right back. Until the guy broke eye contact to look at his watch again.

'Peake, please don't waste any more of my time.'

'You want me to get dressed out here?'

'No, I want you to do the fucking Macarena.'

'You do?'

Sunglasses fully off now, his face twisted in distaste.

'Are you for real?'

Peake rolled his eyes and got to it. Changing clothes. He'd save the Macarena.

'Get in the car,' the man said when Peake was ready. 'Everyone's waiting for you.'

Peake wasn't introduced to the driver, but two minutes later they'd left Peake's belongings and the military base behind, riding in the dirty brown Jeep which jostled and bounced along dusty roads, kicking up clouds of sand behind it. The grumpy idiot who'd met him off the plane told Peake to call him Chief, which gave little away about his real role or rank, other than to confirm he was in charge.

They drove for a couple of hours into the center of the capital. The civil war here had ended some six months previously, roadblocks removed, the rebuild underway as people tried to resume their normal lives. But evidence of the conflict remained with entire streets where buildings were nothing but piles of rubble. Others where the buildings were burned-out shells. Bullet holes riddled some of the structures which were fortunate enough to remain standing.

'You know much about what happened here?' Chief asked as the driver wound the car along narrow, twisting alleys.

'A little.'

Chief turned in his seat to send a glare Peake's way. 'My best advice? Forget whatever you thought you knew.'

The driver eventually pulled up outside a sandy stone building, five stories tall. Half the windows were boarded over, a quarter had cracked panes, leaving only a few that looked intact, even if the wood frames were obviously rotten.

'Welcome to your new home,' Chief said to Peake before he opened his door. Then he turned back to the driver. 'Keep moving, I'll let you know when I'm ready.'

Peake stepped out and a moment later the Jeep disappeared down the street.

'Come on,' Chief said.

Peake followed him to the thick-looking wooden door. Not a new fixture, although the two locks looked new and secure enough. Chief opened up and Peake headed into the much cooler interior after him. Cool, but musty.

'No frills here,' Chief said. 'This place does what it needs to do. If it's ever compromised, we move out and move on. Simple as that.'

'Got it,' Peake said.

They ended up on the third floor. Only two doors off the corridor. They went left, toward the one at the street side. Peake didn't ask what lay beyond the other door, but got the impression the building – once apartments – was otherwise unoccupied.

He heard chatter as they approached the door. Chatter which stopped when Chief knocked.

Footsteps, then the clicking of locks releasing before the door opened to show a young man. Casual attire. Thick, dark hair covered his head and his face held a nicely trimmed beard that didn't leave much of his dark complexion uncovered.

'Chief,' he said, before locking eyes with Peake. 'The final piece of the puzzle.'

Neither Chief nor Peake said anything to that. They moved inside into the basic but spacious apartment. Four bedrooms. An open plan area where four other people sat around a table. Three men, one woman. Several glasses sat on top of the wood and even though Peake couldn't see it, he could smell alcohol.

'Bonding?' Chief said.

'Something like that,' said one of the men who sat back in his chair, an arrogant look in his piercing green eyes.

Chief stood, arms folded, glaring, until the woman bent down and plucked a nearly empty bottle of vodka from behind her.

'Sneaked it in my bag,' she said. 'Just in case I couldn't find any here. Want some?' she asked Chief with a cheeky smile on her face.

She looked a little more sheepish as Chief walked up to her and took the bottle and stared at it for a couple of seconds before unscrewing the cap and taking a big glug.

'Enjoy it while you can, folks,' he said, wiping his chin and slamming the bottle down on the table. 'That's the last one you're going to get for a long time unless you distill it yourselves.'

A few grumbles here and there.

'Vodka aside, did they behave themselves?' Chief asked as he looked to the man seated to the right of the woman, who appeared to be the oldest of the group with specks of gray in his stubble. Early forties, perhaps. He got to his feet. All eyes turned to him.

'Yeah, Chief. They all followed the rules.'

'Thank you, Ares.'

A few raised eyebrows at that exchange, which Peake took to mean that the others in the group hadn't realized the older guy – Ares? Weird name – was keeping an eye on them for the boss.

'You're a fucking stooge?' Green Eyes asked Ares, sounding disgusted.

Ares shrugged.

'What?' Chief said. 'You thought I could trust this rabble having known you all for five minutes?'

No one responded to that.

'Everyone take a seat,' Chief said. 'It's time to get this op underway.'

5

OPERATION ZEUS – DAY 1

'Any questions before I start?' Chief asked, looking over at Peake and the others.

'Yeah,' the woman said. 'What the fuck are we doing here? And who are these losers?'

Green Eyes blew her a kiss. A couple others grumbled under their breath.

'For the benefit of our newcomer,' Chief said, 'let's not forget ground rule one here.'

'And that is?' Peake asked.

'It doesn't matter who you all are, where you came from, who sent you here. What matters is that you are here. And while you're here you never discuss your real identities, even in this group. No talk of your unit or your employer or where you're from, your childhood or any crap like that. Get it?'

A series of nods and murmurs.

'Second, I give the orders here. You don't need to know where up the chain those orders come from. Maybe I make them up myself. Maybe they're signed off from God himself. You don't second-guess. You do what you're told.' He paused. Expecting a response? He didn't get one.

'As you probably figured now, Ares is my man on the ground here. Most of the time I'll relay intel, activities through him. So when he speaks, he's speaking for me. Got it?'

'Yes, Chief,' came the replies, though Peake sensed not everyone was happy about that idea.

'Three. I don't know how long we'll be here. Weeks. Months. Years. But you're here, 100 hundred percent. None of you are to have any contact back home. No phone calls, emails, video calls. Electronics? Ares will tell you what you can use and when, but it's never for personal business. You will be compensated for your time here, but that's really the last thing that should be on your minds right now.'

Again no particular response when he paused this time, though a couple of the faces had turned more sour.

'Four. If this op doesn't go as planned... I'll do what I can to get you out. But understand this. We have no jurisdiction here, even if our troops are in that base down the road. Unofficially the British government helped to support the rebels in the war. Those rebels now run this country, but their victory wasn't without a shitload of bloodshed, and even more bad blood generated between the opposing sides to this endless fucking tit-for-tat sectarian fuckabout. Even if we have a few troops hanging around, out of sight, our government has now officially distanced itself from the new boys in charge, at least while the idea of war crimes is still fresh in the international press. My point is, I know this place. I've been here for years. Forget about good and bad, don't even get started on ideology. Today's good guys are tomorrow's genocidal maniacs. We don't have friends. We don't have allies. Concentrate only on this op. You're here for a reason, that's all you need to know.'

'And that reason is?' Green Eyes asked.

'I'll get to that. But first, back to the basics. Ares?'

All eyes turned to him. Even before he started up, it hadn't escaped Peake's attention that most likely Ares was a code name, particularly given the name of the operation. Zeus, the chief deity of the ancient Greeks. Ares, the god of war. Apt?

'Only ever refer to yourselves and each other by the names I'm about to read out,' Ares said. He looked at the woman. 'Hera.'

She shrugged, looked like she couldn't care less.

'She's the queen of the gods,' Green Eyes said, looking impressed, as though she'd just gone up in his estimation.

'Talos,' Ares said to Green Eyes.

'Who the fuck is Talos?' he asked.

'If you must know, he's a giant, forged from bronze,' Ares said. 'Given by Zeus to his lover as her personal protector.'

Talos nodded now, apparently happy with that. He lifted his arms up to show his huge biceps. 'I mean, I think I should have been a god, but that'll do.'

Hera smiled at him. Peake thought he understood the look.

'Minos,' Ares said to the bearded guy who'd earlier opened the door.

He simply nodded. Did he know the name? From what Peake could remember of Greek mythology, Minos was one of Zeus's sons. A king in the real world, a judge of the dead in the underworld after his death.

Then Ares turned to the other man at the table who hadn't yet spoken. Young. Not as confident or arrogant-looking as Talos. Even sitting down Peake saw he had a slighter figure with wispy hair and buck teeth that made him look a little rabbit-like.

'Hermes.'

The young guy nodded and looked a little pleased with himself.

'Hermes?' Talos piped up. 'He's one of the main gods, isn't he?'

'God of communication, language,' Ares said.

'Ah, OK, so he's the brains,' Talos said. 'Tech guy. Bet you're a computer hacker or something.'

Hermes shrugged.

'And finally,' Ares said, turning to Peake. 'You're Hades.'

Peake's heart skipped a beat and he realized everyone was staring.

'The original badass,' Hermes said, almost in awe?

'Him?' Talos said, looking and sounding bemused. 'He's the fucking badass? King of the underworld? This is messed up.'

'Alright, big balls,' Chief said as he got to his feet. 'Don't get your panties all twisted. There may or may not be reasons why we chose those names, but you don't need to know them. Remember my first rule. These are your only names now for as long as you're here. Understood?'

'Yes, Chief,' came the chorus of replies.

'So how about you tell us why we're here now,' Talos said.

'I suppose I probably should,' Chief said, looking as though he was trying to hold back a smile. 'Quite simply, we're here to help stop another war. And, as long as the people at the top of the chain still want that, we'll do anything to achieve that aim.'

6

Peake sat mostly in silence, in his thoughts for several hours, waiting for the next chapter while the world turned around him. Sooner or later it'd send a signal out to let him know what to do next.

A knock on the door.

Was this it?

He could think of only a small number of people that he expected to see through the peephole. None of them were particularly welcome visitors, even if he'd wanted the development.

No, that wasn't true actually. Katie. She'd be a welcome sight, even despite Harry's clear warning.

Jelena?

He saw neither of them, but a familiar face, nonetheless. Two, in fact.

'Peake, open up. I know you're there,' came the screechy shout and heavily accented English of the diminutive man who Peake knew only as Chan.

His landlord. He'd heard others refer to him as Jackie, but

Peake thought the first name was only in reference to the famous movie star, who Chan bore little resemblance to.

As for the lump of meat behind him? Chris. Or, more accurately, Christine, though Peake had heard to never call him that to his face. The story relayed to Peake was that Chris's parents were first generation immigrants from China. Like many of their compatriots they'd taken on Western first names as part of their assimilation into American life, and had done the same with their children. Apparently, Christine was in reference to the Stephen King novel – or, more specifically, the film adaption – about a car with psychotic tendencies. Perhaps in the Mandarin dubbed version it wasn't obvious that the car, and its name, was 'female'. Or perhaps it wasn't obvious in the English version, either. Peake wouldn't know; he'd never seen the film or read the book. Though he did, in any case, find it odd that parents would choose to name their son after a crazed killer.

But then, to look at the guy...

Chan thumped the door again.

'You're pissing me off now, Peake. Open the damn door!'

Peake reached for the handle and opened up.

'You're late,' Chan said. 'Again. You have my money?'

'Soon. I'll have it soon.'

'No. Not soon. I want it now. Two months, you owe me.'

'I need a couple more days. Just trust—'

Chris stepped forward, reached out and grabbed Peake by the neck and lifted him off his feet and pinned him to the wall.

'You lie to me,' Chan said.

'No... I... need... time,' Peake choked out.

'More time? Why should I give you more time? I have other tenants waiting.'

Peake wasn't sure about that. As far as he knew, Chan owned the entire floor. A few other apartments in the block too. Peake had no clue how he'd come to be in that position. A few backhanders when the building was first completed, perhaps. But the other apartments on this floor were currently all empty, other than his and Jelena's. Largely because they were dumps that Chan spent zero dollars on maintaining. Hence the sewage that occasionally rose up through the shower from the shoddy drains. The intermittent gas and electric. The air-con unit that was so dangerous Peake preferred to fry in the summer than attempt to turn it on.

But what Chan did offer was cheap rent, cash only, in return for a tenancy that required no official paperwork, and no questions asked. Except when rent was overdue.

'How much you have?' Chan asked.

Chris used his free hand to pat down Peake's pockets. He tossed the wallet to Chan who opened it up and held the ten dollars aloft.

'Ten dollar? Why you so damn poor, Peake? You need to get a fucking job.'

'I'm... trying.'

'Come on, I'm nice guy. Don't you think I'm nice guy?'

'Y-yes.'

'Look, Chris is hurting you. He's hurting you. It's not me, right?'

'Yes!'

'But I'm nice guy. I ask him to stop, he stop. Chris? Stop.'

Chris let go and Peake slumped down, coughing a couple of times before he straightened up.

'See? But if you don't pay me everything... No, I want everything you owe, and next month too. Tomorrow. Three months' rent, or maybe next time I don't say stop to him.'

Chan threw the wallet back, but Peake was too dazed to attempt to catch it and it bounced off his chest and to the floor.

'See you tomorrow.'

Chan turned and walked away. Chris balled his fist and bobbed forward as though to attack. Peake remained rooted and the big guy looked as surprised as he did disappointed not to get a reaction.

What? He thought Peake was scared of being beaten to a pulp?

'See you, Christine,' Peake said when the henchman reached the stairs.

He turned. Thunder on his face. But Chan grabbed his arm and pulled him away.

'Not yet,' he thought he heard Chan say before they both moved out of sight.

Peake slammed the door shut. Three months' rent. Six thousand dollars. He had less than two hundred in his account. Less than a hundred in cash in the apartment.

Lie? Beg? Steal? He'd done all in the past. Which option would get him the cash the quickest this time?

He hadn't quite settled down on the sofa to contemplate the mess his life was turning out to be when his phone rang. Unknown number.

'Yeah?'

'Peake?'

'Speaking.'

'This is Sean Lafferty.'

Peake didn't say anything.

'You there?' Sean asked.

'Yeah.'

'You were looking for me.'

'Yeah.'

'You want some work, Mr Communicator?'

'I need some work.'

'You have two hands and a right foot on you?'
For some reason Peake actually looked to check.
'Yeah.'
'Glad to hear it. Then get yourself down to the bar at nine.'
The line went dead.

7

The cross-city travel wasn't quite as slick for Peake's second visit in as many days to O'Hare's bar, and despite having left plenty of time – or so he thought – he arrived five minutes late. Sean Lafferty and Joey stood waiting on the outside of the bar, by a parked BMW, its pristine metalwork shining in the electric light coming from above it. Joey nudged his friend and the two of them stared over as Peake walked toward them.

'You're Peake?' Sean said.

'Yeah.'

'I'm Sean. This is my cousin, Joey.'

'We met,' Joey said. 'And you're late.'

'Sorry.'

'Get in,' Sean said. 'You're driving.'

Peake had kind of figured that from the earlier phone conversation. Sean got into the front passenger seat. Joey stepped into the back behind the driver's seat. Peake paused for just a second on the outside. He'd already had plenty of thinking time about where this newfound relationship would take him, but the simple fact was that he needed money. And fast. He didn't have time or opportunity for doubts or second-guessing now.

He opened the door and sank into the driver's seat. A supremely comfy leather seat. The dashboard gleamed, fancy lights, everything plush and expensive.

'Nice motor,' Peake said, running his hands around the soft leather of the steering wheel.

'Yeah,' Sean said. 'And it's got a beast of an engine. But you won't be testing it out tonight. Now off you go. We're heading for the Bronx.'

No further information than that about their destination or what they'd do when they got there. No talk of how much he'd get paid, either. Not that Peake had expected a negotiation or anything like that, but still...

Peake pressed the starter button and heard the distant grumble of the undoubtedly powerful engine, which was somewhat subdued in the cabin given the top-quality soundproofing. He pulled into the road and set off.

'Slow and steady,' Joey said. 'The story of Sean's life.'

Sean glanced back at his cousin with a look of mock offense. 'Live fast, die young, Joey. Your motto, not mine.'

Peake glanced at his passengers a couple of times as he drove. Unlike his snarly cousin, Sean Lafferty had a certain ordinariness to him. No particular distinctive features except for his bright blue eyes which lit up when he smiled. He was a snappier dresser than his cousin, though. Probably very popular with the opposite sex, and he knew it, given his confident swagger. Could he handle himself too, or was that the purpose of Joey?

'So what's your story?' Sean asked Peake after a few moments of silence.

'Story?'

'You turn up at my family's bar, asking for me. You know Jay?'

'I met him inside.'

'That guy's spent half his life inside,' Joey said. 'Because he's an idiot.'

'A drug-addicted idiot,' Sean added.

'He's been clean nearly two years,' Peake said. Jay had got himself off the gear during his last stint behind bars, and stayed clean when he came out. Or, at least, hadn't retreated to addiction. Prison had helped Jay sort his problems. Peake had been the opposite. He'd never smoked until he was behind bars. A habit he'd never thought he'd pick up. 'Everyone deserves a second chance.'

'Yeah. You think?' Sean said.

'Jay's had more than his fair share of second chances,' Joey added. 'The guy's a loser, going nowhere.'

'He thinks pretty highly of you and your family,' Peake said to Sean. 'Which is why I'm here at all.'

Sean pursed his lips and looked away but didn't say anything. Peake didn't know the whole story, but he did know that Jay had known Sean his whole life, a distant cousin, and their dads were apparently friends. Jay would always be close to the Laffertys because of that. But, in truth, Peake also agreed with Joey. Jay was a loser. Even if he stayed clean, stayed out of prison, he'd never make anything of himself. The sad fact was that Jay had nothing about him. No drive. No interest in fitting into society by getting a job or taking responsibilities or anything like that. Was he a true friend of Peake's? Not really. Not anymore. The two of them had shared a cell for more than a year, had looked out for each other, helped each other, and they'd stayed in touch now that both were out. But life outside prison was very different to inside, and they'd never have associated with each other had it not been for the time behind bars.

Peake had no interest in ever going back inside. Jay... In a strange way, prison suited him and he was probably more content inside than out.

'So, you and Katie, eh?' Sean said, looking over at Peake with a devilish glint in his eye.

'I didn't know she was family,' Peake said.

'Yeah, she is,' Joey said, and Peake caught his glare in the rearview mirror.

Sean laughed. 'Don't worry, Peake. She's my cousin, but she's not Joey's sister. Harry's got three brothers. Lots of cousins all over.'

'But I'm the best of them,' Joey said.

'But Katie's the best-looking of them,' Sean said. 'And she knows it.'

'Don't worry,' Peake said. 'I've already been warned off. I won't see her again.'

Sean raised an eyebrow. 'And what if she wants to see you? You're going to listen to the old man over her? She gets no say in it?'

Peake didn't know how to respond to that. Was Sean encouraging him to go against Harry's wishes?

'She's not a fucking trophy,' Sean said. 'The old men in our family are living in the past. Katie's got what it takes up here—' he tapped his temple '—but they don't even give her a chance. No wonder she suffers. And no wonder she tries everything she can to piss them off.'

'Like sleeping with layabouts like you,' Joey said.

Like self-harming, Peake thought, but didn't say.

'But she's her own woman,' Sean said. 'So as far as I'm concerned, she can sleep with whoever she wants.'

Silence. Peake felt their eyes on him. Were they egging him on, trying to get him to slip up somehow?

'There you have it,' Joey said. 'Sean the modern man. But we all know that if you ever hurt her, at all, he'll tear your balls off and shove them down your throat.'

Peake looked over. A serious look on Sean's face as he stared. Intimidating? Enough.

'I'll steer clear,' Peake said. 'I'm here to make money. That's it.'

Silence again. Until Joey laughed. Peake caught his eye in the mirror again.

'You're too trusting, Peake. You don't know us. You never met us. You jumped straight in this car and drove us off, no questions asked.'

He left the comment dangling.

'You either want to tell me what we're doing, or you don't,' Peake said.

'An errand,' Sean said. 'A simple errand tonight. You're on trial. Do a good job and there's always plenty of work in this city. Take this left.'

Peake did so. They'd reached the Bronx already, an area Peake had been to numerous times, but overall it remained unfamiliar, and he'd never been to these particular streets. Like every part of Manhattan, the Bronx had nicer areas, and not so nice areas. Though, by reputation at least, it had more of the latter.

'A trial,' Joey said. 'It's a good way to think of tonight. A free trial, right Sean?'

Once more Peake caught Joey's eye in the mirror. That same glare on his face. Was he trying to goad him?

If they didn't pay him... what would he do?

'Let's see about that,' Sean said with a cheeky wink. 'Take the next right, then pull over.'

Peake did so. He looked out of the window at the run of low-rise buildings. Homes, but not particularly big or expensive ones. An Irish bar took up the corner plot. Is that why they'd come up here? He saw no one in sight around the outside of it. Further along the street though a group of men, hoods and caps on their heads, stood in a huddle. A couple of them glanced over. Gang members? Lookouts? Or just a bunch of guys out chatting? Odd to do that in the middle of the street in the cold rather than at a bar or in one of their homes though.

'Get out,' Sean said.

All three of them did so.

'Stand tall,' Sean said, coming around the car.

Both Sean and Joey looked Peake up and down, as though assessing his suitability.

'He's not exactly the Rock, is he?' Joey said.

'No,' Sean said. 'But we're better being at least a little bit discreet around here.'

Joey said nothing to that.

'You can handle yourself?' Sean said to Peake, who shrugged in response.

'At least try and look a bit tough,' Joey said. 'Just don't go stomping on any kids' heads.' He smirked at his joke.

'And look after the car,' Sean said. 'I don't want anyone making a mess of it.'

'Be ready,' Joey said, giving Peake a light slap on the cheek. He didn't react and the two of them walked across the street, away from the Irish bar.

A surprise, really. On the opposite side of the road stood a Cuban restaurant. A couple of guys stood outside not doing anything in particular. Peake thought perhaps the restaurant was Sean and Joey's destination, but instead they moved along the street to one of the homes. They walked up the stairs to the door. Knocked. Waited. Peake couldn't see the face of the person who opened up but soon his new employers had gone inside.

Peake let out a sigh. He didn't know why. He pulled a cigarette out, lit it and sucked in then blew the smoke into the air above his head. He looked up the street to the group of men. Still there. Still looking over every now and then.

He glanced back to the Irish bar. A sports game on in there, judging by the loud commentary drifting out, though he didn't get the sense that the place was packed for the show.

He looked to the Cuban restaurant. The two men remained on the outside. Looking over at Peake. He stared for a few seconds until movement got his attention. Past the junction. Two figures coming his way. One on foot. One on a bike. Teenagers? Like the men behind him, both had dark clothes and hoods.

They crossed the road toward him. The kid on foot lifted his head when he spotted Peake standing there and the two of them edged up, the cyclist putting his foot to the floor to come to a stop.

'Nice car,' the kid on foot said.

'Yeah,' Peake said.

'What's it make?'

'It's a BMW,' Peake said, not sure if he'd heard the question right.

They both guffawed.

'No, what's it make? Horsepower?'

'Enough,' Peake said with a shrug.

'You wanna swap?' the kid on the bike said, pushing the handlebars toward Peake. The men further along the street were taking more of an interest now, he realized. Did they know these boys?

'Move along,' Peake said.

'You a cop?' bike boy asked.

'Undercover?' the other said.

'No.'

'Then why you hanging here?'

'Business.'

They both stared at him.

'You want us to leave? Give us one of those.'

The kid on the bike indicated the smoldering cigarette.

Peake sighed. Probably easier just to do it.

He took the packet from his pocket but as he went to reach inside for a cigarette the kid on foot bounced forward and swiped the whole lot from Peake's hand and set off down the street.

'Fuck you!' he shouted as his friend furiously pedaled to get away.

Peake bounced on his toes, basic instinct, ready to launch after the pair of them, before he caught himself and held back. The duo raced toward the group of men who were all now edging Peake's way. They held a brief exchange with the teens before the youngsters carried on. Peake looked back at the house. Where the hell were Sean and Joey?

One of the men peeled away from the others and sauntered forward, hands in pockets, his head tilted as though trying to figure what he was looking at.

Peake tried his best to act calm, nonchalant. He leaned against the body of the BMW as he took another drag from his last cigarette. What would he do if the guys confronted him? Stand his ground? Fight? Run into the Irish bar? Call out for Sean and Joey?

A bang somewhere along the street. A couple of the men flinched, cowered. Gunshot? Another bang a moment later. Then two more. Definitely gunshots. Then shouting. Another bang. But this time not a gunshot. A door slamming, or at least a thud of some kind. The man coming toward Peake had stopped moving while his gang huddled, perhaps wondering if they were about to get caught up in something.

The shouting grew louder. So too did the next gunshot. Out in the open now. Peake looked across to the Cuban restaurant where the two men stood a little more alert than before. Both had one hand inside their jackets.

Sean and Joey sped into view from around an alley at the far side of the restaurant.

'Get in the fucking car!' Sean screamed at Peake.

'Look out!' Joey shouted, whipping a handgun toward the two men by the restaurant. He fired off a shot, causing the guys to cower and retreat.

Peake didn't look to see what happened next. He dove into the car. Fired up the engine. Sean wrenched open the door and jumped in.

'Go!'

Peake released the parking brake. Another gunshot before the back door opened and Joey launched himself inside. Peake slammed the gas pedal and the back tires skidded before finding traction and the BMW raced forward.

Peake glanced in his mirror. Four men behind them – including the two from the restaurant. Giving chase for a couple of seconds, but they soon stopped.

The car whizzed past the group of bystanders. Glares. But no action from them. Whoever they were, this wasn't their fight.

Peake took a sharp right. Then a left. Joey and Sean righted themselves in their seats, put their belts on. Sean had a handgun in his lap. Joey clutched on to his still. He also had a duffel bag in the back with him.

'I knew they'd try to screw us!' Joey shouted, smacking the back of Sean's seat.

'Yeah. Well, they won't get another chance. We're done with them.'

Peake didn't say a word as he carried on driving at speed, glancing at the two passengers every now and then. Both were fuming.

Flashing lights behind them.

'You fucking idiot!' Joey said. 'Slow and steady, you moron.'

'Too late now,' Sean said, staring in the side-view mirror. 'Peake, you better have a fucking good plan from here.'

Plan? No. How could he have a plan? He hadn't been told anything about what they were doing tonight. So he didn't say anything as he floored the gas pedal.

Were the police after them because of his driving? Or because of the gunfight in the middle of the street in the Bronx? The answer didn't really matter that much. He only knew they were all in the shit, and it was down to him to get them out of it.

8
―――

With some hellishly fast turns and white-knuckle dashes across red lights, Peake managed to lose the police car. But they were hardly home free. They were in Manhattan. How many police officers, patrol cars were there on the island? Undoubtedly the car type, the license plate, had been captured and by now relayed to every nearby unit.

'We need to ditch this thing,' Peake said.

Sean and Joey said nothing as they both looked out of the windows in all directions, searching for heat.

'I said—'

'This is my uncle's brand-new car,' Sean said. 'We can't just...'

He trailed off. Peake slowed his speed. No point in alerting anyone who wasn't already on alert. He took turns onto more familiar and quieter streets as they neared the Upper West Side.

'What happened?' he asked.

'Fucking Cubans didn't want to pay,' Joey spat.

Peake's eyes fell on the bag. The Cubans didn't want to pay. It looked like they had.

'It was supposed to be a simple pick-up,' Sean said.

Did that explain why they'd ridden uptown in a car registered to a family member, rather than a clunker on false plates? Yet the idea of a 'simple pick-up' didn't really explain why they both had guns.

'I thought Harry didn't like guns,' Peake said, nodding to the piece on Sean's lap. He only received a glare in response.

Peake pulled over to the side of the road.

'Get out,' he said.

Sean stared at him. Joey lifted his gun as though unsure of Peake's intentions.

'Take the subway home,' he said. 'An Uber, whatever. Call the car in stolen to give yourself a story. I'll sort it out this end.'

'Sort it out?' Joey said. 'You're the reason we're in the shit. Driving like a fucking psycho.'

Peake didn't bother to argue that one.

'Consider your trial over,' Joey said. 'If we don't get out of this one? No, consider your whole fucking life over.'

'OK, OK,' Sean said. He wrapped his fingers around the door handle. 'Joey. Come on.'

Then he paused. Peake heard it before he saw it. Then the police car rolled into the intersection behind them and stopped. The cops were searching. And they'd found their quarry.

'Go!' Joey shouted.

Peake's foot had already hit the gas. He flicked the drive select switch to put the car into sport+ mode, turning off the traction control which had flummoxed him a couple of times before, sapping energy to the pedal whenever the car's computer thought a slide was imminent. This time he didn't even bother to brake as he tugged the wheel to swing out the back end to take the next corner. Sean held on to the dashboard. Joey grasped the seat-back in front of him. Both of them were thrown left and right as Peake weaved through traffic and took corners blindly and at speed. The cops had no chance.

Clear sight in front of them and behind, Peake slammed the brakes and the tires screeched as the car came to a sudden stop, shooting all three occupants forward until their seatbelts locked to keep them in place. Joey lost his gun in the process and the bag on the seat next to him went flying.

'You fu—'

'Get out!' Peake shouted.

Sean was quicker than his cousin, who spent a couple of seconds scooping up his things before stepping out into the night. Joey's door was still swinging when he opened up with another volley of abuse, but Peake didn't stop to listen. He floored the accelerator again and soon the two Irishmen were out of sight behind him.

Peake didn't let up. He found Riverside Drive and hurtled along the road that weaved gently alongside Riverside Park, the Hudson River not far beyond. No sign of the police anywhere still, but Peake knew he couldn't stay with the BMW forever.

He swerved right, bouncing up over a curb and crashing through a hedgerow into the thin strip of scenic parkland that stretched several miles along the western edge of Manhattan. Busy during the day with walkers, joggers, cyclists, but quiet late at night, except for the odd few – rebellious teens and others up to no good mostly.

He passed under the cement behemoth of Henry Hudson Parkway and the black water of the Hudson came into view in front, a short drop down from his elevated position. He hit the brakes and the car came to a rest on a grassy verge. He looked around. No one in sight, although he was sure onlookers had spotted his crazy maneuver. He left the parking brake off, left the car in gear, and stepped out and the BMW rolled forward.

He saw something. On the back seat.

'Shit.'

He moved forward with the car. Tried the back door but it wouldn't open. He dove back in through the driver's door and reached into the back.

A small bundle in the footwell, neatly bound. Cash. $10,000 read the paper band holding it together. Peake's eyes opened wide as he snatched for the notes before he scrambled back out of the still-moving car. He straightened up on the outside and his eyes rested on the money in his hand as the BMW picked up speed, heading down, down and soon out of sight a moment before a splash echoed into the night.

'Police! Don't move!'

Peake ignored the instruction, pocketed the cash and ran. The flashlight beams jostled off to his left as he raced up the hill. He ran across grass. Into a thicket. Branches scraped his legs. He ignored the pain. He pulled himself through onto a tree-lined path, nearly pitch-black because of the canopy shielding the moonlight. He raced away, pumping his arms and legs as quickly as he could. He passed by a dog walker with a light on their head like a miner. The man shouted something Peake didn't catch. He looked behind every few steps. He'd pulled away from the police. But then up ahead another searching flashlight, strobes of blue and red beyond it on the road...

His brain scrambled for an idea. Yes, he could race back onto the city's streets, but was being out in the open really the best option now?

He spotted a hut nearby. A refreshment stall, boarded up for the night. He ran that way and pulled to a stop. The shack was little more than a fancy trailer. A wooden panel ran along the bottom like a skirt, hiding the wheels.

Peake crouched down and grabbed hold of the panel and

tugged. The wood came loose with a creak and a strain and soon the gap was big enough for him to slide inside. He pulled the panel back into place as best he could and lay back on the cold tarmac and waited.

His breathing, his heart rate soon settled. He heard footsteps outside. Voices. He didn't make a sound...

Soon he heard nothing but distant traffic. He let out a long and nearly silent sigh. But still he didn't move. Not for a long time. More than two hours before he finally decided to pull himself back out into the open.

The park still steeped in darkness, he could see little around him. But that was a good thing because he definitely couldn't see the flashlights of the cops. Nor any other indication that the NYPD was still scouring the area looking for him.

His hand rested on the bundle inside his jacket.

$10,000. A lot of money, for him at least. How much had been in Joey's bag?

More to the point, when would he notice the money was missing?

It didn't matter. The money belonged to Peake now. Payment for his services for the night.

With his newfound lifeline tucked safely away, he set off through the darkness.

9

OPERATION ZEUS – DAY 14

Peake looked down to see the dazzling sunlight on his shirt sleeve once more. He pulled his arm back into the shade. Even a few seconds in the blazing sunshine and he felt the heat searing his skin underneath his clothing. Yet each time he inched back into the shade, the sun found him again a few minutes later.

How much longer would they have to wait here?

'Is that him?' Talos asked, nudging Peake in the side as they stood next to each other by the wall of a closed-up store at the edge of the market.

'No,' Peake said.

'Fucking looks like him,' Talos said.

'Next you'll be saying everyone here looks the same.'

'They don't to you?'

Peake didn't answer and a moment later Talos laughed.

'Jesus, Hades, you think I'm actually that much of a dickhead, don't you?'

Peake still didn't respond.

'I know you think you're superior—'

'I don't think I'm superior.'

'Yeah you do, even if it's subconscious.'

'That wouldn't be thought then, would it?'

'You know what I mean.'

'Not really.'

'What I mean is, don't underestimate me. I'm not a meathead. Do you really think Chief would have me on this op if I had nothing in here?' Talos tapped his temple.

'That's him,' Peake said, indicating the young man who came around the corner in front of them.

'Hermes, you have a visual?' Talos asked.

'I've got him,' came Hermes's voice in Peake's ear. 'Heading west to east, toward your position.'

'Minos, you should see him in five seconds,' Peake said into the microphone hidden in the fabric of his shirt.

A short pause, then. 'I see him,' Minos confirmed.

A few seconds of silence. Then Minos's voice came through again. 'I'm following. You're good to go.'

'Hermes, confirm?' Peake asked.

'Confirm I've visual on Minos and Delta.'

His visual being from the camera on the drone he had high up in the sky. So high that Peake couldn't see it at all, nor could he hear its distinctive whir.

'Confirm we have Red location in sight,' said Ares, who together with Hera was keeping watch on Delta's home from the opposite apartment building. 'Nothing on thermal.'

'Let's go,' Talos said, and he and Peake peeled away from their positions.

They arrived outside the apartment block two minutes later. The block more or less resembled the one where their safe house was located, except this one had all of its windows intact. Nothing on thermal? Perhaps not inside Delta's apartment, but most if not all of the apartments here were occupied.

Talos picked the outer lock while Peake kept his eyes busy on the street outside.

'We're in,' Talos said.

The two of them slipped through the open door.

'Second floor,' Peake said.

They saw no one on the way up, but the sounds of voices and TVs gave away that people were home.

'Careful,' Peake said as Talos went to work on the apartment door, feeling all the more nervous this time than he had downstairs. Booby traps were not at all unlikely, though Talos didn't seem to even hesitate.

At least until it came to pushing open the unlocked door.

'Wanna stand back?' he said, turning to Peake with a grin on his face.

Peake did so, but only a half step before Talos whipped open the door with a shout of panic. A mock shout.

He turned back to Peake again and laughed.

'Really fucking subtle,' Peake said, looking over his shoulder.

'The king of the underworld's scared of snuffing it and going back home?'

'God,' Peake said. 'Hades is a god, not a king.'

Talos shook his head. 'I really don't see it.' He turned and stepped inside.

'Minos, where you at?' Peake asked.

'We're good,' came the voice through the headset. 'He's in the market still.'

'Let's get this done,' Talos said, and he and Peake got to work.

Talos roamed the place, looking for any data to glean: electronic media to copy, paperwork to photograph. Peake set up a series of wireless cameras.

'You know, it'd be pretty funny if he already had some of those in here,' Talos said. 'And he was watching us right now.'

'Funny?' Peake said, screwing the light fitting in the lounge back in place.

'Get a load of this,' Talos said, holding up a notepad.

Peake climbed off the chair and looked at the page. Arabic. Not a full scrawl but what looked like short notes.

'Shopping list?' Talos said.

'Locations,' Peake said.

Talos raised an eyebrow. 'You read Arabic now?'

'Minos is a good teacher.'

'You've been here two weeks.'

'Who said it's my first ti—'

'That's enough,' came Ares's voice in Peake's earpiece. 'Remember rule one.'

'So what locations?' Talos asked.

'Take the picture. We'll figure it out later.'

'OK, Delta is speaking to someone,' Minos said.

'Who?' Ares asked.

'Don't recognize him. A local. But he looks nervous.'

'Don't get too close,' Hera said. 'There could be others watching.'

'They're at a spice stall. I'll buy some for later.'

Talos continued to flick through the notepad as though not really listening.

'They're spooked,' Minos said.

'I told you—'

'Not me,' Minos said, cutting Hera off. 'Two police. Closing in.'

Police. Not the most accurate description. The police were simply the military in less aggressive uniforms, but with just as unforgiving and deadly an approach.

'Delta and his friend are coming back your way,' Minos said. 'Toward Red location.'

'The police are following?' Peake asked.

'Yeah. I'll hang back.'

'We done here?' Peake said to Talos.

'Done.'

Except when Peake stepped forward, the floorboard beneath his foot creaked and moved ever so slightly. Both he and Talos froze and looked at each other.

'They're out of the market,' Minos said.

'Hermes, you still see them?' Ares asked.

'I do, but there's a chopper coming over.'

'Military?' Hera asked.

'Yeah. Nothing to indicate it's related but—'

'Doesn't matter,' Ares said. 'Take the bird home.'

'Fuck,' Hermes said. 'Understood.'

'I'm standing down,' Minos said. 'It's too quiet that way. They'll be back in your sights in a minute or two.'

'Talos, Hades? Get out of there,' Hera said.

Neither of them responded. Peake prized the floorboard up.

'Shit,' Talos said.

Peake had been about to say the same thing.

He reached in and pushed the bundles of US dollars aside. Handguns. Grenades.

'C4?' Talos said.

Four blocks of it. Enough to flatten quite a few buildings. But not the usual choice for terrorists and the like who often had to resort to more improvised explosives.

'There,' Talos said, indicating the scruffy bundle of papers.

'I see Delta,' Ares said. 'Just turned onto the street. Red location in two hundred yards.'

'Talos, Hades, you need to move,' Hera said.

Talos took the papers out and gently unfurled them.

'We don't have time,' Peake said.

'What is this?' Talos asked.

'A hundred yards. The police are still on them.'

'Phone numbers?' Peake said.

'Co-ordinates?'

'Guys, get the fuck out of there before you screw everything!' Hermes said.

'No one's saving your asses,' Ares added.

'We gotta go,' Peake said.

'Shit. Take it?'

'No. Come on.'

Talos growled but quickly put the papers back in place. Exactly the same place? Not really. Hopefully good enough.

Peake stamped the plank back down. It didn't quite sit flat.

'I need to see your ugly faces on the outside right now or we're packing up,' Ares said, his voice raised, his nerves clear.

Peake left the floorboard as it was and he and Talos rushed for the door. Peake pulled it shut behind him. Talos dug his hand into his pocket.

Peake closed his eyes for a second in silent prayer.

'Twenty yards...' Ares said.

'We're out,' Peake said. 'Locking up.'

'Fucking leave it!' Minos said.

But Peake stayed right by Talos's side as his colleague locked the door.

'They're outside,' Ares said.

'We'll go up,' Peake said, and he and Talos rushed for the stairs and hotfooted it up to the third floor.

'They're inside.'

'Why has Delta come home if the police are on his tail?' Peake asked.

'I don't see the police now,' Ares said. 'But I do see Delta and friend on thermal on the ground floor still. I think they're waiting.'

'For the police to go past?' Talos asked.

'One of them has a weapon in hand,' Hera added.

Talos and Peake exchanged glances. They hadn't expected to be in a firefight this afternoon. Neither of them was armed.

'It's OK. The police have definitely gone,' Ares said.

What the hell?

'Delta and friend moving up now.'

Peake listened to the sounds of the footsteps coming up. He focused on controlling his breaths. Slow and calm. Talos looked cool as anything too. Ready for a fight? Yeah. But Peake just wanted to get on the outside and leg it back to the safe house.

A door opened and closed below them.

'They're in,' Peake said. 'Come on.'

As he and Talos peeled away, the apartment door behind them opened. Peake glanced over his shoulder as he reached the stairs. A middle-aged man stood there, glaring.

Peake said nothing. Talos said nothing. They moved quickly down. Peake glanced at Delta's door as they passed the second floor. Closed now. Perhaps he was standing on the other side, staring at them through the peephole.

Peake had a flashing thought of the floorboard, the rearranged items underneath, none of which were left quite as they'd found them.

Seconds later they reached the outer doors.

'Are we good?' Talos asked before he opened up.

No reply.

'I said, are we—'

'You're clear,' Ares said.

Talos heaved a sigh before he pulled open the door. He and

Peake stepped outside into bright sunlight, took one look along the street before quickly walking away.

10

The message from Sean came through on Peake's phone as he stood on the jostling subway, heading across Downtown.

> Come to the bar

He arrived outside O'Hare's little more than fifteen minutes later, the time not quite 10 a.m. He carried an extra-strong coffee. He needed the caffeine. He hadn't slept much. He'd not lain down in bed until after 3 a.m., and his brain had remained wired for a couple of hours after that as he went over and over the night's escapade. Mostly he thought about the money. He'd awoken at eight and headed straight to see Chan, who'd been more than a little surprised to be given the wad of cash. Four months' rent, rather than three. Keep the guy off Peake's back for a while.

'You steal this, you piece of shit?' Chan had asked, bleary-eyed himself from a late night, or just a rude awakening perhaps.

Peake hadn't confirmed or denied. Chan had no need to

know how Peake had come into the money. And so what, anyway? It wasn't as though Chan operated above board.

Peake had hidden the rest of the money around his apartment. Better hiding places than the cashbox in the kitchen this time.

The bar looked closed up from the outside, though the three cars parked on the curb suggested activity beyond. Peake walked up to the door and tried the handle. Locked. He knocked and waited. After a few moments he heard locks release before the door inched open. Chops.

'That was quick,' Chops said. Then his skinny face broke out into a wide grin as he opened the door more fully. 'But then I heard that about you. And I'm not talking about your night with Katie.'

He winked. Peake didn't react as he stepped inside. The bar area was dark, no one in sight.

'They're out back,' Chops said, moving ahead and to the door in the far corner. They entered a brightly lit corridor. Past a store cupboard. A toilet. Another room of unknown use. Finally they stopped at the door right before the fire escape. Chops opened and beckoned Peake inside and a moment of doubt washed over him – ambush?

No. He walked in. A big office space. Bright. Tastefully decorated. Like Peake would expect to see for a lawyer or an accountant or something. All the crew – at least, all the ones Peake had met – were there: Dolan, sunken into a leather sofa with a scowl on his face; Joey and Sean sat around a small meeting table; at the back of the room, Harry sat on the big oak desk, rather than at it.

'Here he is,' the older man said, his eyes narrowing as he clocked Peake.

What was that look?

'A little earlier than expected.'

'I was on my way over anyway,' Peake said.

'Yeah?' Dolan asked. 'Why?'

'Why not?' Peake answered.

'Tell me what happened last night,' Harry said, and Peake's heart drummed a little more quickly in his chest as all eyes turned to him. Expectant eyes. As though they all really hoped he'd slipped up.

'I took Sean and Joey uptown. To the Bronx. A collection.'

Harry looked over to the two young men. Both remained staring at Peake, though neither looked quite as confident as they had the night before when he'd first picked them up. He wondered how much they'd already been chastised by their boss.

'And do you know what they were collecting and why?' Harry asked.

Peake paused a moment. 'Money, I'd say, but I don't know for sure, and I haven't a clue what it's to do with.'

'You never thought to ask?'

'I decided if I needed to know, someone would tell me.'

Harry nodded as though pleased with the response.

'But all I saw was a bag. That's it.'

'You sure about that?' Joey piped up.

'Button it,' Harry said to him, even if his gaze remained on Peake.

'They collected the bag. Then what?'

'Joey collected the bag,' Peake said. 'He was the one who had it.'

Joey snarled but didn't say anything.

'I waited by the car the whole time,' Peake continued. 'That was my job. Driver. I have no idea what happened other than after a few minutes I heard gunshots.' He paused a moment, wondering if Harry would ask about who was firing. Peake decided not to go into that. 'Then Joey and Sean came running for the car. I got us all away as quickly as I could.'

'We told him slow and steady,' Joey said. 'We told you that, right?'

Peake didn't even bother to look at him. 'We took some fire from a couple of Cubans outside a restaurant. There were more of them chasing too. There was another gang altogether halfway up the street. I'd no idea whose side they were on. So yeah, I put my foot down rather than get us all involved in a firefight with people I didn't know.'

Harry nodded slowly. 'And then?'

'The cops were on us. I took some initiative. Sean and Joey... weren't exactly giving me much of a cue, so I did what I thought was the best call. I lost the cops. Then I ditched Joey and Sean. To save their asses. And I took the car. Putting my ass on the line.'

'And you dumped the car in the Hudson right in front of the NYPD's eyes,' Sean said.

Peake thought. Had the police actually seen?

'They dredged the car out a few hours ago,' Harry said. 'Right after sunrise.'

OK. So yeah, the police had seen.

'I suggested Sean call it in stolen,' Peake said. 'To give some cover.'

'I did, bu—'

'And the fake plates give us a bit more of a backup,' Harry said.

OK, that was something Peake hadn't known about.

'No,' Joey said, getting to his feet. 'The fake plates should have given us a complete get out. All he had to fucking do was to get the car somewhere safe so we could swap them over again. Instead he drives the Bimmer into the fucking river.'

'And the police quickly matched the VIN to the real registration,' Sean added.

'Which is why we've already had the cops at our door this morning.'

'Alright, boys, that's enough from you two,' Harry said. 'Sit down.'

They looked unsure but then did so, before Harry faced Peake again.

'All they told me was that it was their uncle's car,' Peake said. 'I thought ditching it made most sense to back up the claim that it was stolen. If I'd known about the fake plates... obviously that would have—'

'It's done now,' Harry said, holding his hand up. 'The police sticking their beaks in is hassle we don't need, but I think this time I can keep them off our backs.'

Which sounded like confirmation that he had cops on his payroll. Peake thought again about Wyatt.

'But my biggest immediate concern is the missing money,' Harry added.

Peake swallowed hard. Tried to remain calm as Harry glared at him.

'You're going to have to explain that one to me,' Peake said.

'It didn't take the cops long to pull that car out of the water,' Harry said. 'And not very long for them to find that it belonged to my brother. What they didn't find was any money in that car. Except when Sean and Joey counted up last night, we're forty short from the Cubans.'

Forty short? Forty thousand? The comment threw Peake and for a moment he lost himself and only hoped his reaction hadn't given anything away.

'That's a lot of money,' Peake said.

'Yeah,' Joey said. 'And I bet you took it, you slimy prick.'

Peake tried his best to look offended as he turned his palms outward and shook his head.

But he'd only seen the one bundle of $10,000 in the car. Perhaps the Cubans had actually screwed them for thirty. Perhaps the rest of the missing cash had come loose and fallen on to the floor and Peake just hadn't seen it. But then, wouldn't the police have found it? Unless they'd pocketed it themselves, the dirty bastards.

There was another option. Joey had figured they were $10,000 short, but he'd taken another $30,000 for himself. Greed, but also to try and put Peake even more in the shit.

'Or he really is an undercover cop,' Dolan said. 'He's playing us. The cops have our money.'

'He's not a cop,' Chops said, somewhat to Peake's surprise.

'We already checked his background,' Harry added.

'A curious past,' Chops continued, coming in front of Peake and looking at him like he was studying a specimen in a lab. 'Eight years ago, dishonorable discharge from the British army. Quite a black hole of time before that while he was serving, but I don't think we're going to find out much about that, are we, Peake?'

Peake said nothing.

'Which only goes to show we can't trust him,' Joey said. 'A man with a secret past?'

'Except the last eight years aren't secret,' Chops said. 'He spent time going from crappy job to crappy job before doing his five years in prison. He's only been out six months. So either he's playing the longest of long plays here with the Feds or whoever else, to get on the inside with us, or he really isn't a threat. In that sense.'

'I hate to say it, boys,' Harry said, 'but I'm really not important enough for the Feds or anyone else to play a long game like that.'

Joey said nothing but shook his head and Peake knew he didn't agree. In fact, he clearly hated that no one else saw whatever it was he thought he saw.

'I'm going to ask you this once, and once only,' Harry said, before he paused and held Peake's eye. Neither blinked. 'Are you a cop? An agent. Whatever.'

'No,' Peake said. 'I told you before – I'm just a guy who needs a job.'

'Which brings me to the second, perhaps more obvious question. Did you take that money?'

'No,' Peake said without a thought. 'I didn't take your fucking money. And you know what? I didn't even get paid for last night. So how about that?'

He looked at Sean and Joey. Harry glared at them too.

'Is that right?' Harry said to them.

Neither said a word.

'Joey, take out your wallet.'

Joey didn't respond.

'Do what he says,' Dolan piped up.

Joey still didn't move. Dolan got to his feet and moved over. 'Take your wallet out.'

Joey did so but the moment he had it in his hands, Dolan swiped it from him and shoved Joey back and opened the wallet up to flick through.

'Two hundred... sixty-five.'

'Give it to Peake,' Harry said.

Dolan took the cash and rolled it up and dropped the wallet on the floor before stepping over to Peake and slapping the notes into his palm.

'And now you've been paid,' Harry said.

'This is ridiculous,' Joey said.

Sean put a hand on his cousin's shoulder to try to reel him in.

'But I'm still in two minds here,' Harry said. The room fell silent and all eyes turned to the boss as though awaiting a verdict of some sort. Kind of like the crowd in the Colosseum, awaiting the thumbs up or down from the emperor.

'Sean said you drove like a madman,' Harry said.

Peake said nothing.

'Answer him,' Dolan said.

'I didn't realize it was a question.'

'I meant it as a compliment,' Harry said. 'Where'd you learn to drive like that?'

'Nowhere,' Peake said with a shrug. 'I was told to do something, I did it.'

'Even if he's not a cop, the guy's a fucking liability,' Joey said.

'Boy, clamp that mouth shut,' Harry said, 'before I have Dolan do it for you.'

Joey sneered but once again backed down.

'You like driving?' Harry said to Peake.

'I guess.'

'Peake, do you want a damn job or not?' Sean said.

'Yeah. I do.'

'Then you can drive for us,' Harry said. 'Whenever we need you, you're the man.'

Peake didn't say anything.

'Is that a fucking yes or a fucking no?'

'It's a yes.'

'Good, I'm glad we finally got there.' Harry turned to address the others. 'Boys, we need to talk about our former friends in the Bronx and forty thousand missing dollars. Peake, for now, go home. We'll call you later.'

Peake nodded. 'Thanks.'

He turned for the door.

'But Peake,' Harry said, when Peake was about to step out into the corridor. Peake turned around. 'If I find you're lying to me... about your past... about that money...'

Harry didn't finish the threat. He didn't really need to. The five sets of eyes glaring at him told him the story.

Peake carried on out.

11

He headed back to his apartment. Where else did he have to go? It looked like Harry Lafferty still saw use in him, but the Irishman was the one calling the shots, so Peake had little choice but to sit and await his next instruction, whether it came from the boss himself or one of his lackeys.

He was walking along the corridor to his door when he first heard the noise. Groaning, moaning coming from Jelena's apartment. Peake cringed. He hated the sound. Hated what it meant for her.

He paused with his key in the door. Definitely more moaning than groaning. Fake pleasure, he was sure, but not a pained sound at all.

Peake carried on into the apartment. Went about fixing himself a drink. He had the coffee machine running when he paused, staring at the bottle of bourbon on the counter. Early in the day... but so what?

He poured a large measure and worked a good mouthful around his mouth, enjoying the burn. He swallowed and went for another mouthful but paused with the glass to his lips.

OK, so he kind of had nothing to do for the rest of the day, except... What if Harry or Sean or whoever else did call him, most likely for him to drive them around on some other dodgy errand?

Just one more then. He downed the amber liquid, it barely touching the sides of his mouth this time. He slammed the glass down and was about to set about making the coffee when he paused.

Because of the noise next door.

That last sound had definitely not been a moan of fake pleasure. A panicked yelp. A meaty thud. Another meaty thud after, except that one wasn't accompanied by any sound from Jelena at all.

Then came shouting. A man. Peake balled his fists.

He could let it go, like he had before. He'd wait for the scumbag to leave then go and comfort her.

Or...

'Damn it,' he said before rushing for the exit. He threw open his door, then paused in two minds. Knock on the door? No. What was the point in alerting the guy to Peake being there?

And breaking the door down would only cause Jelena a problem.

He went back inside, took only a few seconds to grab the basic tools he needed – two paperclips.

A second later and he'd worked the ends of the clips around the innards of the lock, releasing each of the levers.

He turned the handle and quietly opened the door and winced as another thud came. Then Jelena shrieking.

'Get out!'

Not at Peake.

They still had no clue he was there. He moved along the corridor to the bedroom. Door open. He glanced in to see Jelena huddled in the corner, naked, curled up with her knees to her chest, her arms wrapped around her legs. Her hair strewn across her face. Blood dribbling from her nose.

'Yeah, I'm going, you stupid fucking wh—'

Jelena's eyes found Peake's and caused the guy to pause. Standing there in nothing but his jeans the near-side of the bed, he turned to Peake. Jolted in shock.

'Who the fuck—'

Peake strode forward.

'Peake, no!'

He didn't listen to her. The guy backtracked and grabbed the nearest object he could – a vase – and launched it at Peake who easily dodged the flying object before he swiped the man's legs from him, took hold of his wrist and twisted it up behind his back.

'Try anything and I'll break it,' he whispered into the man's ear.

He squirmed, but only a little.

'Peake, please!' Jelena shrieked in between sobs.

But he wasn't listening.

'Tell her you're sorry.'

'W-what?'

'Tell her you're sorry!' Peake yelled and then threw his fist into the guy's kidney.

He keeled to the side, teeth gritted in pain.

'And make it convincing,' Peake added.

'I'm... sorry.'

'And you'll never come back here again. Right?'

Peake pushed the wrist a little further to breaking point.

'Right!'

'And you'll never do this to anyone again. Right?'

'R-right,' the guy said with a feeble nod.

'Now get dressed and get the hell out of here.'

Peake let go of him and kicked him down to the carpet. He moved to put himself between the man and Jelena but then her eyes sprang open.

'Watch out!' she yelled.

Peake spun and saw the glint of the knife in the man's hand as he rushed forward.

Peake stooped and side-stepped and a swivel kick knocked the knife free. Perhaps broke a couple of fingers too, although the guy hadn't yet got the idea and launched himself for Peake one last time.

Peake ducked and swooped under the intended blow and again grabbed the guy's wrist as he went flying past. Somehow found the resolve to not just snap it there and then. He pulled the man up.

'You're dumber than I thought,' Peake said.

He pushed the guy out of there, to the door. He opened up and kicked him to the floor outside. Stomped back to the bedroom to get the man's shirt and jacket. Paused in the corridor a second as he checked his own pocket.

Yep. Got it.

The guy faced off with Peake again when he opened the door.

'Give me my damn things,' he said.

'What, these?' Peake said, holding the clothes up.

But he didn't toss them. Instead he went through the pockets.

'This yours?' Peake said holding the phone up.

No answer.

Peake tossed it and the guy ducked as though he thought it was an attempt to attack him. The phone clattered along the corridor and over the edge of the stairwell and banged and clanked to the bottom.

'I guess you weren't too good at baseball.'

'You idiot!' the guy yelled looking from Peake and to the stairwell a couple of times. 'Just give me my—'

'Car key?' Peake said, holding that up. 'Mercedes. Nice.'

He tossed that too. Higher than before. This time the man did try to catch it, though it went over his hands and ended up the same place as the phone.

'I'm gonna—'

'What are you gonna do... Eric Gregerson?' Peake said, reading from the driver's license that he'd taken from the man's wallet. 'Ah. Upper East Side. Nice area. What do you do for a living?'

Now Gregerson had nothing to say.

Peake noted the ring on his finger.

'Your wife know you come over this way to pay for sex?'

No answer.

'Because she will do if I ever see you here, or even on the streets around here again.'

No response to start with but Gregerson slumped as though finally realizing his predicament.

'Just give me my damn things,' he said, a lot less feisty than before.

'These things?' Peake asked, holding the clothes up. He took out his lighter and lit the end of the jacket sleeve.

'No, my...'

'Get out of here,' Peake said. He stepped forward to encourage Gregerson to step back.

'But! My...'

'Get the hell out of here,' Peake said, stepping forward again and again until Gregerson was backtracking on the stairs. Peake let go of the smoldering clothes which fluttered down toward the first floor.

'Off you go, then,' Peake said.

Gregerson rushed off down, mumbling and cursing as he went.

Peake turned back around and paused. Jelena was there in the doorway. Robe on now. Face like thunder.

'What the hell is wrong with you?'

'I—'

'Who do you think you are?'

'Jelena—'

'You have no right to-to invade my—'

'I'm not going to sit in my apartment listening to some asshole beat you up!'

'He's a client! He pays to come here! He pays well.'

'It's worth it, then?'

She didn't answer.

'And what if one day they take it too far? What then? You want me to sit and wait it out when one of those shits has his hands around your throat?'

She slammed the door shut without another word. He moved over and put his face close to the wood.

'Jelena, I—'

'Peake, just leave me alone. Please.'

He thought about that for a brief moment, then did exactly what she asked.

12

OPERATION ZEUS – DAY 35

Another long day in the heat with little to show for it. Three weeks ago they'd placed cameras in the apartment of one of their four prime targets, the man they referred to as Delta. Alpha, Beta, Gamma, Delta, all four of them were former officials in either the exiled government or the army. Peake and the rest of the Zeus team had instructions to keep close tabs on the quartet, learn about their movements, their associates, their plans...

The problem was, Alpha, Beta and Gamma were well-protected men, in hiding. Out of the four Delta was the obvious best place to start. Except it looked like Delta had known about the break-in at his apartment after all. As Peake had watched the camera feeds from what remained of that day, Delta hadn't shown any overt signs of being spooked, of finding the cameras or the misplaced floorboard. He'd simply left the apartment later in the evening and never returned.

Three weeks later and Peake and the others had made no inroads on any of the four prime targets, working off scraps the whole time. Recce after recce, traipsing around the capital and beyond, using the little intel they'd gathered from that initial foray to Delta's apartment, scoping out each of the addresses listed on those handwritten sheets. The addresses comprised a whole host of disparate places – apartment blocks, individual homes, markets, shops, office blocks. They had no clue what it all meant.

More frustratingly, they had no idea where Delta had gone, nor had they ever identified the mystery man who they'd seen him with in the market that day, who they'd simply called Zeta.

Peake pulled open the door to the safe house building and heaved a sigh as he stepped into the cool interior.

'You should be used to it by now,' Minos said, who'd been on the recce to the arms factory with him.

'I am,' Peake said. 'But I still hate it.'

'Hate it? You probably know more about this city by now than people who've lived here their whole lives.'

Which was true. The amount of times he'd walked the streets... In some areas he knew every nook and cranny, every market, every shopping center, every office block, every factory. Even in a city of several hundred thousand he recognized many of the same faces too. People who hung about in the same places at the same times each week. He took in everything he saw, but so far the knowledge had added little to the operation. An operation which had become little more than endless observation with no obvious goal.

The truth was, he was bored out of his mind, and he knew the others were too – the ever-headstrong Talos in particular, whose grumbles against the op, Chief and his rules grew more frequent and more forceful day by day.

'You're right,' Peake said. 'I know pretty much everything about this city now. One of the reasons I hate it so much.'

He didn't really know why he said that. Hate it? Did he? Either way, he thought Minos looked a little offended at his words. Clearly the guy had roots in the Arab-speaking world and over the last five weeks he'd wondered over and over about the man and his past yet Peake didn't even know which country the guy originated from, what side of the religious divide he and his family sat. On the one hand he understood Chief's need for secrecy even between the team members. Most crucially it meant that should any one of them be caught and taken prisoner, they'd have little to give away about the op, about their colleagues, if placed under duress. On the other hand it didn't exactly help bonding and morale to have no clue about the people he was risking his life with.

'We're a bit early,' Minos said as they moved up the stairs. Two hours before their planned daily debrief, to be precise, but quite frankly Peake had had enough of the recces.

'Perhaps we should head out to a bar and sink a few ice-cold beers,' Peake said.

'Sounds fucking good to me.'

'The nearest place is only a thousand miles away.'

'I'd walk it just for a single beer right now. Served tall. Frozen glass, crusty ice slipping down the side.'

Peake's mouth went dry at the thought. Of all the things he missed, beer had to be right up there. When he got home – if he got home – he'd go on the bender of his life.

'So you not teetotal then?' Peake asked Minos. A simple question really. The locals were. In fact, alcohol was entirely banned in the country under the new regime. Previously, posh hotels had a special dispensation, largely to cater for the traveling Western businesspeople and diplomats, but that had all gone now.

'No,' Minos said, with a strange look on his face, as though again offended about the insinuation, or just feeling awkward having to answer a personal question, as if Peake now knew too much about his private life and his past.

Peake opened the door to the safe house then paused a second. He'd expected the place to be empty. Ares and Hermes were out together on the west of the city, Talos and Hera in the south. But he heard soft, muffled voices inside.

Immediately more alert, he turned to Minos whose face had taken on a steely determination. In more than a month in the capital, the nearest they'd come to confrontation was that day in Delta's apartment. But thoughts rumbled now as to whether their covers had been blown. He imagined all sorts of sights as he tiptoed through the apartment. His colleagues bound and gagged, as their captors tortured them, awaiting the return of the rest of the crew. Or a cadre of militarized police, searching.

He held his empty hands out at the ready – he had no weapon on him. Chief had always insisted on no weapons. If they were caught by the police or the military carrying anything, even a combat knife, the repercussions could be huge. Not just for the op team, but for the wider political landscape.

Still, weapons or not, Peake would be ready to fight when needed. He'd never seen his other colleagues in action, but he knew none of them would shy away from conflict...

No one in the lounge.

'In there,' Minos whispered, indicating the partially open bedroom door. The bedroom Hermes shared with Ares.

Peake stepped forward and put his hand to the door. Then he pushed it open quickly, crouching down into a defensive pose.

The room was empty, but the noises had grown louder...

At the far side of the room, beyond the beds, through the open doorway of the bathroom...

He caught their faces in the mirror. Two naked bodies. Hera, bent over the sink, Talos behind her, thrusting for his life, his eyes closed, face all screwed up with concentration. Hera caught

Peake's eye in the mirror and smiled then laughed but didn't make any attempt to stop Talos or to cover herself.

'Fucking hell,' Minos said.

Talos opened his eyes in surprise and his face burst red with rage.

'Piss off!' he bellowed, and Peake grabbed the door handle and pulled the door shut, moving about as quickly as he'd ever moved in his life. He stood there like a chump for a few seconds, staring at the ground, trying to erase the images from his head.

Then Minos laughed and Peake couldn't help himself.

'Inevitable really,' Minos said.

'Yeah,' Peake agreed. One confident, young woman, four arrogant and single men, excluding himself, of course. At least he assumed they were all single. Yet for Hera to have picked Talos...

'Now I really need a fucking drink,' Peake said.

'I'll make some coffee,' Minos said.

'Not really what I meant.'

'Yeah, but what can you do?'

He slapped Peake on the back before sauntering into the kitchen like he didn't have a care in the world.

* * *

Half an hour later Talos emerged. Still no sign of Hermes and Ares by that point. Minos and Peake were both at the dining table, a second coffee for the two of them. Neither said a word to Talos as he strode in with a sullen looking face, boxer shorts and T-shirt on. He set his grumpy sights on Peake.

'What?' Talos said, clearly up for the challenge.

'Nothing,' Peake responded.

'Good.'

Talos turned and went to the fridge and took out a bottle of water. He took several swigs straight from the bottle before scrunching up the empty container.

'You can stare at my ass all you like, Hades, but I'm not interested in you.'

Talos glared back at Peake again.

'Do we have a problem?' he asked.

'I dunno,' Peake said. 'Shall I check with Chief?'

Talos stormed forward but Minos shot up from his chair and the big guy seemed to think better of whatever he'd planned to do.

'You breathe a word to Chief and—'

'What?' Peake said, standing up from his seat too.

'Boys,' Hera said, walking into the room, fully clothed now, with about the widest grin Peake could imagine. 'Not fighting over me, are you?'

She clearly loved that idea.

'Mr Underworld here is a bit jealous,' Talos said.

Peake shook his head. 'I'm not jealous, you prick – I'm pissed off that you two are screwing while we're out working. And don't get me started on the potential for your little sex-fest to jeopardize our op.'

'I'm not jeopardizing anything,' Talos said.

'Yeah? You think Chief would agree?'

'Don't even—'

'And what about if it comes down to a choice between her and the op?'

'Excuse me,' Hera said. 'Her? I'm in the fucking room too.'

'No,' Peake said. 'This isn't the fucking room. Apparently, that's Ares and Hermes's bathroom. Have you got zero respect?'

He got no response to that. Just a snarl from both Hera and Talos.

'Nothing to say? Is that some sort of power trip?' Peake said to

Talos. 'You swing your dick about in other people's private spaces for kicks?'

'You need to watch your mouth. Or we're gonna have a problem.'

'Problem? You're the problem here.'

Talos looked ready to bite back again but the sound of the front door opening and closing got everyone's attention. Minos retook his seat. Hera and Talos and Peake remained standing as Ares and Hermes walked in.

'Afternoon,' Ares said, already looking suspicious. 'What did we miss?'

All eyes turned to Peake. As though he was the one causing problems. No one answered the question.

'I said—'

'It's fine,' Peake said. 'There's nothing wrong here.'

'It's just the heat,' Minos said as though the peacemaker.

Talos and Hera said nothing at all, as though they genuinely believed they'd done nothing wrong, and the only person out of line was Peake.

Whatever. He would keep quiet for his own benefit, if not for theirs. He moved forward. He just wanted some space. But Talos stepped into his path and Peake thudded into the big guy's shoulder – deliberately, really.

'Watch your step,' Talos said.

Peake said nothing in return as he carried on out of the room.

13

Peake had little else to do but sit and await the next call from the boss or Sean or whoever else from the gang needed him. He watched TV. Listened to the radio. He didn't relax. Mostly he sat in silence at the dining table, thinking over last night, the stolen money, thinking over what had happened with Jelena and that prick Gregerson. He thought about going back next door and trying to appease her, not for his own sake but because he really just wanted to make sure she was OK. He certainly hadn't heard any more noise from over there. That was a good thing, he hoped.

For more than an hour, deep in his thoughts, he stared at the view outside the window. Not a particularly good view – simply the bricks and windows of the apartment block that his backed directly onto, only a few yards away.

Unable to put any of the world's wrongs to rights, he shook his head to escape his trancelike state and went into the kitchen and refilled the coffee machine and set it going, standing watching the drips almost in a daze. But as the low rumble of the machine heating up water slowly died down, he focused on a noise outside his apartment. Not out of the window, where he'd been staring before, but outside the front door. Voices. Soft.

He moved that way, walking lightly so he could concentrate. Jelena, he was sure. Another voice too. Neither was angry. Almost whispers. The other voice was... female too.

Peake looked through the peephole.

Katie.

He pulled open the door and she jumped then smiled and laughed.

'Hey, Si,' she said.

'Si?' Jelena said, stepping out of her open door and fixing Peake a teasing look. At least she didn't seem as pissed with him now. 'That's a new one. How cute.'

'Pet names for us two already, right, babe?' he said.

Katie hit his arm.

'Huh,' Jelena said. 'Who knew? Maybe there is something under that tough exterior after all.'

'Thanks, Jelena,' Peake said. 'I think I've got this from here.'

She winked at him before moving back inside. 'Have fun,' she called before her door banged shut. Yes, she was definitely no longer mad at him.

'She seems nice,' Katie said, still all full of smiles.

'She is.'

'Should I be jealous?'

'What you should be is nowhere near here.'

Her smile faded. She put her hands on her hips. 'Let me guess. Dolan? Or Harry?'

'Both.'

'Fuck, Peake. Are you a baby or something?'

He didn't respond.

'Whatever.'

She turned to move away but Peake grabbed her shoulder.

'Do you want to...' He trailed off. He didn't know why.

Her anger didn't last long as she stared into his eyes. And he really didn't want her to go either. Honestly? He was more than pleased to see her, and she looked great. Tight jeans again, leather jacket over a halter neck top. No makeup – she didn't need it – and the gentle waves of her hair framed her face so perfectly, a look cover stylists would take hours to achieve on their model clients. And her eyes...

OK, enough of that.

'You want some coffee?' he asked.

She lifted her head slightly as she sniffed. 'Do you actually have some, or is this like the other night?'

'I actually have some.'

'Shame, we could have gone straight for the heavy stuff.'

'Still could.'

'But it smells nice. Why not.'

They both headed in, Peake's eyes searching along the corridor, half expecting the Laffertys to be right there, spying. They weren't. He shut the door.

'You been here long?' Katie asked as she stripped off her jacket. She caught Peake staring and he looked away sheepishly.

'A few hours.'

She laughed. Kind of. Looked at him like he was an idiot.

'Oh. I mean... not too long. A few months.'

'Since you got out of prison?'

How much did she know? Had her family told her about his past? What they knew of it, at least.

'Pretty much,' he said.

'It's nice,' she said, and she sounded genuine enough.

'It does a job.' He hated it. Perhaps more so because he hated Chan though.

'And Jelena...' She held his eye and he tensed a little as he awaited the rest of the statement. 'She likes you.'

'You think?'

'I definitely do.'

'We're just... neighbors.'

Katie looked at him dubiously.

'We look out for each other,' he added.

'That bruise to her face? Not you, I guess.'

'Of course not.'

'You know who did it?'

'Why are you asking that?'

She shrugged. 'Don't really know.'

'You probably shouldn't be here,' Peake said.

She rolled her eyes. 'I thought we did this bit already. So come on, tell me what they said.'

Peake thought then sighed and walked to the kitchen and poured two coffees to waste some more time.

'How do you take it?' he asked.

'However you want.'

He dropped a cube of brown sugar in each and moved back over to her. She took the mug and cradled it and stared at him.

'Nice delaying,' Katie said.

'They told me to stay away from you,' Peake said.

'Who?'

'Harry first.'

'So you've met my uncle now?'

'More than just your uncle.'

Did she know anything about the night before, he wondered? What he and her cousins had been up to?

'You're working for him now?'

'Apparently. I'm their new driver.'

She laughed. 'Wasted talent, I think.'

'It's a start.'

'So my uncle told you to stay away from me. Why?'

'He didn't say why.'

'But you agreed.'

'I don't think he gave me a choice.'

'You realize I'm a grown woman. And you're a grown man.'

'Yeah.'

'You don't think I should be allowed to make decisions for myself?'

Peake sipped from his coffee.

'Of course you should,' he said. 'But I also wonder... do you sometimes make decisions just to piss him off? I'm not sure I need to be caught up in that.'

'So you think I came here to cause trouble. To cause you trouble?'

'Did you?'

She shook her head, smile gone again now. He knew if he didn't soften up he'd get on her wrong side. In a way, that could be for the best.

'No,' she said. 'I came here because even though I knew Harry would tell you not to see me, I want to see you. I want to know more about you.'

He stood and thought for a moment and took another sip from his mug.

'Why don't we sit?' he suggested.

They did, both of them on the sofa, up against opposite arms, although Katie folded her legs over so she was pointed toward him. She directed the subject of chat away from her family, onto banal things. Probably what they both needed, but Peake wanted to know more about the Laffertys too, about how she did or didn't fit in.

'You're the only girl,' he said.

'Girl?'

'All your cousins are boys.'

'They all act like boys.'

'I'm still trying to figure out the relationships.'

'Who have you met?'

'Harry, obviously—'

'My dad's younger brother.'

'But Harry's in charge?'

'He is now.'

'Your dad's—'

'In a care home.'

She sank a little in her seat. 'For nearly a year now. He's... It's dementia. You know, when I was growing up, Harry and my dad were like superheroes to me. Before I really knew about... their other sides. They were just so big and strong and confident, and I didn't think anything or anybody could ever hurt them. Or me.'

She paused and put her mug down on the table. Peake sensed she wasn't finished talking so he waited for her to carry on.

'To see him now... His mind's just... gone. He doesn't even recognize most of us. But he does know me still. Every time. And I think...'

'What?'

'Dad and Harry never wanted me to be part of the business. Honestly? They're sexist dinosaurs. But they really love me, I know that... They always made me feel... like I couldn't be part of that, but they didn't want me to go my own way either. I've always felt so trapped.'

Peake nodded, the raw emotion in her voice was unmistakable. He thought again about the marks on her wrists. Had the strong wills of the older men around her pushed her to that, or was there more to the story?

'What about your mom?' he asked.

'Never knew her. She died when I was a baby.'

'Sorry.'

'Yeah. I've been in this world of men my whole life. The odd one out. I don't think I ever wanted to be like them, really. I just wanted to be... me.'

She unfolded her legs and shuffled a little along the sofa before curling her feet under her and leaning toward him, her elbow on the chair-back, her chin on her hand.

'What about you?' She glanced away from him and at the sole picture frame in his apartment.

'My mom,' he said.

'She's still—?'

'In England. I was born there. But I've not been back for a long time.'

'You speak to her?'

'Not in years.'

'Why not?'

'It's... complicated.'

'You should. Because one day you may regret not doing it.'

'I know.'

He hung his head. He didn't want to go there. They sat in silence for a few moments. When Peake caught Katie's eye again, she looked a little more upbeat. At least more upbeat than he felt.

'Who else?' she asked.

'What?'

'Which of the boys have you met?'

'Joey, Sean. Dolan, Chops.'

'Basically all of them then. Family, anyway. Anyone else is just a mercenary.'

Is that how she saw him?

'But I'm struggling to figure the relationships,' he said.

'Just as well you got me as your insider then,' she said with a devious wink. 'Dolan is Joey's big brother...'

That made sense. They both had the same sneery face. And the way Dolan had chastised Joey earlier with the wallet... Definitely a big brother move.

'But there's quite an age gap,' Katie added.

Which again made sense as Dolan looked late thirties, Joey probably ten years younger at least.

'And their dad is?'

'Sam. He's dead now. Heart attack. Five years ago. He was by far the oldest brother. And Chops is Liam's son.'

'And Liam is?'

'In prison. And I don't think he'll be getting out. And, before you ask, it was nothing to do with the business.'

'No?'

'He strangled his girlfriend. An act of madness. Or love. A bit of both, most likely.'

She said it all so matter-of-factly.

'Why is Chops called Chops?'

She raised an eyebrow and looked taken aback.

'That's his real name,' she said.

'Seriously?'

Her face remained deadpan a moment before she burst out laughing.

'Of course not, you idiot. His real name's Gavin. Much more boring. Just like him.'

'He does seem... uptight.'

'I think he was born with a metal rod up his ass. He doesn't fit in at all with the others. But he is... clever. More so than the rest of them combined.'

'So why Chops?'

She laughed again. 'Have you ever seen him eat?'

He shook his head.

She blew out her cheeks. 'He looks like a dumb squirrel with a mouth full of nuts. It's stupid, but there you go. I've no idea who started it, but he's been Chops as long as I remember.'

They fell into silence. Comfortable at first, but then Peake felt more and more awkward as she gazed at him coyly. Like a teen boy sitting next to his crush, her wanting him to make a move but him terrified to do so.

'You want another drink?' he asked.

'Something stronger than coffee...?'

He sighed. 'I would, but I might...'

'What? Need to drive later?'

'Yeah.'

'Don't worry. From what I heard, I don't think the cops would catch up with you anyway.'

Again with that look, like she enjoyed that she knew more about him than he did of her. Which of the guys had she spoken to about him?

'Unless I'm wasted and wrap the car around a streetlight.'

'Suit yourself,' she said, and she jumped up from the sofa and to the kitchen where she started to rummage around. At least he'd put the bourbon away earlier, knowing if it sat looking at him, and him at it, he'd have been unable to stop himself having more. 'You must have something good here somewhere.'

He watched her for a few moments, entertained by her boldness. Entertained just by the sight of her, really. She seemed so carefree and full of life... so at odds with the other side of her he knew lay somewhere within...

She opened the cupboard door where the day before Chops had found the red tin. Did she know about that too? Was she looking for it?

He stood up from the chair and she paused and looked over and he couldn't read the look in her eyes.

'Come on, give me a clue,' she said.

He moved closer and she got to work again. Went low this time. She opened the door of the corner unit and he paused and watched as she gazed inside. She wouldn't see the cash. It was hidden beneath the panel at the back which peeled away if you knew how to angle it.

'Seriously?' she said. 'You haven't got anything good?'

'You're so close,' he said, before flicking his eyes upward when she looked his way.

She straightened up and he moved closer to her, and as she reached up to open the cupboard door he wrapped his arms around her waist and kissed her neck and she sighed and tilted her head to him, her hair falling into his face.

She still went for the door. She opened it.

'I knew it,' she said. 'Vodka, brandy, tequila, whiskey? Yes please.'

She took the bottle of tequila and spun around in his grip to face him, the bottle between their chests.

'Glasses? Or straight from the bottle?'

He didn't answer before she ducked down and slipped out of his arms and bounced a couple of steps before turning and opening the bottle and taking a large swig. Her face scrunched up as she swallowed, and she handed the bottle over to him. He took it and paused for a moment as he stared at her.

Why say no, really?

The bottle was to his lips when his phone buzzed in his pocket. He took a swig anyway and swallowed hard, enjoying the burn at the back of his throat. He could quite happily get wasted with her... again.

But then...

When he looked over, her face didn't seem quite so relaxed and playful as a moment before.

'You want to check, don't you?' she said.

He didn't say anything.

'Why?' she asked.

'Why what?'

'Why do you want to be part of... that.'

'It's not about what I want. I need the work. I need the money.'

She shook her head. 'I don't believe you. You're not that... simple.'

'Meaning what?'

She didn't answer. His phone weighed heavy in his pocket.

'Are we drinking that bottle or not?' she said with a playful pout, clearly not yet ready to give up on him. She struck a pose, hip out, chest up and he tried to stop the smile – to stop the arousing thoughts – but failed.

Still, the next moment he had his phone in his hand.

A simple text from Sean.

> You're needed.

He sighed.

'So that's it?' Katie said, not trying to hide her agitation.

'I'm sorry.'

'Are you?'

'I don't know how long I'll be, but... you can wait here for me if you want?'

Did he trust her?

Except she looked even more irritated by that idea.

'No, Simon. One thing I will definitely not do is sit around waiting for you, or anyone else.' She stormed up to him and grabbed the bottle of tequila. 'For the journey home.'

She pushed past him. She grabbed her jacket and was at the door in a flash. She opened up and turned back to him.

'I'd like you better if you were just yourself,' she said. 'Rather than trying to be like them.'

Real venom in the last word.

She strode off, swigging from the bottle as she went.

14

Trying to be like them? Peake didn't think he was trying to be like anyone. What did Katie not get about his predicament? OK, so she didn't have a job, perhaps wasn't allowed to pursue whatever she wanted to pursue in life because of the overbearing Harry and his out-of-date views. But she was still pretty well-kept given her swanky apartment. Peake didn't have that luxury. He didn't have any luxuries. He had to get on in life on his own. Like he always had.

Did he want to be working for the likes of Harry Lafferty and his family of misfits? No. But he would, if it paid the bills.

'Relaxing afternoon?' Joey asked, a glint in his eye as Peake approached the bar. Did he know about Katie? It really wouldn't come as a surprise.

Joey remained standing there, propped up against the wall with a man Peake didn't recognize. Similar age to Joey, similar style about him, a cocky look in his eye.

'This is Tom,' Joey said. 'Tom, this is our chauffeur for the evening.'

Joey cackled and tossed Peake a key fob.

'Get in,' he said. 'I'll rally the others.'

Joey disappeared into the bar. Peake pressed the clicker and saw the blinking lights in the corner of his eye. Across the street. A shining black Mercedes GL. A beast of an SUV.

He didn't say a word to Tom, whoever he was, just headed across the road and opened the door and sat down in the opulent cabin. Even nicer than the drowned Bimmer.

After a few moments he heard chatter and looked out of the window to see four men striding his way. Joey, Sean, Tom, and another young man.

'How you doing, Peake?' Sean said with a pleasant enough smile as he jumped into the front passenger seat. 'This is Tom and Owen.'

Peake nodded to the newcomers. Newcomers to him, at least.

'So what have we got in store for tonight?' Peake asked.

'Tonight? We party,' Sean said, to which the other three cheered and whooped.

'We party,' Joey said with his usual sneer. 'Not you, Peake. You drive. So get to it.'

'Yes, sir,' Peake replied, with a salute that drew a laugh from the other three and a deeper scowl from Joey. 'Where to, your highness?'

Joey didn't answer.

'Greenwich to start,' Sean said.

Peake got them on the way, enjoying the effortless drive of the Merc, a lot more than he enjoyed the boyish banter of Sean and his cousin and their friends.

'A replacement for the Bimmer?' Peake asked Sean while the three in the back were huddled in a chat.

'Yeah,' Sean said.

'Another one in your uncle's name?'

Sean fixed him a look.

'Yeah,' he said.

'Which uncle?'

'Katie's da.'

'Pretty decent of a man with dementia to keep buying cars for his nephews to run around in.'

The chat in the back had stopped.

'What do you know about our uncle?' Joey asked.

'Not much,' Peake said.

'Power of attorney,' Sean added. 'The only reason he needs his money now is to pay for his care bills. What's left... we use.'

'You think it's not what he would have wanted?' Joey asked. 'He loved us like we were his sons.'

'I wouldn't know.'

'No. Because you don't know him. Or us. So keep your mouth shut about our family, yeah?'

'Message received,' Peake said.

Joey looked away and Peake decided to leave the conversation there. He didn't like Joey. Not at all. But it probably wasn't a good idea to deliberately get on his wrong side. At least not if he wanted to continue getting paid.

'Take the right here,' Sean said.

Peake did so.

'Pull over.'

Again Peake complied and the four piled out in front of a trendy-looking cocktail bar.

'Be ready for us,' Sean said before he shut the door.

'There's no parking here,' Peake replied.

'You're parked, aren't you?'

Sean slammed the door and Peake watched as he and his friends sauntered to the bar. They only stayed inside for twenty minutes on what turned out to be the first of many stops. And the stops weren't in any obvious or even logical order either, nor contained to one neighborhood. Greenwich. Upper East. Meatpacking District. Lower East. Soho. Midtown. A mixture of establishments too. Swanky cocktail bar, sports bar, craft ale bar, Irish. More than once Peake had a cop at his window, insisting he move on as he waited at the roadside. More than once he wasn't in the right place at the right time because of that, meaning he took an earful from an increasingly drunken Joey.

Actually, all of them were becoming increasingly drunken, but while Sean and Tom and Owen became more jolly and animated, Joey became more sullen and sneery. If that were possible.

At quarter to one they arrived outside a nightclub on 36th Street. Eternal. Peake didn't know it. He hadn't been clubbing for… a long time. But it looked like a big place, from the outside at least. Three bouncers stood by the door. A red rope barrier stretched along the street behind which a crowd of forty or fifty youngsters stood waiting to get in.

Sean, Tom and Owen stepped out. Joey opened his door but then hovered. Peake turned around to face him, sure the guy had something to say.

'I know you took the money,' he said.

He glared. Peake held his eye.

'You're not even denying it now?'

'I already denied it. To Harry.'

'You lied to Harry.'

Peake said nothing.

'Just tell me you took it.'

'I didn't.'

'You want to know what else I know?'

'Joey, come on!' Sean shouted over.

'I know she was at your apartment earlier.'

Again Peake said nothing.

Joey smiled, though it was a callous look.

'Yeah, Peake. You might think I'm a dumb runt, but don't underestimate me. I know she was there. I won't tell Harry. This time. But do you know how I know?'

'Humor me.'

'Because I had a guy watch your place.'

Peake gritted his teeth.

'Wanna know where my guy is now?'

'In bed. It's late.'

'No, Peake. He's in your apartment. Looking for that money. And when he finds it...'

Joey drew a finger across his throat before he laughed.

'Shit, buddy, I see the dilemma on your face. You want to speed over there right now, don't you? How long would it take?'

'Joey, for fuck's sake, come on,' Owen said, grabbing his friend's arm.

'But you want this job, right? So you're not going anywhere,' Joey said. 'See you soon.'

Peake remained frozen as Joey slammed his door and joined the others as they walked toward the bouncers. A brief exchange followed, which interestingly Tom led, before the four were let inside ahead of the waiting line.

What the hell was Peake supposed to do? Race home to check everything was OK, and hope he got back in time for them coming out?

That assumed that Joey had even told the truth.

Anyway, there was little he could do, even if he got back to his apartment to find someone in there. He could beat the shit out of them, but if they were connected to Joey, that was hardly the best idea.

A tap on the window shook him from his thoughts. He pressed the button and the glass slid down in silence. One of the bouncers, who had a large, round face to match everything else about him.

'No stopping,' he said with a gruff voice.

'I'm waiting for those guys,' Peake said. 'Sean Lafferty and—'

The bouncer raised an eyebrow and looked really unimpressed.

'Definitely no stopping for you then,' he said. 'Five seconds and I call the cops.'

He moved away. The other two bouncers glared too. Not the response he'd expected, given Sean and crew had just been let inside so easily.

Peake pulled away. He circled the block. Pulled over on the opposite side of the road for a few minutes until he spotted a police squad car coming down the street. He moved on again, performed the same maneuver a few more times. All the time his brain rumbled.

He could have been home and back already.

But then... they surely wouldn't find the cash now. He'd re-hidden what remained of it already. And it wasn't as though he had the full $10,000, still neatly bundled up. Joey and his pals had no way of proving any cash they found had come from the missing batch.

Did they?

Another tap on the window. Actually, more like a thud.

'Hey, I told you before,' the bouncer shouted from outside. 'If you don't move...'

He didn't finish the sentence, because the next moment shouting spilled out from the club entrance. Joey came out through the doors, stumbling about, another bouncer – who'd obviously shoved him – hot on his heels. Then Sean, Owen... no Tom. Another bouncer though. Five against three once the bouncer by Peake's window rejoined his friends.

Joey turned around and hurled abuse. Sean and Owen were angry too, gesticulating with the bouncers who huddled together around the entrance.

Peake stepped out of the driver's seat, debating whether to go over or not.

'I'm going back in,' Joey shouted, chest puffed as he strode toward the wall of bouncers. Sean and Owen joined him, but the bouncers stood their ground, shoving the drunken men back.

Eventually the door opened and Tom staggered out, hand to his nose which streamed blood. One of the bouncers turned and grabbed his shoulder and hauled him away from the entrance.

Joey didn't take kindly to that and lunged for the bouncer...

No, he was simply trying to push past and back into the club.

He shoved the bouncer. The guy stumbled back. The one next to him went to take a swing but Joey suddenly burst into action. The fighter in him. He ducked under the shot, jumped to the side and threw a fist into the big guy's kidney which caused his face to crease in pain. A punishing uppercut made his legs wobble and he collapsed to his knees. The one he'd shoved came back at him but again Joey easily moved out of the way before an arcing right caught the guy on his temple and he collapsed to the tarmac. Didn't even put his hands out to protect himself, out cold from the moment of contact. Sean jostled with the other two bouncers. Tom and Owen pulled him away. Joey bounced on his toes, ready for more. Peake had thought Dolan – the older and taller, more muscular brother – looked like an experienced and well-schooled fighter, but apparently his little brother was far from a novice. Put together with his temperament, it made for a lethal combination.

'Come on!' Sean shouted, as if suddenly seeing sense, and the four of them turned and sprinted for the car.

Peake jumped back in. The other four did the same a

moment later and Peake hit the throttle and the Merc blasted off down the street.

Silence for a few moments as the others settled in and caught their breath.

'You OK?' Sean asked, turning to look at Tom who'd tilted his head back to stop the flow of blood.

'Yeah.'

Then a smile spread across Sean's face. Owen's too.

'Fuck, you caught him there,' Sean said to Joey, mimicking the right hook.

'Bastard was begging for it,' Joey said, pure arrogance, before he looked at Peake. 'Some fucking help you were. Standing watching like a chump.'

All eyes turned to Peake.

'I thought I was just a driver,' he said.

'Yeah. But not for long if that's your attitude.'

'If you want my help...' He shrugged. 'Next time, you got it. Just shout.'

No one said anything to that.

Peake had no idea where they were going next. He was sure they'd all had more than enough to drink. And Tom's nose looked a mess.

'So we're done now?' he asked after a couple of minutes of aimless driving, hoping for an affirmative. Would Katie still be awake?

'Done?' Sean said.

'No, we're not done,' Joey said, a devilish smile spreading across his face. 'Not by a long way. This night's only getting started.'

15

Bullish words from Joey. The alcohol talking. Alcohol mixed with what seemed like a non-stop supply of testosterone. But the night was, in fact, over – at least for Tom and Owen. Even though Peake drove them all onward to another club, Tom's nose wouldn't stop bleeding, not just from the nostrils, but from a gash on the bridge.

'He needs stitches,' Peake said, looking at the back seats through the rearview mirror.

'He'll be fine,' Joey replied. As a fighter himself, he should have known better really.

'He's a mess,' Sean added, sounding and looking disheartened.

'There's an ER not far from here,' Peake said.

Tom didn't like that idea at all. 'I'm not going to a hospital.'

'No bar'll let you in like that,' Sean said.

'Just take me home then.'

Peake waited a moment to see if anyone else would chip in with their thoughts. They didn't.

'OK. Tell me where.'

Not far, as it turned out. Tribeca. Both Tom and Owen got out there. Peake didn't know whether that meant they shared a place, or if Owen was simply going to look after his friend.

'We done now?' Peake asked.

'I told you the answer to that already,' Joey said.

'So where to then?'

Sean looked at his cousin. Joey nodded as though the two of them were on the same wavelength.

'The Bronx,' Sean said, facing front.

Peake didn't move. He had more than a sneaking suspicion why they'd be going there again.

'So come on then, driver,' Joey said. 'Drive.'

Peake did so. Joey's head lolled as they moved up through Midtown, to the Upper East Side. He was wasted. Sean seemed a little more alert. But not much more.

Peake decided to go for it. Hit them when they're down.

'What happened in the club?' he asked Sean. Start small.

'It was nothing.'

'Tom looked pretty bad to me.'

'Some asshole tossed a drink over him. Thought Tom was getting too close to his lady.'

'And then?'

'Joey stuck up for him. Only the bouncers didn't listen to any of that. Threw us out instead.'

'And Tom's nose?'

'The bouncer. The one Joey floored.'

Peake had seen plenty of drunken brawls. Had got himself caught up in them too. He'd rarely seen someone like Joey who not only had the bravado, but the skills to back it up too. The bouncer he'd felled was lucky. As he'd fallen to the asphalt he'd landed on his shoulder rather than his head, which could have been a fatal blow.

'We're going back to the Cubans' place?' Peake said.

'Yeah.'

'Why did they owe you so much money?'

'It wasn't that much money,' Sean said.

'Forty thousand missing. So how much was it in total?'

Sean didn't answer straightaway but Peake felt the guy's eyes on him.

'What do you know about our business?' Sean asked.

'Nothing.'

'The Cubans are new to us, but we deal with anyone who wants to play. The Italians, Chinese, Mexicans, Russians, Serbs, Kurds.'

'Americans?' Peake asked jokingly.

'There's a reason immigrants form gangs,' Sean said, before sighing as though trying to find the words in his drunken state. 'You come to a country that's not your own and most of the locals look down on you. See you as leeches. So immigrants band together.'

'Safety. Familiarity,' Peake said.

'Yeah, but you treat a group of people like shit and you always get the same result.'

'Which is?'

'They take what they want. What they need. They fight back. Through gangs and criminality? Yeah, if that's their only choice.'

While Peake tended to agree with much of that, he didn't believe that Sean and Joey necessarily fitted into that bracket of oppressed immigrants. Their fathers possibly did, when they'd first come to the US, but not the boys. Plus, Sean made their endeavors sound almost noble too. Peake wasn't so sure about that.

He glanced in the mirror, glad to see Joey was fast asleep and snoring.

'So what was the money for?' Peake asked.

'From the Cubans? Gambling. Sports betting, mostly.'

'Is that the main business?'

'No. We're like... a financial insti... institution... for people in need. Money in, money out. We lend money to businesses who can't get loans from the big banks. We take deposits from businesses to keep their money safe. We offer insurance to businesses too.'

So illegal gambling, loan sharking, money laundering and extortion. But Sean described it all as though they were the good guys, helping out the unfortunate.

'My dad's very clear,' Sean said. 'What we do is help people who need us. And apart from the gambling, we steer clear of vices. No drugs, no weapons, we don't traffic people, we don't run prostitutes. Too much harm.'

No harm from illegal gambling, loan sharking, extortion and money laundering? Peake decided not to question that.

'The Cubans came to us,' Sean said. 'They're new around here. We helped them set up a new outlet in the Bronx in exchange for access to our... services. We take a percentage of their take. They agreed to it... then tried to renegotiate.'

Peake turned onto the street. No one in sight tonight.

'Keep going,' Sean said. 'Around the next corner.'

Peake did so then pulled to a stop.

'So what are we doing here tonight?' Peake asked.

'Tonight we get what's owed to us from those bastard wetbacks,' Joey blurted.

Peake hadn't realized he was awake.

'These are Cubans, not Mexicans,' Peake said.

'Cubans, Mexicans, who gives a shit. Sweaty, slimy South American fuckers.'

'Neither Cuba nor Mexico is in South America.'

Joey thumped the back of Peake's seat. 'OK, Mr fucking Geography.'

Peake smiled when he realized Sean was too.

'It didn't look like anyone was home when we passed,' Sean said.

'So what about it, Peake?' Joey asked.

'What?'

'We're missing forty grand because of you. So you can come and help find it.'

Peake turned around to look at Joey but didn't respond.

'You want to be a no-good driver all your life?' Joey asked.

'All my life? This is day two.'

'You owe us. You help us.'

Peake glanced at Sean, wondering whether the calmer of the two would see sense, but he only saw a determination in the man's eyes.

'Three of us is better than two,' Sean said.

'How much?' Peake asked.

'How much?'

'If I help, how much extra will you pay me?'

Joey sneered but didn't say anything.

'If we get the full forty back, you get 25 percent,' Sean said.

'Ten grand.'

Ten grand? Had to be worth it, surely? But then the offer of that specific amount…

'You know how to pick a lock?' Joey asked.

'No,' Peake lied.

'Then come and watch and learn.'

Joey stepped out. Sean did too. Peake waited a moment…

Seconds later and the three of them were walking casually along the darkened street to the house. Peake's eyes scoured the scene around them. No one in sight, and most of the homes were bathed in blackness, the faint glow of lighting beyond windows visible every now and then. They stopped at the stoop to the house where Joey and Sean had previously fled in the midst of a gunfight. No weapons on them tonight.

'Sean, keep watch,' Joey said.

He and Peake moved up the steps to the door.

'Paying attention?' Joey said as he took out his basic tools – small torsion wrenches. Within seconds the lock had released – he was actually pretty skilled – and Joey tried the handle. But the door caught on a chain.

'Fuck.'

'Someone's home, then,' Peake whispered.

'Unless they put the chain on and went out the back.'

'Let me see.'

Peake peered in through the small gap.

'You have a screwdriver?'

Joey held one up.

'Your hands are smaller than mine. If you can get the angle, you can unscrew the panel from the frame.'

Joey didn't look impressed with the suggestion, most likely because he didn't like being told what to do. Still, he got to work. Peake looked over the house. He could hear nothing from within. Over the next minute or so Joey became more and more frustrated, until he dropped the screwdriver.

It landed on the inside, out of reach.

'Fuck this!' he said, not particularly quietly.

'Did you get any?' Peake said, reaching in and pulling on the chain.

'Two screws out. One loose. One I didn't get to.'

Possibly good enough. Peake grasped the chain as tightly as he could in the small space and yanked down. It gave some. He did it again and this time the chain pulled free, but not without a soft clatter as pieces fell to the floor.

He and Joey froze, staring at each other.

'Boys?' Sean whispered from the street.

'We're in,' Joey responded.

Sean bounced up the steps to them.

'Stay here,' Joey said to him. 'Peake, they keep their money upstairs. Back room. A closet. Underneath the floorboard in there.'

'And you know that how?'

'Because that's where it was last time, dickhead. I'll keep watch downstairs.'

Peake didn't move.

'Come on!' Sean prompted.

Peake took a deep breath and headed for the stairs. He made three in silence before a creak on the fourth. He paused. Looked back at Joey in the hallway who willed him on. Peake got moving again and made it to the top with only one more, lighter creak.

He glanced back down below. Joey remained there, Sean out of sight at the front. No sounds from within the house other than from Peake's ascent.

He carried on. Past two closed doors. Snoring beyond one, he thought. He reached the final door at the back. Ajar. He pushed it slowly. The bottom scraped on the rough carpet and his body went more and more rigid.

He slipped through the gap as soon as it was big enough. Too dark to see anything. But he could hear someone inside. Light breathing. Someone asleep.

He took out his phone. Not for the flashlight – too bright. He unlocked the screen and turned the brightness down as far as it would go and tried his best to see what lay in front of him. He really couldn't tell. Two people? It sounded like two. A glint of metal at the far side. Closet handle.

He moved that way. Loose floorboard. Another creak. A heightened snore and shuffling. He froze for several beats. All good. He carried on. Edged the closet door open. He sank to his knees. Felt around in the darkness. Bare wood on the floor. An empty space.

Nothing loose. The boards were locked in place. What the hell?

'Peake, you little prick!' came a top of the lungs shout from below. 'Get down here now, you naughty boy!'

Joey. The bastard.

Peake jumped up. Smacked his head off the top frame of the closet. Movement in the room. Shouting. Confusion. Peake didn't wait for them to grab a phone light or a weapon or whatever else. He ran for the door. Into the hall. A woman stood there across from him, wide-eyed.

'Move!' he shouted, barging past her.

More shouting from behind. Angry. Spanish. A gunshot. He ducked and cowered and jumped most of the stairs, rolling into a heap at the bottom.

He sprang to his feet. No sign of Sean and Joey.

But a man rushed out from the front downstairs room. Nothing on but a pair of white boxers. A hunting knife in his hand which he swung through the air.

Peake blocked with his lower arm and sent his elbow into the man's face. The guy fell sideways, smacking his head on the wall. Peake instinctively ducked again when another gunshot rang out from above. The bullet thwacked into the floor by his feet.

He spun around and raced as quickly as he could out of the front door.

He sprinted along the street. Glanced once, then twice behind him…

As he rounded the corner he saw the gunman emerge…

'Shit!'

Peake ran faster still. So fast he almost lost the rhythm in his arms and legs, and he stumbled, arms flailing, before somehow righting himself.

'Come on, Peake!' Joey shouted from the car, both him and Sean laughing their heads off.

Peake unlocked the car. They jumped in. He followed soon after. He pressed the start button. Floored it. The Merc shot off and away.

Sean and Joey were still laughing a couple of blocks later as Peake's breathing finally calmed.

'Good work, Peake,' Joey said. 'You were like fucking Bambi.'

'You set me up,' Peake said. 'Is that all that was?'

'Cash in a closet? Under a floorboard? How the fuck would I know?'

Peake said nothing.

'Yeah, we set you up,' Joey added. 'Call it part two of your trial.'

'We set you up,' Sean said, holding up a bag. 'But only a little bit.'

'Good distraction,' Joey said with a wink.

Peake didn't know whether to laugh or rage.

'How much?' Joey asked.

'Eight,' Sean said.

Joey grumbled.

'Better than nothing,' Sean said.

'Until they come back after you guys,' Peake said.

Neither responded to that, but both glared at him.

'So what do you reckon?' Joey asked Sean. 'How much does our driver earn for tonight.'

'A grand,' Sean said. 'What do you think, Peake?'

Not exactly 25 percent, but...

'I'm happy with that,' Peake said.

'A grand?' Joey said. 'I was thinking a hundred. After all, he still owes us a fortune. Isn't that right, Mr Driver?'

Peake didn't say anything. None of them did. Not until Peake was parked up in the Lower East Side.

'You can take the car,' Sean said. 'Easier that way.'

Sean slapped some money down on the center console before he and Joey got out.

'Oh, and Peake,' Joey said. 'Sorry about the mess in your apartment.'

He chuckled to himself as he slammed the door shut.

Peake pocketed the money and got on his way. He didn't drive slowly. Shackles off, he wanted to get home as quickly as possible. A small part of him still wondered whether Joey was simply playing him about the earlier threat of his 'associate' raiding Peake's place. Hoped, more than anything, that his apartment remained untouched.

He parked the car on the road around the corner – the closest spot he could find. He strode back to his building, bounded up the stairs. Paused a split second on the sixth floor. His heart sank. The door was closed to, but the splintered wood around the lock was obvious. He moved forward, more slowly. Joey hadn't been tricking him. The asshole had sent someone to break into his home.

He stopped at the door for a couple of beats before slowly pushing it open.

The hallway looked fine. Barely even any mess on the floor

from the forced entry, just a few tiny bits of wood and paint chippings.

It didn't make sense.

His body primed and ready, he moved forward toward the open plan living space. Stopped again when he reached the doorway.

Not the mess he expected at all. But there had been a mess. He knew that because of the small remnants of his broken and torn belongings that remained on the carpet here and there, and because of the three bulging bin liners that sat around the room.

The shape on the sofa moved.

'Simon,' Jelena said, stirring and opening her eyes and groggily sitting up. 'What time is it?'

'Late.'

'I heard them... I... waited for them to leave. I'm sorry.'

He walked to her and sat down on the sofa.

'Thank you,' he said. He reached forward and slightly opened the nearest bag and peered inside. 'You didn't have to do this.'

'I couldn't leave it like they did. It's... This is your home.'

Peake didn't say anything.

'Anything I thought could be saved I left over there,' she said, pointing to the pile of broken things in the corner.

Peake looked over to the kitchen where several doors hung off their hinges or had been snapped off altogether.

'Chan's going to lose his shit,' Peake said.

Jelena laughed. Peake didn't know why. But for some reason he did too.

'But they didn't find it,' she said. 'They never came anywhere near my place.'

He'd expected the same, which was why he'd asked her if he could stash the money over there that morning. Before the scuffle with her client.

'You should get to bed,' he said.

She looked at him and held his eye and the sadness he saw tugged at his heart...

'You had a bad night too?' he asked.

'You know how it is.'

'Not Gregerson?'

'No. I'm sure he won't be back, not after what you did. But you can't change the world, Peake.'

He wasn't sure what she meant by that.

'I'm sorry for... how I handled it,' he said. 'I just... I don't like seeing you hurt.'

'And I'm sorry for shouting at you.'

He patted the torn cushions, only half as thick as they used to be. 'Comfy enough, I guess.'

'And enough space for two.'

She lay back down on her side, legs curled up. Peake sighed and went and spent a minute securing the front door as best he could before he returned and squeezed into the small space on the sofa behind her. After a few seconds she took his hand and pulled his arm to wrap it around her like a blanket.

Moments later her breathing softened and he was sure she was already asleep.

He closed his eyes too. Only wishing he could sleep. But he couldn't. Not at all. Not after what had happened, and with thoughts of Joey's grinning face burning so brightly in his mind.

16

OPERATION ZEUS – DAY 40

'Another day, another bunch of nothing,' came Talos's fed up voice in Peake's ear.

He looked over at Hera, hiding with him in the shade of the arched doorway to the closed-down department store. The way she'd wrapped her headscarf left nothing of her face showing except her eyes. Not just a means of 'fitting in', given her gender, but more importantly making her more unrecognizable.

'Nothing, right?' Peake said to her.

Even with her face so well-covered, he knew the look she gave him in return was far from friendly, and he knew damn well what she and Talos had been up to whenever they got the chance. Peake hadn't breathed a word to Ares or Chief, but he had done his best to at least keep them apart when he could. Like right now, when he'd insisted she come with him on the ground.

'Any sign of him yet?' Minos asked.

He and Talos were in the Jeep, a couple of blocks away. Hermes had stayed home to play with his drone which was somewhere overhead. Ares wasn't involved today. At 8 a.m. a driver had picked him up and whisked him off for a meeting with

Chief – Peake assumed – and they'd neither seen nor heard from him since, even though he knew they had this lead to follow today.

An actual, tangible lead. The first they'd had in days.

'He should have been here by now,' Talos said. 'You said he'd be here. His routine.'

'What am I, his secretary?' Peake said.

Hera sniggered, making her eyes sparkle – apparently she'd forgiven his earlier jibe already.

'And you're sure it's Zeta?' Talos asked.

'Yes. It is.'

'And remind us, Hades, how exactly did you ID this guy?' Talos asked.

'By doing my job.'

'Is that him?' Hera said, nudging Peake in the side.

He studied the man walking along the street for a couple of seconds.

'No,' he said. 'Not him.'

The street went deadly quiet after that. A real, tangible lead? Perhaps Peake had been wrong about that. How much longer would they stick it out before calling it quits? Although he could well-imagine the stick he'd take from Talos if they ended up doing that.

'I'm taking a piss,' Talos said.

Peake shook his head. When he caught Hera's eye she indicated down to his chin.

She mouthed something to him. Off?

She fiddled under her headscarf. Peake did the same to turn his mic off.

'What?' he asked.

'You're sure about this lead?'

'Sure enough.'

'You see why Talos is a bit... wary.'

'Not really.'

'It's just... you, Hades. You're... a closed book.'

'Rule number one, remember.'

'That's not what I'm talking about.'

'Isn't it?'

'It's... None of us knows each other. We don't talk about where we came from, what work we did. But... this lead...'

'What about it?'

'Out of nowhere you found this guy, ID'd him, figured his routine?'

'Out of nowhere? We've been in this city nearly six weeks.'

She shook her head. 'You can tell me. Are you getting intel from somewhere else?'

He stared at her. He knew what she was insinuating.

'I was talking to Talos and he—'

'Put you up to this?' Peake suggested.

She paused. 'No. I'm asking for me. I want to trust you... but... it feels like you know more than you should. You're not just one of us. And I don't know if that's a good thing or not.'

'If I knew more, I wouldn't be standing out here right now, believe me.'

'I just need to know we're all in this together.'

'I've already kept your dirty secret away from Ares and Chief. Isn't that enough to buy your confidence in me?'

Her eyes narrowed a little, as though his mention of her love affair with Talos had insulted her once more.

'He's not a bad guy,' she said.

Peake had nothing to say to that.

'You know, your problem – your problem with each other – is that you're too similar. Pa—Talos just wants to be top dog.'

She'd been about to say his name... He didn't even want to

ask about that. Rule number one apparently didn't mean too much when you were having sex with each other.

'Top dog? I've no interest in a pissing contest,' Peake said.

'Hades, the entirety of human history is one big fucking pissing contest. It spurs us on. Otherwise we'd all still be sitting in caves, telling each stories about berry picking or something.'

He shook his head. He really didn't have a response.

'You do realize, me and Talos...'

'What?'

'I went with him because he took an interest.'

She held his eye. He said nothing.

'I've seen the way you look at me,' she said. She paused again. 'If only you'd asked.'

'I didn't ask because I don't want to jeopardize this op.'

She reached out and ran her fingers across his arm.

'No,' she said. 'That's not it. You know, if you want something, you just need to go for it.'

He shrugged away from her touch. Turned his mic back on.

'I see him,' Peake said, indicating to Hera the man who'd turned onto the street. And he wasn't alone.

'Zeta?' Talos asked.

'And Delta.'

An unexpected turn.

'OK,' Talos said. 'We're here if you need us.'

'I see them too,' Hermes said.

Peake and Hera kept their heads down as the men approached on the opposite side of the street, then set off after them. They took the next left. The targets slowed.

'It's the next building on the right,' Peake said. 'We'll head on past and wait.'

Except the targets didn't stop at the building that he'd watched Zeta enter several times before.

'What are they doing?' Hera asked.

'Guys?' Talos prompted.

'They didn't go in,' Peake said.

'They've made you?'

'I don't know.'

'Then damn well figure it out!'

Zeta and Delta sped up. Peake sensed Hera becoming more on edge. More fidgety, looking around them.

'There's no one following us,' Peake said.

'Confirmed,' Hermes added.

'Wait,' Peake said, gently tugging on Hera's shoulder. 'They're splitting up.'

'They've made you,' Talos said. 'For fuck's sake. Just leave.'

'No,' Hera said. 'If they've made us, we need to see where they run to. It'll tell us a lot—'

'If Ares was here he'd pull you—'

'Ares isn't here, is he?' Hera said. 'I'll take Delta. Hades, you stay on Zeta, he's your guy.'

'I can't follow you both,' Hermes said.

'Delta is heading west, back closer to the Jeep, so Minos and Talos can back me up. You help Hades.'

'Got it.'

She dashed across the road after her mark. Peake moved away after Zeta. The guy was walking much more quickly now. Peake knew these twisting streets, but if he stayed too far back, he could easily lose his prey if he wasn't careful. Yet if he got too close... A foot chase or worse, a confrontation, was the last thing he wanted.

'Shit,' Hera said. 'I've lost him.'

'How the hell—'

'He must have gone inside somewhere. Hades, what about—'

'I still see Zeta, but he's getting further away.'

'Then move quicker!' Talos said. 'Hermes, you see him still?'

No answer.

'Hermes?'

'I can't fly over here. He's going toward the embassy district. There's too much surveillance.'

'Fuck!' Talos shouted.

'It's OK,' Peake said. 'I'm still with him. Pick Hera up and drive the Jeep this way.'

'Understood,' Talos said.

Peake carried on. Zeta took a series of quick turns. They ended up on the tree-lined boulevard where on either side stood the mishmash of buildings containing embassies of various countries from around the globe. Some of the buildings were big and glitzy, others looked more like mini fortresses. Some had been empty since the last civil war. Was Zeta headed to one of these buildings?

No. The guy soon turned onto quieter and far narrower – eerie – backstreets again.

'Hermes, do you see me?' Peake asked. 'I turned from Ninth Street a couple hundred yards back, right after the Iranian embassy. Then a quick left and right.'

'I'm flying around toward there, but I don't see you yet.'

Peake groaned. 'Hera, have you found the others?'

No response.

'Hera?'

Peake turned the corner then froze. An alleyway lay ahead. Fifty yards long. No way out in front. What he did see that way though were two men, glaring at him, at the ready. Zeta wasn't one of them.

Peake spun on his heel but then spotted another two men lunging his way.

'Code red!'

A long blade swooshed toward him. Peake ducked and blasted into the legs of the man holding the weapon. He lifted him off his feet and tossed him to the ground then turned and...

Stopped dead. The barrel of a handgun only inches from his face. The man holding the weapon spewed venom at him in Arabic. Peake only caught a few of the angry words.

'I seriously need help here,' Peake said, sounding calm as anything as he talked into his mic. He wasn't really. 'Four of them.'

The man became more agitated still. Perhaps because Peake wasn't answering whatever question the man with the gun was asking.

'Guys, I really need some fucking help here!' Peake's voice was slightly less calm than before.

He roared and ducked down and threw his arm up to push the aim of the gun off. The man fired. The blast was deafening. Peake fought through the disorientation and hauled his knee into the man's groin. He grabbed his neck, spun him around. Twisted his arm until something popped, then he swiped the gun. Still holding the man around his neck, Peake fired off warning shots, enough to keep the two men who were yet to join the fight at bay.

But the one with the blade...

He swung the knife at Peake's side. Without releasing his hold, Peake couldn't move quickly enough and the blade slashed across his ribs. He yelled in pain and pulled on the trigger again. Leg shot to one of the guys in front. Gut shot to the other.

He let go of the man he was holding and kicked him away. Then Peake sank to his knee, turned and fired again as the man arced the knife for his head. The bullet splatted into the guy's forehead and he collapsed to the ground, the knife falling from his grip and clattering away.

'Hades, I see you again,' came Hermes's voice. 'Guys, for

fuck's sake. Your Jeep's only a hundred yards way. Take a left then right.'

Peake groaned as he pulled himself back to his feet. The three men he'd floored but who were still breathing groaned even more. Peake used his foot to turn over the one with the broken arm. He pointed the gun at his head.

'You piece of shit,' he said. His finger twitched on the trigger.

Sirens. Close by. Then he heard a fast-revving engine.

Peake scooted to the side of the alley, behind a big green trash can, but then saw the Jeep speeding into view and rocking to a stop.

Peake didn't hesitate. He darted forward, even as one of the floored men behind suddenly shouted out.

The back door to the Jeep opened. 'Hades, behind you!' Hera screamed.

He rolled and turned. A shot came his way. It missed and clanked into the metalwork of the Jeep. He pulled once on the trigger. Another hit. This time the guy wouldn't get back up again.

'Get in!' Hera shouted.

Peake dove forward and Minos floored it even before he'd landed. He righted himself and got his senses back and put a hand to his bleeding side and gritted his teeth in pain.

'Toss the gun,' Talos said, matter-of-factly.

Peake did so then closed his eyes as Minos drove like a lunatic, throwing the Jeep left and right.

After a couple of minutes of breathless driving, the sirens had faded and Minos slowed down.

'Everyone OK?' Hermes asked.

'Two dead,' Peake said. 'Two wounded. No idea on IDs. Not our targets.'

'And Hades is bleeding,' Hera said, looking genuinely concerned for him.

'I'll be fine,' Peake replied.

Talos turned around. A smug look on his face.

'Close call, huh?'

'Yeah,' Peake said. 'You didn't hear my cry for help?'

Talos pursed his lips and shook his head. 'Comms blackout. Dunno why.'

'Bad timing.'

'Something like that,' Talos said with a callous grin, before looking back at the front. 'At least we know you can handle yourself now.'

'Comms blackout, yeah?' Peake said to Hera. 'Is that right?'

'Yeah,' she said. She turned away from him. 'Hopefully it doesn't happen again.'

17

For the second morning in a row, Peake woke up with a woman in his arms. Yesterday it'd been Jelena, on the sofa in his trashed – but at least tidied – apartment. Twenty-four hours later and he found himself in a different apartment and with a different woman and an entirely different dynamic.

He gently pulled his arm out from underneath Katie then peeled his naked body away from hers. She murmured and reached down and pulled the sheet up over her shoulders. They hadn't needed the covers in the night. Not just because of the warmth their bodies had generated but because of the masking effect of the alcohol they'd drunk. Peake winced as he moved and held a hand to his throbbing skull. His eyes cast over the empty bottle of vodka and the nearly empty bottle of tequila on the dressing table and the sticky splashes down the drawer fronts. He couldn't remember bringing the bottles into the bedroom. Couldn't remember much about the night, really. No, not quite true. He remembered Katie. Remembered her on top of him.

Before he made the seemingly mammoth task of reaching for his clothes he glanced over at her. If she was trying to stay asleep she wasn't doing a very good job. She turned over onto her back, her face creased in discomfort.

'Shit,' she said, throwing an arm over her head.

'Yep,' Peake said, and Katie laughed. 'We were wasted.'

'You're a bad influence,' she said.

'Me?'

'I seem to remember it was you who wanted to forget about your day.'

Yes, he had said that. But he hadn't meant it quite so literally. Had just wanted something to take his mind off the Laffertys. Well, the male side of the family at least.

They'd drunk a lot. Too much. He'd long known that his 'off switch' for drinking alcohol was faulty at best, but with Katie around it'd broken entirely. Except at least they weren't just drowning their sorrows together, even if now, with his hangover in full swing, he wondered if their being together was actually helping either of them with their problems.

'I need water,' Peake said, standing from the bed and taking a moment to steady himself and to wait for the swirling in his head to subside. He trudged to the en suite and turned the cold tap on and stuck his face then his mouth under the running water.

He jumped when Katie came up behind and wrapped her arms around him. He turned the water off, glanced into the mirror, her face just poking out around his side as her fingers danced across his thighs, working toward his groin.

'Hair of the dog, or something else to get you ready for the day?' she said before kissing his back.

'Something else,' he said.

He turned, grabbed her and lifted her onto the sink. As she wrapped her legs around him he completely forgot about both his hangover and the Laffertys.

* * *

Half an hour later the coffee and eggs he and Katie had made were further helping Peake energize for the day ahead.

'You never did tell me what got you so uptight last night,' Katie said.

Peake didn't say anything as he took another sip of his coffee.

'So?' she said. 'I know it's something to do with my family. What I can't work out is whether you coming to me is because you like me, or just your way of getting back at them.'

'I like you,' Peake said.

'Would you like me as much if being with me wasn't taboo?'

'I could ask you the same question,' Peake said.

Katie fixed him that devilish smile. 'I never said I liked you. I'm in this purely to piss off the others.'

Peake smiled and shook his head. 'You're bad.'

Her smile faded. He wasn't sure why.

'Seriously though... even if I get about as much information from you as from a piece of wood... I don't... I know there's more going on in there, in your head, than just donuts about your new job driving my family around.'

He chewed through a couple of mouthfuls of eggs.

'So?' Katie prompted.

'So what?'

'What happened to you? Before, I mean.'

'There isn't any one thing,' he said. 'I'm just... This is me.'

'No. It's not true. We're all shaped by our past.'

'Yeah. You too.'

'Absolutely me.'

'So you want to tell me about your past?'

She looked really uncomfortable. 'What do you want to know?'

'About the scars. On your wrists.'

Her eyes flickered, welled a little, and he could sense her inner turmoil, how her brain was battling to keep her emotions at bay. Her demons too, perhaps.

'It was years ago,' she said. 'I was a stupid teenager. I don't hurt myself anymore.'

'Why did you then?'

'Harry said it was a cry for help. For attention.'

'Who gives a fuck what Harry thinks? He's not a psychiatrist.'

'And neither are you. And neither am I.'

'So—'

'What about you? I know about the prison time.'

He sighed. She didn't want to talk. Neither did he really. But... 'Like I said to your cousins, like I've said to everyone, I tried to help that girl.'

'What you did sounded pretty vicious.'

He didn't respond.

'Do you regret it?' she asked.

'Of course I do.'

'Hurting those teenagers, I mean, not the fact that it led to you being locked up.'

'Yeah. I do. Because I know I went too far. But... that's...'

'It sounds to me like what happened with those teenagers was a reaction to something else. Same as me cutting my wrists was a reaction. So tell me about the something else. What caused you to act like that?'

He hated that she seemed to have such a good read on him.

'Until I came to New York, I'd spent my whole adult life in the army,' he said. 'Maybe you can figure how that story goes.'

'You saw some bad shit?'

He scoffed. 'No. I did some bad shit. I was... I wasn't a regular soldier. I...'

'Special forces?'

He scoffed again. 'Yeah. I guess that's a way to describe it.' Except the truth was that the assignments he was given were even more secretive, and even more sensitive, brutal, controversial than what the SAS and the like did. 'The army gave me purpose,' he continued. 'I had a life there. And I was damn good at what I did. Wherever I went, whatever I was asked to do, I did it.' He clenched his fists together as old memories surfaced. 'I got too used to that life. To being that man.'

'What does that mean?'

'It means... I was kicked out of the army for attacking a superior officer. Payback, in my eyes.'

She nodded as if she understood, but didn't say anything, and really he'd told only a tiny part of the story. And it wasn't that final incident, nor that he got the boot after, that tormented him but the events that preceded it.

Operation Zeus.

Everything in the army that came before then had shaped who he was – a ready-for-anything combat machine. Yet every pull of the trigger, every plunge of the knife, every life he took or forever changed had tarnished his consciousness, his soul a little more. Still, he'd been the operative the army needed, and so he'd simply carried on to the next assignment. Over and over. Losing sight of the real world a little more each time.

Then came Operation Zeus... From a personal standpoint, the way that op went was really just a culmination of everything that had come before – an inevitable outcome.

But there was simply no coming back from what he'd done out there, and he'd never not hate himself – and what he'd become – because of it.

'After the army, I had nothing,' he said. 'I couldn't go back home, and I had no friends, no job.'

'PTSD,' she said. 'It's pretty damn obvious, Peake. And you wouldn't be the first soldier to find it hard to adjust—'

'It's not as simple as that.'

'But have you tried getting—'

'Help? Part of my parole conditions is going to a self-help group. It's a waste of my time.'

She didn't say anything to that. Perhaps she'd been to similar groups herself.

'The fact is... this isn't about me getting over what I saw others do. It's about getting over what I did. But I won't forget that, or let it be pushed to somewhere deep in the back of my mind. Because if I do that, if I just get on with my life like nothing happened... then... then I really am a monster.'

'You're not a monster,' she said, moving over to him and taking his hands in hers. She kissed his cheek.

Her words were sweet, heartfelt, but they didn't make him feel better at all. Because she really had no clue what he was, or what he was capable of.

Peake pulled from her grip.

'I've got to go,' he said.

She looked really hesitant. 'Thanks for letting me in,' she said. 'If only a little. I know how hard that is.'

He kissed her forehead.

'I'll see you soon.'

He turned and headed for the door.

* * *

He had some time to kill so headed home, yet the awkward conversation with Katie still rumbled as he made his way up the stairs to the sixth floor of his apartment block. He paused there a few moments while listening for any sounds from beyond either his or Jelena's doors.

Yes, she was in. And she wasn't alone. He could hear her moans, and the grunts of her guest. He gritted his teeth, opened his newly mended door and slammed it shut, a little harder than he'd intended. The doorframe and the wall shook and for a few moments the noises in the adjacent apartment died down.

Peake took another cool shower before dressing and putting some fresh coffee on. As he enjoyed his drink, he heard shouting through the wall before Jelena's front door opened. His willpower to ignore it only lasted a moment before he strode to the hall and stared out of the peephole.

Wyatt, the cop, again. He hurled abuse Jelena's way before storming a couple of yards away. Her door slammed shut then the guy launched himself back there and pounded the wood.

Peake really tried to hold himself back, for Jelena, for Katie, for everyone who'd ever questioned his ability to control himself. But his resolve lasted all of two seconds. He flung his door open.

'Is there a problem?' Peake asked.

Wyatt, fist clenched, stopped banging the wood and set his steely glare on Peake.

'Mind your own goddamn business.'

'This is my business. You're disturbing my beauty sleep.'

The guy opened his mouth to say something but then he shook his head and whispered something unpleasant under his breath before turning and skulking off. Peake watched him go before he gently rapped on Jelena's door. She didn't answer so he knocked again, and when she did open up she left the chain on and only opened the door a couple of inches, showing as little of her face as possible.

'I'm busy, what do you want?'

'You OK?'

'Is that why you're bothering me?'

She went to shut the door but he stuck his foot over the threshold to stop her.

'Simon! I told you before, I don't need you sticking your nose in! You're not my protector!'

She heaved the door and he moved his foot back rather than fight. He stood there a moment, brain swimming. He knew she was still standing there. He could hear her heavy breaths and her lighter sobs.

After a few moments he headed back inside to finish his coffee.

* * *

He arrived outside the condo block on the Lower East waterfront five minutes earlier than needed. He'd never been here before. The building's glitzy glass-rich exterior and lofty, shiny entrance gave away the quality and worth of the units it contained. Peake parked in the drop-off spot at the front of the building, shut down the engine and walked up to the bellboy who nodded in acknowledgement.

'I'm picking up Harry Lafferty,' Peake said.

'Go and check with Juan,' the guy said, indicating the doors behind him.

Peake headed inside. Very nice indeed. The lobby even had a fancy water feature – a wall of thick glass behind which bubbling liquid changed color every few seconds.

He went over to Juan at the reception desk who was on the phone to someone upstairs within a few seconds.

'He says you should go up,' Juan said, pulling the receiver from his ear.

Peake indicated outside. 'The car—'

'It's not a problem,' Juan said, waving away whatever Peake had been about to say.

Did all residents get such leeway or only those in the plushest condos?

Or maybe just Harry.

Peake headed up to the thirty-fifth and top floor. Three penthouses there. The door to Harry's was open and Dolan stood outside, looking as mean and menacing as always.

'Morning,' Peake said with as bright a smile as he could muster.

Dolan said nothing but nodded and stepped aside for Peake to move in and along the marble floor of the hallway.

The door behind him closed. Dolan had followed him in.

'Go on,' he said.

The huge living space came into view in front of Peake, but then he sensed movement behind him and even though Peake was ready he didn't fight back as Dolan grabbed him and shoved him up against the wall and pushed his forearm into Peake's throat to pin him there.

'Lover boy,' Dolan said, a snarl on his face.

'You're not my type,' Peake managed to choke out before Dolan pushed even harder on his throat.

'A comedian too?' Dolan said. 'What were you told about my cousin?'

Peake spluttered, showing he couldn't talk, and Dolan let up ever so slightly.

'Which one?' Peake said. 'You've got a lot of cousins.'

Dolan threw a fist into Peake's gut. A solid shot. Not an unpracticed one at all, his whole bodyweight behind it. Peake's insides churned and his brain swam for a few moments.

'Harry told you to stay away from her,' Dolan said. He hauled his knee up into Peake's groin and Peake winced. Dolan let go and Peake slumped down. 'So fucking stay away from her.'

'Kid, that's enough,' Harry said, stepping into view from within.

'Seriously, Harry, this guy?'

'What?'

'Other than ignoring you, and screwing your niece, he's not up to much, is he?'

Dolan slapped Peake's face lightly, as though trying to entice him into a fight. Peake wasn't dumb enough to try. Not here anyway. Not now.

What was it he was thinking earlier about his ability to contain his monster? Shit, apparently he did have what it took after all. What did that say about the times he'd lost it?

'So?' Harry said to Peake after a few moments of silence, as though he was supposed to have answered Dolan's question himself.

Peake straightened up and focused on the older man. He didn't want to see Dolan's gloating face.

'This is where you say something,' Harry said. 'Like providing an answer as to why you directly disobeyed me.'

'She—' Peake started but then stopped himself.

'Maybe this guy actually wants us to bury him,' Dolan said. 'It would explain why he's fucking about around the Cubans too. You know it'd save us the trouble if you just picked up a gun and blew your brains out yourself.'

Harry remained glaring at Peake.

'I like her,' Peake said. 'And she... she likes me.'

'What are you, twelve?' Dolan said.

'Kid, button it,' Harry said, his eyes not leaving Peake. 'I made myself pretty fucking clear, didn't I?'

'Yeah.'

'But you still disobeyed me.'

'Not to hurt or annoy you,' Peake said. 'I listened to her. Maybe other people should too.'

He saw the gut punch from Dolan coming but he didn't do anything to defend it. He stayed bent over for a couple of seconds before facing Harry again.

'You're saying I don't know what's best for her?' Harry said.

'I'm saying she should get a choice.'

Silence. Peake waited for another cheap shot from Dolan. It didn't come, and Harry seemed to mellow a little.

'I admire your balls if nothing else,' the boss man said.

'He'll have no balls if—'

'Dolan, go and check the weather or something.'

Dolan hesitated before grunting and moving off and out of the front door.

'You must see you've gone about this in a very... strange way,' Harry said. 'It wouldn't have been any more obvious if you'd done it on my couch.'

'Would you be more or less pissed off if I'd tried to keep it a secret?' Peake asked.

'Is that supposed to be funny?' Harry asked.

'No.'

Harry seemed to consider Peake's question for a few moments.

'Maybe I do need to let her make her own decisions. Her own mistakes. But that doesn't mean I'm happy about her decision being you.'

'You don't need to threaten me. You don't need to tell me what you'll do if I hurt her. I get it.'

Harry didn't say anything for a while.

'I'm not sure you do,' he said. 'But you know what? I can't

protect her if I push her away from me. For now... I'll go along with what she wants. This time.'

Silence.

'A thank you might work about now,' Harry said, his voice raised.

'Thank you, Harry.'

'My father once told me... be careful around guys who have nothing to lose. Guys who don't care if they live or die.'

He left the comment hanging. Again Peake wasn't sure if he was supposed to respond or not.

'What I see in you... standing there taking shots from Dolan like you don't give a damn what damage he does... I admire your grit. But I worry that you're a lost cause, who doesn't care what happens to him. And you'll drag me or my boys down to wherever it is you're going.'

'That's not it at all.'

'No? I see how you are, moping around. But you know what?'

'What?'

'I'm not sure my father was right. Sometimes it's the guys who have everything to lose that are the biggest worry. Because they become desperate.'

'I guess I see both sides.'

'You do? So tell me about the Cubans. What the fuck?'

Peake slumped a little. He'd expected some comeback to the antics of the other night.

'I only did what Sean and Joey—'

'If Sean and Joey told you to cut off your weenie with a blunt knife, would you?'

Peake didn't answer.

'So next time use your fucking brain. I love them both but when you're out with them, when you're driving them around at 2 a.m. and they're so out of their minds that they think ripping off my business associates is a good idea... give your fucking head a shake. Understand?'

'Yes.'

'Good. So today you're running errands.' Harry reached into his pocket and took out a piece of paper and handed it over. 'Four addresses. Four pick-ups. A straight two hundred gee total.'

'OK.'

'Take Sean with you. He'll do the intros but I want to see something from you today. Something that makes me want to keep you on around here. When you've got the money, you'll go back to the Bronx and back to the place you robbed and you'll walk up to that door and say whatever you need to say to smooth things over. Pay them back the money you took. Eight grand.'

'Out of the two hundred?'

Harry's face screwed in disgust. 'Out of my money? No, you fucking moron, out of your money. You made this mess, you sort it out.'

'Harry, eight grand? I don't have eight grand. Joey and Sean took—'

'Not my problem, is it? Just like Katie apparently isn't my problem now either. You want to do things your way, don't you? Here's your chance. Now get out of my home.'

Peake stood there a few moments, brain whirring as he tried to think of something else to say.

He came up with nothing.

He walked to the door and opened up. Dolan was there, staring with a smug look on his face. Had he heard the conversation, or did he just know already what Harry had planned?

'Can't wait to see how you fuck this one up,' Dolan said with a wink.

18

Peake needed eight thousand dollars by the end of the day if he was to have any chance of still working for Harry Lafferty. Staying in a position where he could see Katie without grief. Eight thousand dollars to stay alive? Was his life on the line if he failed? He really didn't know, but he didn't want to take the risk.

He could pull together nearly half what he needed from the stash at Jelena's apartment and his recent takings, but without resorting to theft, he didn't have a whole lot of options for gathering the rest.

First up he headed to collect what he already had. He put his ear close to Jelena's door before knocking – all quiet beyond now. He heard her soft footsteps a few moments later and she once again opened the door with the chain in place.

'What do you want?'

'Can I come in?'

'Why? So you can—'

'I need my money.'

She seemed to consider that, as though deciding whether she believed his motive or not. Without saying anything either way she pushed the door closed and took the chain off before opening up, though she still hid herself behind the wood as much as she could.

'Come on,' she said.

Peake stepped in and Jelena closed the door.

'Wait there,' she said before hobbling off. Peake watched her go. She wasn't moving freely at all though he couldn't quite tell what part of her hurt.

He moved forward a little along the hall as he listened to her rummaging beyond. As ever her apartment smelled... homely. Smelled of her, her perfume, her natural sweetness. He liked it. It made him feel so calm and... something else he couldn't describe.

He hated that she shared this place with those bastards. Not just men who used her and who cared so little for her, but men who abused her. He'd scared off Gregerson, even if she'd scolded him for it. He wasn't against scaring off the others too. But perhaps he needed to be more discreet next time...

'This is all of it,' she said as she limped back up to him with the plastic bag in her hand.

'What happened?' he asked.

She kept her head down, avoiding his eye.

'Who hurt you this time?'

'Peake, please—'

'That policeman?'

She shot him a look. A look of fear and desperation.

'You should leave,' she said.

'Tell me what he did.'

'I've told you before, it's nothing to do with you!' she shouted.

'I can't—'

'What?'

Peake held his tongue.

'And what about you, anyway?' she said. 'Want to tell me about that?' She indicated the bag. 'About where you got that? About the men who came looking for it? About where you're going with it now?'

Peake didn't answer.

'See. It works both ways.'

'Telling you would only open you up to danger.'

'Exactly,' she said, reaching for the handle. She opened the door. 'Please. If I need your help, I'll ask.'

Peake stepped out and she closed the door behind him without another word.

As frustrated and angered as he was both by her attitude with him, and the idea of those guys hurting her, Peake didn't hang around. He needed to get moving, even if he didn't yet have the money he needed.

* * *

Peake hadn't been to Sean's place before, which it turned out was housed in an old converted warehouse in ever-trendy Soho – for some reason not the type of place, or location, Peake had expected. He didn't bother to get out of the car, just honked the horn and waited. Not long after he spotted Sean's face at the tall second-floor windows. Sean kind of waved then disappeared from view. A couple of minutes later the thick, oversized entrance door to the building opened.

A tall, leggy woman, flowing blonde hair, strode out first, a confident look in her eyes, her lips in a well-practiced pout as she locked on to Peake's gaze. Sean came up behind her, slightly shorter than her, given her heels. She spun around and wrapped her arms around his neck and the two of them kissed unashamedly in the middle of the street, until Sean broke contact and pushed her away, her giggling like a kid.

She again caught Peake's eye before she pulled a pair of glitzy sunglasses on and strode off along the street, hips swaying along with her designer handbag.

Sean jumped into the passenger seat.

'She's something, right?'

'Girlfriend?' Peake asked.

Sean smacked his arm – not hard. 'Pretty much. So don't go getting any ideas.'

'I wasn't,' Peake said.

He took out the piece of paper Harry had given him earlier.

'Yeah, I know about the collections,' Sean said. 'But we've loads of time. I need to hit up a friend in Tribeca first. It's not far.'

Peake pulled out and headed off in that general direction.

'I know what you're thinking,' Sean said.

'You do?'

'Yeah, she's a model. Proper catwalk stuff. This is New York, right? And yeah, I get it, she wouldn't be anywhere near me under other circumstances. But she's Irish. Her grandfather knew mine. And anyway...'

He trailed off, his demeanor souring a little and Peake wondered what Sean had decided to hold back on.

'That said, she's got a lot of model friends too,' Sean said, face brightening once more. 'Some hotter than her. If it doesn't work for you with my cousin...' Sean winked at him. 'But you know something? You haven't seen high maintenance until you've seen those girls. You think Katie's hard work, think again. You'd slit your wrists after a few days.'

Peake winced a little at the last comment as he thought of Katie. He hadn't considered her as being high maintenance, just... complex. But did he really know her?

'You don't seem as angry about me and Katie as the others,' Peake said.

'It's her life. I'm not saying you're the man for her, or anything like that, but it's not really my business, is it?'

Sean laughed. Peake didn't ask why.

'The thing with Katie... Harry's always been for the hardline approach. His way or the highway. Her dad was the same. But it's never rubbed with her. The more you tell her not to do something, the more likely she is to do it.'

Peake had suggested something similar to her himself. He also noted more than once now Sean's use of his dad's first name. What was that about?

'Is he the same with you?' Peake asked and Sean didn't answer straightaway and when he glanced over Sean had a pensive look on his face. The question had struck a chord.

'I'm out running errands with you,' Sean said. 'While Joey's been given a step up to go off with Dolan to woo the Arabs.'

'The Arabs?'

Sean waved the question away – disdain. 'Chops reckons they're the future of our business. He met this guy at university. Son of a billionaire sheikh or something. Their family has more money than most countries. So we're buttering them up.'

'Meanwhile you get sent out on collection duty with lowly me.'

'Exactly,' Sean said, sounding a little sulky. 'No offense.'

'None taken.'

'Take the right here. Park up on the corner.'

Peake did as instructed.

'The thing with Harry is...' Sean sighed and looked out of his window, as if deciding whether he really wanted to open up to Peake or not. 'He's never seen me as anything other than his little boy. He says, to my face, that he wants me to take over one day, but he doesn't trust me to do anything but the basics.'

'Maybe he's just looking out for you. Protecting you.'

'No, it's more than that. He's a control freak who doesn't like to be challenged. And he's always looking for any reason to keep me at the bottom. It's almost like he's afraid of... being shown up by me. Most fathers would be proud to see their son flourish. Not Harry.'

Peake didn't know either man well enough to comment, though he certainly sensed genuine tension in Sean's words. He felt ever so slightly sorry for him.

'So I get to keep you company for a while,' Sean said. 'At least until Harry gets over the mess with the Cubans.'

'The Cubans?' Peake said. 'Harry's blaming you for that?'

'Me and you.'

'What about Joey?' The way Peake saw that night, Joey was the bad influence, the unhinged one not caring if his actions caused problems for Harry and the others.

'Joey's got a way with words,' Sean said. 'He knows how to play the old man.'

'He left you in the shit? You let him do that to you?'

Sean shot Peake a glare. Perhaps he'd stepped out of line.

'I know Harry asked for the money back,' Sean said. 'Eight grand, from you.'

'Yeah.'

'You're not going to ask me about that?'

'Ask you what?'

'Ask me to give it to you. So you're not out of pocket.'

Peake stared at his passenger for a few seconds but said nothing.

'You know what I find curious about you?' Sean said.

'What?'

Sean laughed. 'Actually, pretty much everything. But you came to us, desperate for money. We gave you a little. Then ten grand went missing. We got you a little more from the Cubans. Know you owe us. But you haven't cried about it. You haven't complained. So what's the game?'

'I'm not sure what you're asking me.'

'I know Joey had your place turned over. And they didn't find the missing money.'

Was that why Harry was insisting on Peake paying back the eight thousand himself? A further test to see if Peake had the stolen cash or not?

'So are you good for eight?' Sean asked.

'No. Not all of it.'

Sean smiled. 'I'm kinda glad to hear that. But you haven't asked me to help you out either. To give you the money I'm sitting on from that night. Why?'

'Mostly because I thought you'd tell me to piss off.'

Sean laughed again. 'Yeah. And if you'd asked Joey he'd probably have knocked you out. And I'm sorry, Peake, but you're not getting my share from that night. But that doesn't mean I won't help you out.'

'Then what?'

Sean winked. 'Wait by the car,' he said. 'You see a big Black dude coming down that fire escape, you grab him for me.'

And with that Sean got out of the car and moved up to the door of the building in front of them. Peake waited until Sean opened the door and disappeared inside before he stepped into the open, his brain whirring with the guy's words. He lit up a cigarette, hoping the hit would help him think straight.

He spotted an NYPD squad car coming his way. Peake kept one eye on the car as it approached. The passenger locked eyes with him for a moment... then the lights flashed on and the car sped up and shot off down the road.

Peake let out a long exhale. Then heard shouting from within the building. Banging too. Crockery smashing. A thud. A woman's scream. What the hell?

The window by the fire escape shot open and a pair of legs poked out. One bare foot, the other with a white sock. More shouting and the feet disappeared a moment then a grunt of pain. Sean?

Peake stubbed the cigarette out with his foot as the man blasted out of the window above him. One white sock. White boxers. Nothing else.

He ran down the creaky metal stairs. A woman appeared in the window and tossed out a pair of jeans. Then a shirt. Then a shoe, followed by another. The second one smacked the big guy on the back of his head but he didn't take notice.

Was she attacking him or helping him?

The door to the building burst open.

'Stop him!' Sean shouted.

Peake rushed for the guy. Despite his size he looked... startled.

'OK, OK!' he shouted, backing up, hands out in defense as Peake and Sean circled.

'You alright?' Peake asked Sean who had a dribble of blood coming from his nose.

'His woman isn't as friendly as he is.'

'Sean, I'm sorry,' the big guy said, looking like he might wet himself. 'She didn't know.'

'But you know,' Sean said. 'So why'd you run?'

'I'm sorry.'

'Just give me the fucking money.'

'It's here,' the man said, crouching down for his jeans, still holding his hands up to show he wasn't reaching for something.

'Go on then,' Sean said.

The man, hands shaking, took out a rolled wad of bills and tentatively handed them out to Sean. He swiped them and pocketed the money.

'Peake, give him a slap.'

'What?'

'Slap him.'

Peake looked at the guy who cowered away. He took a step forward.

'We haven't got all day,' Sean said. 'Come on!'

'Sean, please,' the man said.

Peake took another step and pulled his hand back and slapped the guy across his cheek. Not too forcefully. He felt like such an idiot.

'Fuck, Peake, is that all you've got? This is a slap.'

Sean stormed forward but the next moment a woman came darting out of the still-open door wielding a bread knife.

'Leave him alone!' she screamed as she rushed forward.

'Baby, no!'

She lunged at Sean who side-stepped, avoiding the half-hearted swipe.

'Come on,' Peake said, pulling on Sean's shoulder and indicating the two uniformed NYPD fifty yards away who'd just turned onto the street.

Peake and Sean rushed for the car. Peake fired up the engine and swung the Merc around as the woman wrapped her arms around the big man.

'Bitch!' Sean shouted as they set off down the street.

'What the hell was that?' Peake said after a few moments, content they were in the clear.

'He owed me. Apparently, his missus didn't agree.'

'Owed you for what?'

'Something on the side,' Sean said. 'Something Harry doesn't need to know about.'

Sean took the cash out and unrolled it and flicked through. 'Five thousand, two hundred.'

Peake said nothing.

'How much do you need?' Sean said.

'About four.'

Sean rolled the money back up and tossed it at Peake and it bounced off him onto the car's floor.

'There's your day's takings, too.'

'Thank you,' Peake said.

'Like I said. This is something Harry doesn't need to know about. There's plenty of money in this city, Peake. You stick with me, I'll help you get your hands on it. What do you say?'

'I'm happy if you're happy.'

Sean nodded and chuckled.

'Now that, my friend, is a good fucking answer.'

19

The first three pick-ups of the day, all in Manhattan, went smoothly and without incident. On each occasion Sean waited in the car while Peake did the business. A chance for Peake to get to know Harry's 'clients', according to Sean. Or was it only that Sean wanted Peake to take the risks? It wasn't as though seemingly straightforward pick-ups always went to plan. Just look at what had happened the first time they'd tried to collect from the Cubans.

Perhaps it was that this set of collections was so routine, so lowkey, in the grand scheme of Harry's business, that any old idiot could do it...

'Brooklyn next?' Peake said when Sean had finished counting the last haul – sixty thousand off the Kurds.

'Yeah.'

Peake headed off in that direction for the longest journey of the day.

'What happened with the Cubans?' Peake asked.

'What do you mean?' Sean said, sounding a little defensive.

'That first time. When they underpaid. When you and Joey ran out of there.'

'They were trying it on, that's all.'

'But Harry still wants to work with them.'

'Whatever morals he says he has, Harry works with anyone who makes him money. As long as it's on his terms.'

Peake wasn't really sure that answered his question.

'Do you trust them?' Peake said.

'The Cubans?'

'Yeah. We could be walking into a trap later.'

'We?' Sean said, smiling. 'I'm sending you out there on your own.'

Peake had already guessed as much.

'But can we trust them?' Sean added. 'Honestly? I don't know for sure. But Harry's done a lot of legwork, according to him at least, to clear the air. The main guy... Gonz... he's alright. It's the youngsters around him that are a bit... feisty.'

Kind of like Harry and the youngsters around him then, Peake thought, but didn't say.

'Gonz...' Peake said. 'As in, Gonzalez?'

Sean gave Peake a curious look, eyebrow raised.

'It's a Spanish name,' Peake said with a shrug.

'Think his real name's Pinto or something.'

'So why Gonz?'

Sean smiled. 'As in, Go NZ. Go New Zealand.'

'I thought they were Cuban?'

'Apparently it's an in-joke.'

'An in-joke you know?'

Sean shrugged. 'Not that exciting, really. They were watching the New York Marathon. It goes right past where they live. This other group had signs and T-shirts all saying "Go NZ". The old guy got all excited cause he thought maybe a Cuban was running or something. Gonzalez, like you thought. So he's shouting for Gonz all morning until one of them tells him they were cheering on some New Zealand runners.'

Sean laughed. Peake didn't say anything.

'I guess it probably made more sense to them. Perhaps you had to be there.'

'Generally the case with in-jokes and nicknames.'

'Probably. You ever have one?' Sean asked.

'A nickname?'

'Yeah.'

Did Hades count? Not that Peake wanted to go there.

'No,' he said.

'Huh,' Sean said, as though he didn't believe him.

'You?'

'Donkey,' Sean said.

'Donkey?'

'Donkey schlong. Donkey Kong. Get it?' Sean winked again, looking pleased with himself. 'Another reason why I can keep a supermodel interested.'

Peake really had nothing to say to that.

They'd soon passed through most of Brooklyn, edging closer and closer to the coastline at Brighton Beach.

'The Russians still run most of this?' Peake asked.

'Russians?' Sean said. 'This is NYC, not Moscow.'

'But—'

Sean laughed. 'Jesus, Peake, yeah they're Russian. They don't call it Little Odessa for nothing. Now these guys...'

'What?'

'Some people work for Harry, some people work with Harry. Here... we work for them. These guys have connections you wouldn't believe, and they're sadistic bastards when they want to be. So keep it calm and easy.'

'You're really selling it to me.'

'You wanted a job,' Sean said. 'And you are fucking Harry's niece. You could call this payback.'

They stopped outside a shabby-looking brick tower block. A huddle of beefy men stood on the outside.

'It's all you,' Sean said.

Calm and easy. Peake got out and casually walked up to the group, who parted a little to stand their ground around the building's entrance.

'Afternoon, gents,' Peake said. 'I'm collecting for Harry Lafferty.'

The oldest and shortest of the group cupped his ear and rattled off something in Russian.

'I'm collecting for Harry Lafferty,' Peake said again, as clearly as he could.

With that the old guy whipped out a handgun and lunged a couple of steps to push the barrel close to Peake's eye. Peake didn't flinch. The Russian shouted vitriol in a strange combination of English and his mother tongue.

Peake still didn't react, just slowly held his hands up to – hopefully – show he wasn't a threat.

Silence. A standoff. One of the others patted Peake down, then the old guy laughed and the others joined in. Peake didn't.

'You're a cool guy,' the man said in accented English.

'Thank you.'

'You Irish?'

'No.'

'So why are you driving around with Sean Lafferty?'

The guy looked over Peake's shoulder, back at the car.

'It's a job.'

'A job. You do whatever they tell you to do?'

'Yeah.'

'So you like taking orders like a little bitch?'

'Don't we all?'

The guy's face twitched like he couldn't decide whether to smile or not. In the end he did neither.

'He too scared to come and say hello?'

'No,' Peake said. 'They wanted me to get to know the rounds. Call it my... initiation. I'm only here to collect. Not to socialize.'

'Huh.'

The guy continued to stare at Peake.

'So have you got anything for Harry or not?' Peake asked.

The old guy turned and nodded to one of the others who scuttled off into the building. No one said a word before the man came back out with a small black holdall which he dumped by Peake's feet.

'Is it all there?' Peake asked.

'You tell me.'

Peake took the bag. 'I guess I will. Nice meeting you.'

He held his hand out. The guy didn't take it. Just spat on the floor. The globule landed all of an inch from Peake's toes.

He said nothing as he turned and moved back for the car.

'They give you shit?' Sean asked once Peake was back in the driver's seat.

'Not much. I don't think they liked that you didn't say hi.'

Sean huffed. 'They're only soldiers. Otherwise I would have. Let's get out of here.'

He sounded far less relaxed than at any other point during the day.

Peake pulled away, his eyes busy in his mirrors.

'You recognize that SUV?' Peake said, indicating the Grand Cherokee a couple of cars back.

Sean whipped around in his seat.

'Shit,' he said. 'Feds, do you think?'

'No,' Peake said. 'But I'm pretty sure I saw the same car earlier too.'

'You serious? Why didn't you say anything before?'

'Because it wasn't suspicious then. Only now that I've seen it again.'

'And how do you know it's not the Feds then?'

'I don't know for sure. But if it's the Feds, if they were planning a sting, they'd have swooped when I took the bag from the Russians. But they weren't even in sight then.'

'You're not filling me with much confidence here.'

'Any reason why anyone else would follow us?'

'No,' Sean said, taking out his phone. 'But I'll get someone to run the plate.'

He spent a minute or so on his phone. Peake had no idea who he called, and he decided not to ask.

'They still there?' Sean said to Peake when he'd finished.

'Yeah.'

'OK. Time to do your thing. Lose them.'

'With pleasure,' Peake said with a smile as he thumped the accelerator.

Not even hard. He lost the tail before they made it back to Manhattan, Sean finally letting go of the dashboard as Peake slowed and they headed across Brooklyn Bridge.

'Time for the final call,' Sean said.

Peake glanced at the clock. 'You don't want to drop this lot off with Harry first?'

'Who says it's going to Harry?' Sean said with a determined stare which lasted a couple of seconds before he smirked. 'You should see your face. I'm not going to screw him. But this money stays with me. You don't need to know what for. So let's just get this business with the Cubans done. Then we both go home happy.'

'If you say so.'

The sun rested on the horizon as Peake wound the car through the ever more familiar streets of the Bronx. One more stop, then Peake could start to think about the evening. Katie?

'May as well park right outside tonight,' Sean said.

'Yeah,' Peake said, pulling the car over not long after.

He turned the engine off, but neither of them got out.

'What are you waiting for?' Sean said.

'All me again?'

'Whatever I might think about what happened before, this is your mess to clear up. Plus, I'm looking after these.' Sean tapped the bag beneath his feet. The other three remained out of sight in the trunk.

'Fair enough,' Peake said.

No one in sight as he made his way to the entrance. Although he didn't get there before the door swung open and two angry-looking men came out. He kind of recognized one of them from the previous night. And he didn't look happy.

Much like in Little Odessa, Peake stayed calm as the men showed their weapons. The one Peake had struck the last time had a handgun which he held casually by his side. The other held on to a machete which he swooshed through the air, bringing the blade to a stop a hair's width from Peake's neck.

The guy launched into a tirade in Spanish – pendejo the only word Peake caught. Not the worst insult ever, but certainly delivered with a bit of venom.

'On your knees.' He finished his monologue in English that was so heavily accented the words were almost unintelligible.

Peake did as he was told without question and the machete followed him down. The other man checked Peake for weapons. Satisfied, he resumed his casual position with his gun.

'You're the one who came into my home?'

'Yeah,' Peake said.

'You wanted to hurt me? My sister?'

'No.'

'Then why?'

'You owed us money.'

'We owed you shit.'

'My mistake.'

'You shouldn't have done that.'

'I'm sorry,' Peake said, rather than launching into the whole story of his night with Joey and Sean and their involvement and how really it had started with the Cubans trying to screw Harry in the first place.

'You have our money?'

'Yes,' Peake said.

'Hector, Leo,' came a gritty voice from inside and all eyes turned to the old man who stepped out. Wiry gray hair, a walking stick in one hand which wobbled in his shaky grip as he tried to keep his steps steady.

'You must be Harry's new man,' the old guy said, his voice hoarse.

'I guess so,' Peake said. 'And you must be Gonz.'

For some reason he took a slap to his face for that comment, from the man holding the gun.

'Leo, it's OK,' Gonz said. 'This is our friend, yes?'

'Yeah,' Peake said.

'Come on, get up.'

The other guy – Hector – moved the machete away from Peake's neck and he slowly rose up.

'The last time was... a misunderstanding, yes?' Gonz said, placing a hand onto Peake's shoulder.

'Yeah. One that I'm very sorry for.'

He reached for his back pocket and Hector and Leo tensed a

moment until Peake very carefully pulled the envelope out into the open.

'Eight thousand,' Peake said. 'Repayment.'

'Eight makes us even, it doesn't make this right,' Leo said.

Gonz took the envelope and all three of them stared at Peake.

'This is what Harry agreed,' Peake said.

'But Harry's not here, is he?' Hector said.

'Then what are you suggesting?'

Hector leaned over and whispered into the old man's ear. Gonz nodded, as though he understood, and agreed with whatever was said. Peake glanced over his shoulder a couple of times, thinking through his moves if he needed to make a break for it...

The car was right there. He couldn't see Sean at all from his angle though. Did the Cubans know Peake wasn't alone?

'Look—' Peake said.

But he didn't say anything more when he – and the three Cubans – all turned their attention to the fast-approaching car that had turned into the street, engine growling. The old man instinctively stepped back as the black SUV burst toward them. Tires screeched and two men – balaclavas on their heads – jumped out of the passenger side. Both were armed. Uzis.

'Get down!' Peake shouted as the men opened fire, peppering the stoop with bullets.

Peake spun and launched himself for the old man, grabbing him and hauling him down behind the trash cans at the front. Hector returned fire but wasn't even checking his aim as he cowered for cover.

Peake yanked the machete free from Leo's grip and jumped up before vaulting the trash cans into the open. One of the shooters spotted him but he didn't spot the spinning blade that Peake launched through the air until too late. The curved edge slashed across his thigh and he yelled as he pulled his Uzi up in panic to fire uselessly into the air.

'Peake!' Sean shouted from his left. He was out of the car. A third man stood there, handgun to Sean's back.

Peake didn't stop. He ducked and weaved and grabbed the now bloody machete from the road and swiped at the second shooter. The blade caught him on the shoulder as he struggled to keep up with Peake's speedy and erratic movements, his aim off right up to the point the Uzi came free from his grip as he clutched at the gaping wound. Peake grabbed the man around the neck and pushed the blade to his skin.

'Let him go!' he shouted to the man by Sean.

'The money or he's dead!'

'Let him go or you're all dead,' Peake said.

A moment of doubt... Sean made his move. Peake smacked the butt of the machete onto the back of the man's neck and swiped his legs and his head crashed off the metalwork of the SUV as he fell. Peake rushed forward again. Sean wrestled for control of the gun. A wayward shot splatted into their car. The barrel of the handgun twisted toward Peake...

A single swipe with the machete put an end to that. The ultra-sharp blade sank through bone and flesh, severing the arm just below the elbow. The man screamed in pain and panic and Sean let him go and with the red mist fully descended Peake was about to deal a further blow before a shout from behind.

'Don't!'

The driver. Half out of the car. Gun pointed, but he didn't fire.

'Come on!' he shouted to his friends.

The two by the car scrambled back in. They called to the man by Peake's feet but then Gonz's men finally rejoined the battle, firing on the SUV. With the renewed onslaught the driver didn't hesitate and a moment later the Grand Cherokee shot off down the street, leaving the armless man screaming in agony on the tarmac.

Only then did Peake become aware of the cries of pain from by the house where Gonz lay sprawled by the open door.

'He's hit!' a young woman shouted out as she rushed from the house.

'Get him inside,' Peake said.

'What about him?' Sean said, indicating the man in the road.

'Him too.'

Together with Hector and Leo they took both injured men through the house into the kitchen at the back.

'He's dying!' the woman said as Hector and Leo stood guard over their bleeding prisoner.

Peake ripped Gonz's shirt open. A single bullet hole.

'Collapsed lung,' Peake said as Gonz rasped and gasped for breath, a horrible sucking wheeze accompanying each attempt. 'We need to release the pressure from his chest cavity.'

'We need to call 911!' the woman sobbed.

'No,' Gonz somehow managed to say, grabbing her hand.

'No police. No ambulance,' Hector confirmed.

'Unless someone else has already called,' Peake said.

'No one around here will call.'

Spoken confidently enough.

'We have a doctor,' Leo said. 'But it could take time.'

'He doesn't have time,' Peake said. 'Get me a skewer. A ball-point pen.'

Everyone looked at him.

'Do it!'

The woman set into action and thirty seconds later had the two items.

'Hold him steady.'

Several sets of hands grabbed Gonz.

'I'm sorry,' Peake said. 'You won't like this.'

He put the skewer through the plastic case from the pen then used his fingers to find a spot between Gonz's ribs. He placed the tip of the skewer against the skin before pushing with a short, sharp thrust. The skewer pierced the skin and within seconds several inches of the metal disappeared as Gonz writhed and cried out. Peake pushed and twisted the plastic case through the hole. Not an easy task, not a pleasant task, but he managed it and pulled out the skewer to leave the tube in place and everyone kind of froze as they stared at Gonz, listening to the whistle as the air escaped through the hole in his side.

'He's not fixed,' Peake said. 'Not by a long stretch. But he won't die just yet.'

'Thank you,' the woman said, tears streaming down her face.

Neither Hector nor Leo said anything but both held apologetic – if slightly shocked – faces.

'What about him?' Sean said, indicating the one-armed man on the floor who'd lost so much blood he was barely conscious.

'You don't need to worry about him,' Hector said. 'Don't worry about him at all. We're all good here.'

'You're going to kill him?' Peake said, surprised that he cared. Moments ago he'd been about to deliver a fatal blow to that man – but that had been in the heat of a gunfight, not in cold blood.

'You should probably go now,' was the only response he got to the question. 'Tell Harry thanks for the money.'

Peake didn't move. Hector's face soured. He edged forward.

'Come on,' Sean said, hand on Peake's shoulder.

The two of them turned and walked out, and were soon back by the car.

'Check the bags,' Peake said. 'Just in case.' They'd been in the house several minutes, the car unattended.

A couple of moments later they'd done so. All the money remained.

'You saved him,' Sean said – in awe? – as Peake started up the engine and pulled away. 'In fact, I think you saved all of us. The money too.'

Peake said nothing.

'And I'll make sure Harry knows it.'

'Thank you,' Peake said, happy for the compliment, but trying his best not to dwell on the fate of the one-armed man.

20

OPERATION ZEUS – DAY 41

Peake took a seat on one of the uncomfortably hard chairs in the dining area of the safe house, wincing as he did so. No chance of him slouching down in a sofa with the recently stitched wound in his side. The knife wound wasn't the worst injury he'd ever had, and it'd heal quickly enough, but the awkward position meant any kind of twisting or bending pulled at the seams of the wounds, sending prickly pain spreading outward.

A few of the others took notice of his agonizing movements but no one offered any sympathetic words. Not that he needed their sympathy. Although he didn't quite understand the obvious animosity from Talos, Ares, Hera either.

'The man of the moment,' Chief said, staring across the table.

The room fell silent. Peake looked over the crew. Minos and Hera at the table with him and Chief. Ares and Talos on the sofa – the grumpiest looking of the bunch – surprise, surprise. Hermes stood at the breakfast bar.

Was Peake supposed to respond to Chief's words? Of course, the boss already knew what had happened yesterday from the debrief with Ares the previous night, but he'd only arrived at the safe house a few minutes ago and Peake was sure he would want the full explanation regurgitated in person.

'So who's going to start?' Chief asked.

'I think the man of the moment should do the honors,' Talos said.

All expectant eyes on Peake once again, but he still kept his mouth shut. Like an obviously guilty suspect on the stand in the courtroom. No point in blathering and inviting trouble. If anyone thought he'd done something, they had to prove his guilt. Not that he felt he was guilty of anything.

'Let me start this off from my perspective,' Chief said. 'I've been firefighting calls from all corners for the past twelve hours, trying to allay concerns, fears. Trying to figure if we have a diplomatic crisis or worse. Debating if we'll see more bloodshed because of yesterday afternoon. Trying to determine whether we're already burned out here and whether we can even make it out of this county in one piece.'

'Burned? We're making progress,' Peake said.

Chief raised an eyebrow. Ares guffawed and Talos looked pleased by the response from the number two. When did they become two peas in a pod, anyway? Would Ares be so happy with the big guy if he knew what he'd been up to with Hera?

'Progress?' Chief said. 'You killed two people in daylight in the capital city. Left the two dead bodies in the streets.'

'It was very nearly my dead body,' Peake said. 'Not helped by the lack of assistance I got from this lot. Comms blackout, was it?'

He switched his focus from Hera to Talos but neither of them said anything to that. Chief looked confused for a moment but his natural angry – or was it agitated – state soon took over once more.

'I really shouldn't need to say this, but this op has to run cleanly, otherwise it doesn't run at all. Dead bodies on show is not what we need. Especially dead bodies in the street with witnesses to the killings.'

'The only witnesses were the other two guys who attacked me,' Peake said.

'You're sure about that? You checked over each and every premises in that alley to make sure no one was watching?'

'They lured you there, Hades,' Ares said. 'Specifically there. It'd be a surprise if they didn't have someone watching that space.'

'Can you imagine the fallout if a video of you taking out two locals appeared on YouTube?' Chief asked.

'Has it?' Peake responded.

Chief paused.

'Has it?' Peake asked again. 'Otherwise what's the point in even bringing that up—'

'Excuse me, but—'

'And what exactly would be the problem anyway? These guys, our targets, aren't the good guys. What's the problem if—'

'The problem is this op is covert for very simple reasons that I've explained to you already.'

'Do you want to find yourself behind bars here for the rest of your life?' Ares asked grumpily. 'Because we could always hand you to the authorities here.'

'Is that a threat?' Peake asked.

'It's a warning,' Chief said. 'If the police do come looking for you now—'

'What you both seem to be forgetting, what you're all forgetting, is that this was a lead. We had two of our targets, Delta and Zeta, and they—'

'And they knew you were following them,' Chief said. 'Whatever lead you thought you had, it's already fucked.'

'That's crap and you know it,' Peake said. 'The fact they were ready to attack shows exactly who these guys are. They're organized, but they're on edge. We've hit on something here.'

The room fell silent. Peake's eyes fell on Hermes. He'd hoped out of everyone there that he – or Minos – would have said something to back him up, but so far not a word.

'So no one else is going to address the big stinking elephant in this room?' Talos said.

'That's one way to describe you,' Peake responded.

'Hilarious.'

'What elephant?' Chief asked.

'How'd you find Zeta at all?' Talos said to Peake. 'And how did you ID him?'

Peake glanced at Hermes but the guy was looking down, as though deliberately avoiding his eye.

'I did my job,' Peake said. 'And since we ID'd him, me and Hermes have managed to build up quite a profile. Hermes, do you want to—'

'No,' Ares said. 'We'll get to that. Talos asked you a question. How did you ID Zeta?'

'You want the truth?' Peake said. 'I got lucky.'

He left it at that but no one looked convinced.

'You're going to have to do better than that,' Chief said.

Had Ares already been behind Peake's back, talking to the boss about this?

Talos looked so goddamn smug...

'I found Zeta by chance,' Peake said. 'We've been out on so many recces, of the key areas, target locations, that it was only a matter of time, really. When I found him... I followed him. To a cafe. I stood in line right behind him. I caught a glimpse of his ID in his wallet. Simple as that. From there, Hermes—'

'Bullshit,' Talos said.

Peake glared but didn't say anything.

'Sorry, but that is a load of crap,' Talos said. 'I know what you two have been up to. You're about to start telling us that this guy is our way in. An ex-government adviser in exile who's part of some fucking attempted coup or something. And there he is prancing around in the capital, in a coffee shop, waiting in line with his ID on show for all to see.'

Peake gritted his teeth as once again focus turned his way.

'He's got a point,' Chief said. 'That's a stretch.'

'Hades is getting intel from somewhere else,' Talos said. 'I know it. What I don't know is why he won't tell us where it's coming from.'

'You want to be on this team?' Chief asked Peake.

'Yes,' Peake said.

'Then you've got one more chance to tell it straight.'

Peake took a deep breath.

'I happened upon Zeta by chance on a recce—'

Talos threw his hands up. 'Here we go—'

'Talos, shut up,' Chief said.

Silence. Peake carried on. 'I happened upon him by chance. And he did go to a cafe. Maybe not a very public place, but he met Delta there. I waited outside. I had Hermes on comms. When they were done, I snuck in there and I cleared their cups away. Took them with me. I managed to get a couple of decent prints for Zeta and later that day I sent images to a contact I have to ID him.'

Talos looked really suspicious still. Ares looked incredulous. Chief looked… a little more understanding, surprisingly.

'Who's your contact?' Chief asked.

'I can't tell you that,' Peake said. 'Rule number one, remember? Giving away this contact would give this whole group far too much information on my own identity.'

'What a cop-out,' Talos said.

'No one ever said we can't use sources outside this crew,' Peake said. 'Right, Chief?'

Chief seemed to chew on that. 'Right. I didn't. But from now on, that's exactly what I am saying. If anyone wants to communicate with a third party over details of this mission or our targets, you get my approval first.'

'I knew he was working with someone else,' Talos. 'How can we trust—'

'Talos,' Chief said. 'I admire your bullishness, but sometimes just learn when to keep your mouth shut.'

Ares nudged the big guy in the side as though further confirmation that it was time to leave it.

'You know what I'm most disappointed about?' Chief said.

No one answered.

'The lack of cohesiveness in this team. You're all supposed to be highly trained. Elite. Ready for anything. Yet this bickering and cock-swinging.'

'Boys will be boys,' Hera said.

'Thanks for that psychoanalysis, sweetheart. But I need to know, before this gets any more fucked up, each and every one of you, tell me... Can you work together, professionally, on this?'

He turned to Minos first.

'Absolutely.'

Next Hermes.

'You know it.'

Ares.

'You don't need to ask me that.'

Hera.

'One hundred percent.'

Chief paused before he looked at Peake.

'Hades?'

'I'm the one out there chasing these leads.'

Chief said nothing but glared a moment before finally looking at Talos.

'You can trust me,' Talos said. 'You know that.'

The way he said it... They had a past.

'Good,' Chief said. 'So, Hades and Hermes, you have another development, I understand?'

Peake indicated for Hermes to carry on. He picked up his tablet and flicked across the screen.

'I'm not just a drone operator,' he said, 'even if that's what you lot seem to make me do day in day out.'

'Boo-hoo,' Hera said.

Hermes blew her a kiss before he carried on. 'Since we ID'd Zeta I've been doing everything I can to understand this guy's past, and to break down his life now. As Hades already mentioned, we know he used to be a government adviser. Not very high level, but high enough to give him some connections. Connections which I think we can exploit.'

Hermes turned the screen for everyone to see. A little bit unnecessary as all he showed was a string of messages that Hades – and presumably the others – couldn't read at distance.

'And that is?' Chief asked.

'Zeta is part of several groups on chat sites on the dark web. I've managed to piggyback on some existing, but little used, accounts in a couple of those groups—'

'Piggyback?' Talos said. 'You mean hack into.'

'Basically, yeah. And I've already built up quite a rapport with this guy and a few others, although I don't know the IDs for those yet. Zeta isn't in charge. But he is worth pursuing.'

Chief nodded as though impressed. 'So what's he up to?'

'Specifically? They're readying to fight back.'

'A coup?' Hera suggested.

'Not as organized as that. Yet. Not these guys, anyway. They just want to hit back.'

'With what?'

'He's looking for suppliers. Components for explosives.'

'They already have C4,' Talos said.

'They've more than that. And I've already set up a first run deal with him for a batch of electronic detonators.'

Silence, which surprised Peake a little. He'd expected enthusiasm, and the fading optimism on Hermes's face suggested he had too.

'You actually want to help arm these people?' Talos said.

'This is as good a way as any to infiltrate this group,' Peake said. 'This is just a starter. We build some trust here and we can unpick what these guys are actually planning with the weapons they're gathering.'

'Or you deliver a batch of detonators and three days later kaboom, we're responsible for thousands of deaths,' Hera said.

'They're already armed,' Hermes said. 'Whether they get further weapons and components from us or someone else, they will continue with their plans. This gets us close to them, quickly.'

No one said anything but Peake sensed plenty of apprehension still.

'Chief?' Peake prompted. 'We've been here more than forty days. Recces aren't going to get us the answers we came here for.'

'This is good,' Chief said after a while and Peake saw the relief spread across Hermes's face. 'It's not without risk, no, but this entire op is risky.'

'What spec of detonator?' Ares said.

'Pretty basic stuff,' Hermes said. 'Equipment I know we can source quickly and cheaply.'

'And what's your ruse?' Chief asked. 'Who does he think you are?'

'Like I said, I piggybacked on real accounts. The one offering the goods belongs to an American mercenary who used to be over here, but who's currently serving time back home. He's going to be inside for a while. He won't know.'

'And what if Zeta and his guys do their homework on your mercenary?' Talos asked.

'It's a risk. But this is the dark web. It's not that easy for them to peel back the layers and find out his whole life story.'

'You managed it,' Talos said.

'But I never said it was easy.'

'An American?' Hera stated. 'It's a bit... in your face, isn't it? You want this guy to trust you?'

'He trusts me enough. You give me the go ahead and the budget and I can get this delivery set up within forty-eight hours. Then we wait and watch what happens next.'

Chief glanced around, as though gauging the mood of the room, though it was already clear from the satisfied look on his face what his answer would be.

'You're good to go,' Chief said. He got to his feet. 'Hades, a word.'

Peake didn't look at anyone as he got up and followed the boss out of the room and to the door.

'So come on then,' Chief said quietly, checking over Peake's shoulder as he spoke. 'Who's your source?'

Peake considered the question but didn't answer.

'I understand your reluctance in front of the others, Hades, but don't forget I know where you came from.'

Peake still said nothing.

'I'm privy to a lot more information than you probably give me credit for,' Chief said. 'I know about your group, Hades. I know about the deep-behind-cover, no-holds-barred shit you all get to do there. And let me put it this way... Given what I know about that team, you wouldn't have been on my op at all. Because guys like you spend so long without rules, you really do come to think they don't apply to you. But to me, that just makes you liabilities.'

'I've followed your rules, haven't I?'

'I'm still trying to decide on that. Tell me, who's your source?'

'An asset,' Peake said.

'Civilian?'

'No.'

'Then who?'

'Jordan Special Royal Guard Command.' He watched Chief's reaction for a few seconds but couldn't glean anything. 'I won't give you any more than that, even if it means you pull me out of here.'

'That's the problem though, isn't it?' Chief said. 'I can't pull you out without someone else's say so. But if I ever think your actions are going to jeopardize me personally...'

'You'd be well within your rights to react,' Peake said.

Chief snorted and kind of glared, but also looked a little... fearful. Was that it? Certainly uncomfortable.

'You know, the nickname I gave you wasn't without reason,' Chief said. 'And standing in front of you... I don't know what disturbs me the most. The things I know about your little cohort, and the things you and they have done... or the fact that when I look into your eyes, I don't see a man capable of that at all.'

And with that he opened the door and walked out.

21

'If it isn't GI Joe,' Harry said as Peake walked into the gargantuan and sleek lounge of the boss's penthouse.

Peake was the last to arrive. Sean and Joey were sat together on a cream leather L-shaped sofa. Dolan sat on a stool in the bar area, slicing an apple. Chops sat by a small writing desk, glasses propped on his nose as he stared at his tablet. Harry stood by the floor-to-ceiling windows.

'What a view,' Peake said, moving closer to Harry. Not an empty platitude – the view truly was spectacular. He'd been to the penthouse before but hadn't paid much attention the last time when he'd barely made it out of the hallway.

'The big boy's getting ideas,' Joey said. 'One good turn and he's getting ready to take over from you, Harry.'

Harry laughed and moved up to Peake and slapped him on the shoulder.

'Seriously, kid, you did good the other night. Sean told me everything, even before I had the call from Gonz.'

'He's OK?' Peake asked.

'Fucking kiss-ass,' Joey murmured under his breath.

'Button it, or get out,' Harry shouted at his nephew. Then he stepped back as though ready to address the room. 'Gonz is alive, my son too, thanks to Peake.'

Dolan looked as disgusted as his brother. 'Harry, I—'

Harry held a finger up to stop the protest. 'Whatever problems any of you had with the Cubans, or even with this guy... it's done. I've been in business longer than the lot of you combined, and one thing I can tell you for a fact is that adversity, shared suffering, helps to build bonds...'

Peake agreed, though he wasn't sure Harry had suffered anything at all in this case.

'That close escape in the Bronx means Gonz trusts us more now than ever. I went to visit him yesterday. He's on the mend and he'll be back at it in no time, because of Peake. To say he's grateful is an understatement. He's pretty much ready to hand his daughter over to one of you knuckleheads if you wanted it.'

Sean smacked Joey in the ribs. 'There's someone for everyone.'

'I'm not dating one of them,' Joey said with genuine disgust.

'Casual racism,' Chops said without looking from his screen. 'Yeah, that's cool.'

'I didn't mean because they're Latino or Cuban or whatever. I meant because of their family.'

'The point is,' Harry interjected, 'I can see a good future here. We're going to do some good business together. And Sean... you can run it.'

All eyes turned to him. He looked... shocked.

'Yeah,' he said. 'I will. Maybe Peake should help?'

'No,' Harry said, with unexpected force that caused even Chops to break eye contact with his screen.

'I'm going to keep Peake a bit closer to me for a while.'

Was that a good thing? Peake couldn't decide, but no one in the room looked at all pleased by the prospect.

'First move, son... find out who tried to rob us.'

'You're sure they were targeting us, not the Cubans?' Dolan asked.

'I'd seen the same car following us earlier in the day,' Peake said.

Dolan raised an eyebrow. 'You saw them,' he said. 'And what? Just carried on, driving around the city with two hundred grand until they decided to make a move?'

'No,' Sean said. 'Peake spotted the car and we didn't know if it was the Feds or what, so we called the plate in to Alessi...'

Alessi? Peake had no idea who that was.

'...then I told Peake to lose them. He did.'

'Sorry,' Dolan said looking at the ceiling as though deep in thought. 'You lost them? Was that before or after they shot the Cubans to pieces?'

'Before,' Peake said. 'We thought we'd lost them. We had no reason to believe they were still tailing us.'

'Maybe you're just really stupid then,' Joey said.

'Or maybe whoever this is knows more about us, our rounds, than we would like, and that's how they found us again.'

'We? Us?' Dolan said. 'He actually thinks he's fucking Irish all of a sudden just because he hangs around here and drinks Guinness at the bar.'

'Did I ever say that?' Peake said, glaring at Dolan, and for a moment the room went silent before Joey grunted.

'This guy's got balls.'

'Yes, he has,' Harry said. 'But that's enough of the petty bickering. However this happened, it could have gone a lot worse. I could have lost my son. We could have lost two hundred grand and a very good income stream. All in all, we got a good outcome here. But we follow through to make sure it doesn't happen again. Sean, what did Alessi give you?'

'Stolen vehicle,' Sean said. 'Two days ago in Queens.'

'Has it been found yet?' Dolan asked.

'Not that I know of.'

'Then find out,' Harry said. 'What about the attackers. What do we know?'

'All four wore balaclavas,' Sean said. 'So I don't know anything really except for the one the Cubans took. He was a white guy. Just a plain old white guy. Average height, build. Thirties maybe. Not sure how else to describe him.'

'Peake?' Harry prompted.

'I don't know anything more than that.'

'You sure it's not one of your mates?' Dolan asked.

'I tend not to cut arms off people I like.'

'I'm just saying,' Dolan continued, looking at Harry, 'we didn't have this shit before he arrived, did we?'

'Kid, we've had shit our whole lives.'

'What have the Cubans told you?' Peake asked. 'They had the guy. What have they done with him?'

'And why do you care?' Dolan asked. 'You worried for your friend?'

Peake didn't answer.

'After they killed him, they most likely chopped off his fingers and toes, took out his teeth and sank him in the Hudson,' Chops said, matter-of-factly.

'The guy is dead,' Harry said. 'According to Gonz he bled out in the house. Before they found out anything. And yes, I'm sure the body is long gone.'

'Did they get his fingerprints or anything so they could try and ID him?' Peake asked.

'Wow, get you, detective,' Joey said.

'I don't know,' Harry said. 'They didn't say so.'

'They're lying,' Chops said. 'Unless they're really stupid they wouldn't just dump the guy without doing what they could.'

'What are you suggesting?' Harry said.

'Maybe Gonz isn't telling you everything. Maybe they did find out who he is.'

'And they're going to take care of it themselves?' Sean suggested.

'Or maybe they knew all along,' Dolan said. 'Maybe they organized that hit in the first place and Gonz getting shot was just a mistake.'

Harry's face soured. He didn't like the idea of that at all, and he obviously realized it was a possibility.

'Sean, do what you can to find out more,' he said. 'And I want you all to keep an ear close to the ground. See if that body shows up. If we find out who he is, we can find out who's on our backs. Until then, stay vigilant.'

'And if you think you've got a tail at any point,' Dolan said, 'don't just fucking carry on your merry way.'

'What then?' Sean said. 'Attack first, no questions asked? What if you end up taking out a federal agent?'

'What is it with you and Feds?' Dolan asked.

'This meeting is over,' Harry said, forcibly enough to get everyone to shut up. 'Go and enjoy your weekends.'

Peake was the first to the door. He had no reason to stay and chat. Even if his position was more cemented now than before, he would never be one of them. That was fine, he didn't need or want to be. He only wanted the pay.

'Hey, Peake,' Sean said, coming up behind before he glanced back toward the lounge, as though wary of the others seeing or hearing.

'I'm taking Ell out tonight. Some posh steakhouse in Midtown.'

'You want me to cover something for you?'

'No. I'm asking you to join us. Bring Katie along. I haven't caught up with her in ages.'

Peake opened his mouth but he really didn't know what to say.

'Eight, yeah? I'll text you the details.'

Sean turned and headed off. Before he left, Peake spotted Joey peeping around the corner, face sullen, but the guy said nothing before skulking off out of sight.

* * *

Peake messaged Katie on his way back home. A double date with Sean Lafferty? A few days ago Peake would have laughed at the suggestion. He didn't know whether he was pleased or horrified to be in that position now. One thing he did know: spending more time with Katie couldn't be a bad thing.

She replied to say she was available. Peake smiled and put his phone away as he climbed the last few stairs. He heard the voices before he saw them. Chan and Chris, standing outside Jelena's open door.

'Gentlemen,' Peake said, edging toward them.

'Ah, look who it is,' Chan said, turning from Jelena who looked seriously unhappy about the two men on her doorstep. 'Mr Big Guy. Mr Rich. You got some more piles of cash for me?'

'I paid you for four months,' Peake said.

'Did you? Sorry, I forgot to count. You see, I still can't believe you managed to get all of those dollars so quickly. So what's your secret?'

'Hard work.'

Chan laughed. Chris didn't. So Chan turned and hit the big man in his stomach and he let out a forced laugh-come-grunt.

'See, he thinks you're funny. Right, Chris?'

'Right.'

'So what's the truth, Peake? Where you get that money?'

'Nothing to do with you. Jelena, you OK?'

'She's fine. We were just talking. I asked you a question. Where you get that money?'

'And I told you, it's nothing to do with you.'

'But it is. You live in my apartment. I don't want you doing anything illegal in there.'

'At least not without giving you a cut, eh?' Peake said with a wink.

Chan didn't like that at all. His round face turned red and creased.

'I have my eye on you,' Chan said. 'Jelena, see you soon.'

Chan and Chris left, but not without Chris sending an obligatory death stare their way.

'Don't even say it,' Jelena said.

'What?'

'Are you OK? Or whatever it was you were thinking.'

'Are you?'

'I said don't ask.' Though she kind of smiled as she said it.

'Why was Chan giving you grief?'

She held his eye but didn't answer.

'You owe him rent?'

She still didn't answer.

'I can help you out,' Peake said.

'I don't need money.'

They stared at each other a moment. She looked so... broken.

'OK... Well, just shout if you need anything at all.'

Peake moved up to his door. Had the key in the lock when she spoke again.

'Simon?' she said.

'Yeah?'

'Maybe we could just... hang out. Talk.'

'Whatever you want.'

'Your place,' she said.

He'd have preferred hers. More of an escape. More homely, somehow. Perhaps she felt the same way about his apartment.

'Sure.'

Peake opened up and headed in. Jelena followed a few moments after. She still wasn't moving smoothly, and he was sure she'd deftly covered yet another bruise on her cheek with makeup – he could see the faintest hint of the darkened skin.

'Quiet day today?' Peake asked, feeling horribly awkward for the question. He wondered if it were best to ignore her 'work' or to treat it like any other paid job?

'It's Saturday,' Jelena said. 'A day for spending time with wives and girlfriends and kids.'

Peake didn't say anything to that. Was it really the case that most of her clients were married or in relationships? Peake didn't know whether that was a surprise or not.

They moved into the lounge. Jelena seemed to relax a little, her shoulders loosening, her face brightening.

'You want a coffee?' Peake asked.

'Something stronger?'

It was past midday at least, but he'd have to be careful if he was meeting with Katie and Sean and Ell later.

'Whiskey, brandy, vodka.'

'You choose.'

He chose brandy and coffee. They sat back on the sofa.

'It looks like you're moving out,' Jelena said, glancing about the room. It did look... a bit too empty now.

'I'll get it back to how it was eventually,' he said.

'Why were those men looking for your money anyway?'

'It wasn't really my money.'

'You stole it?'

She didn't seem too bothered by the idea.

'Not exactly. They left it behind. I thought I needed it more than they did. But it turns out maybe I was wrong.'

'Will they be back?'

'For that money? No. At all? I can't say.'

'Are you in trouble?'

Peake thought back over the last few days.

'Actually, if anything, I think things are looking pretty good now.' Though he was sure most people looking in probably would never come to that conclusion based on what had happened.

What did that say about him?

'Good for you,' Jelena said, and she reached out and pinched his cheek then laughed.

'My mom used to do that all the time,' she said.

'I think mine probably did too.'

They fell silent. Peake felt she had more to say but he didn't know whether to probe or wait.

'Those guys...' Peake started. 'Your clients... you shouldn't have to—'

'Peake, I don't want to talk about that. Let's just pretend... Let's just talk about something else.'

Except neither of them really seemed to know what to say, until Jelena took a large sip of her coffee then pulled a face and put the cup back down on the scratched-up table.

'You don't like it?' he asked.

'It's not bad. Just not how I normally take it. The first time I tried American coffee, I...'

She waved the comment away, as though it wasn't worth finishing.

'The way we make it back home, it's completely different,' she said. 'Thick and sweet and... the smell. We use a cezve. It's this tiny little coffee pot.' She pinched her fingers to indicate the size of it. 'It's—'

'Like Turkish coffee?'

'You know it?'

'Yeah. But you're not—'

'I'm from Serbia. But our coffee is pretty similar. Same all over the Balkans. I guess from the Ottoman Empire. I don't know. Some of my friends here manage to find what they need to make it like that, but I never have.'

Initially enthused, her demeanor dropped as though settling on unwelcome thoughts.

'You've never told me about where you come from before,' Peake said.

'It was a long time ago.'

'But you were born in Serbia?'

'I left when I was very young. During the war. I don't really remember much about it. Just the soldiers on the streets and the fear in my family's eyes. That's what I remember the most... the fear.'

'You fled?'

'Me and my mom. I was six. My dad, my brother... I don't know for sure. I know they died. I don't know how. I think my mom knows but I never asked. Really? I don't want to know. Even if we left as soon as we could, I saw what the war did to her. She never talked about it but there's just this... emptiness in her.' She turned to Peake. 'Kind of like what I see in you.'

Peake closed his eyes but didn't respond.

'You've seen bad things,' she said.

Done bad things. He'd done horrible, unforgivable things.

Operation fucking Zeus.

'Yeah.'

'In war? The army?'

'Kind of. Where's your mom now?' Peake asked, hoping to switch the subject back to her.

'Still in America. California. She has a husband. Two children.'

'You don't see her anymore? Any of them?'

'Not for a long time.'

'Why?'

'Because... she's not the same woman now. We came here to get away from our past. To start something new and happy. She got all that for herself, and I'm really pleased for her. But when she sees me... it only brings all the demons back. I can't do that to her.'

She swallowed the rest of the brandy and put the empty glass next to her half-finished coffee. She curled her legs up underneath her and in doing so shuffled closer to Peake, her head just resting on his shoulder.

'What about you?' she asked.

'Me?'

'You're not from New York. I don't think America either, right?'

'England. Originally.'

'Ah, right, I guess you kinda almost sound like that. In a weird way.' She laughed. 'And your family?'

'Just my mom. She still lives there.'

'But you're not in touch with her either?'

'No.'

'Why? Something bad happened between you?'

'No. Not really. I lost touch because... I guess I'm embarrassed. Ashamed, really, of how things turned out.'

She twisted her head to look up at him.

'Why would you think that?'

'Because I know her. And I know me.'

'I don't know what happened to you in the past,' she said, shuffling closer to him still. 'Perhaps one day you'll tell me.'

'Perhaps.'

'But what I do know? You have a kind soul, Simon. And... you make me feel safe.'

He didn't say anything to that and they sat in silence for a few minutes while Peake slowly finished his drink.

'You want another?' he asked.

'No.'

'You want anything at all?'

She looked up at him again.

'Just to sit with you and... that's it. Can we do that?'

'Yeah,' he said. 'We can do that.'

22

The steakhouse in Midtown was even more extravagant than Peake had expected, consisting of a huge open space at the bottom of a skyscraper. The lofty single story had a massive, shiny gold and black bar in the middle. White tablecloth and white-gloved waiters finished off the high-end look.

All of it to sell big slabs of meat cooked for a few minutes on a grill.

'Two hundred dollars for a steak,' Katie said, wide-eyed as she stared at the menu. 'And have you seen the wine?'

'That's not the Katie I know,' Sean said. 'Seems like Peake is rubbing off on you already.'

Sean smirked and Peake really didn't know whether to be offended or not.

'Anyway,' Sean said. 'I'm paying. So get what you want.'

Peake and Katie glanced at one another and he couldn't help but give her a wide grin at the cheeky look she gave. In fact, he could barely take his eyes off her. She was wearing a low-cut black dress and a glitzy necklace and matching earrings, and she'd obviously spent time and effort on her hair too. Even in the dim light of the restaurant everything about her seemed to glow. In Peake's eyes at least, she easily outshone even the supermodel Ell.

As for Peake? He'd made as much of an effort as he could, given his limited wardrobe, going for dark jeans, brown leather shoes and a white long-sleeved shirt, but he felt seriously out of place.

'So, Ell, you haven't got bored of Sean yet,' Katie said. Peake hadn't specifically asked beforehand, but he got the impression the two women had met previously and weren't that fond of each other. Or maybe just didn't know each other very well.

'How could she get bored of this?' Sean said, pouting and puffing up his chest. Katie laughed but Ell just looked a little bit put out.

'I have to say, Sean,' Katie said, before taking a big swig of red wine, 'this is a bit out of the blue, asking us out with you. A few days ago Harry—'

'I'm not Harry, am I?' Sean said, face souring.

'No, you're not,' Katie said. 'And you're all the better for it.' She raised her glass to that. No one else did.

They managed to get through two bottles of red wine before any food arrived and although the conversation, led mostly by the cousins, flowed smoothly enough, Peake sensed an unspoken tension not far under the surface.

'What about you, Simon?' Ell asked, shaking him from his thoughts. It was the first time she'd spoken directly to him.

'Sorry?'

'Did I forget to tell you, he's a bit of a daydreamer,' Katie said, playfully nudging him.

'Sean told me you're from England,' Ell said.

'Originally.'

'You don't exactly sound like the Royal Family. It's a shame. I like the accent.'

'I bet you can still do it, though, right?' Sean asked.

Peake shrugged. Sean laughed.

'Oh wait... you put it on sometimes, don't you? To get girls?'

Peake glanced at Katie, expecting to see a sour face, but she looked as amused as her cousin.

'What about you?' Katie said to Sean. 'When I've heard you on the phone to Grandma, you put on your most polished Dublin accent. You've never even been there.'

Ell laughed at that – perhaps a little too heartily. Sean blushed a little and tried to hide it behind a long drag from his goblet wine glass.

'I'm proud of our heritage, that's all,' he said when he'd recovered.

'You see, I know pretty much everything there is to know about this guy,' Katie said, focused on Peake as though this was information he needed to know.

'Yeah, yeah, we grew up on the same street as kids,' Sean said. 'Saw each other all the time.'

'He ever tell you he flashed me once?'

Ell nearly spat out her wine. 'Please, go on,' she said.

'We were only six years old,' Sean hurriedly added.

'And apparently Sean was already pretty curious by then. It was a real I'll show you mine if you show me yours moment.'

'And did you?' Ell asked.

'Fuck no,' Katie said.

Ell laughed again and Peake sensed just a little bit of genuine snideness toward Sean who was looking more and more grumpy now.

'If we're going for embarrassing stories, how about your first kiss, Cuz?' Sean said.

Katie shrugged, as though she didn't care.

'Wait,' Ell said, switching her gaze from Sean to Katie. 'You two? No. That's disgusting.'

'To be fair, it was a very dark room,' Sean said.

'And I thought you were someone else,' Katie said.

'How old were you?' Ell asked.

'Fourteen.'

'One moment I'm sitting there all innocent...' Sean said, 'the next I've got a tongue down my throat.'

'You weren't that quick to complain.'

'I was stunned.'

'You gave some back.'

'Fuck off did I.'

'You definitely did. And actually it wasn't my first time. I just really hope it wasn't yours given your technique.'

Katie mouthed a horrendous open-mouthed kiss and Peake laughed, but the other two looked put out.

'Hopefully he's learned something since then,' Katie said to Ell, who didn't respond.

'Whatever,' Sean said, shaking his head.

'Maybe we should move this on,' Ell said. 'Before we get totally put off our food.'

Mere moments later two waiters headed over balancing four plates. The sides arrived soon after and Peake managed two mouthfuls of supremely tender meat before his phone vibrated in his pocket.

'You're not taking that?' Katie said.

'It can wait.'

But the phone rang again. And then again.

'Just answer the goddamn thing,' Sean said.

Peake apologized to everyone as he took out his phone. An unknown number. He turned away from the table to answer.

'Where the hell are you?'

'Joey?'

'I messaged you an hour ago.'

'I'm out with Sean.'

'Well you fucking shouldn't be. You need to get over to the airport.'

'Airport?'

'You're our driver, aren't you? The sheikh's got his family arriving in about... twenty minutes. JFK. Don't mess this up for us.'

He ended the call.

Peake stared at the phone for a couple of seconds. Then to Katie whose disappointment was clear.

'Joey?' Sean said.

'Yeah. I'm needed.'

'Seriously? Screw him,' Katie said.

'Alright, Katie,' Sean said, indicating with his hand for her to calm down. 'What did he want?'

'Pick-up. At the airport.'

'The Arabs?'

Peake nodded.

'Sean, come on?' Katie said. 'Whoever it is, get them a taxi. A chauffeur. Whatever.'

'You'd best go,' Sean said to Peake.

He wiped his mouth and got up.

'I'm really sorry,' he said to Katie, hand on her shoulder.

'Yeah,' she said. 'Of course you are.'

'I'll call you when I'm done. You might still be out.'

'No. I won't be.'

Peake hovered a moment, not knowing what else to say.

'Just go already.'

* * *

Peake surprised even himself how quickly he managed to race across the city to JFK airport, all the while wary of the alcohol he'd had. Not that he felt drunk, but he'd surely fail a roadside test if the police stopped him. He felt keeping on side with the Laffertys was probably worth the risk.

He parked as close to the terminal as he could and strode quickly into the building, checking his watch and the flight details Joey had texted him. The plane should have landed already, but he'd hopefully be fine, given the likely time it'd take to clear through immigration.

He scanned the arrivals board, looking for the flight.

Not there. He re-read the text…

Then he called Joey.

'I'm here,' Peake said.

'You've got them?'

'No. I don't see their flight number.'

'What do you mean you don't see it?'

'It's not on the board.'

'Give me a minute.'

Peake continued to scan the information, and also the people moving by around him, as though he might suddenly spot the arrivals.

Joey came back on the line with a chuckle. 'You'll never guess what,' he said.

'What?'

'I gave you the wrong info. Maybe it's the time difference or something.'

'Yeah. Something.'

'It lands in two hours. Oh, yeah – and it was an em, not an en at the start of the flight number.'

Peake looked at the board. He spotted the flight right at the bottom.

'Sorry about that, buddy. At least you're there now. Hope I didn't spoil your night.'

Joey ended the call mid-chuckle.

'Bastard,' Peake said a little too loudly, causing several people to glance over.

Two hours. He wanted to race right back off to Midtown to meet up with Katie and the others... but instead he had a strong coffee, then another, then bought some mint chewing gum to at least freshen his breath – from the red wine, more than the coffee.

He hastily prepared a sign and stood by the arrivals doors. He called and texted Katie, but she ignored each attempt at contact.

Well over an hour after the flight had landed, and finally a man clocked Peake's sign and walked toward him. The man wore a white suit, gold chain around his neck, and had frizzy black hair – kind of like a Miami Vice look overall, but trendier and certainly more high-end. The woman was dressed more casually – perhaps more appropriately for the long flight – in sweatpants and a hoody. Although the lounge gear still had a designer emblem and her hair was neatly styled, makeup perfect, and she wore several items of obviously expensive gold jewelry. The guy wheeled a Burberry bag which he kind of thrust toward Peake.

'You're our driver?' he said, sounding edgy and agitated.

'I'm Harry's guy.'

The man smiled. 'Yeah. Of course you are.'

'My name's Peake.' He held out his hand. The man reluctantly took it.

'Khalid. And my wife.'

No name for her apparently.

'The car's this way,' Peake said.

No chat at all between them as they headed outside and neither of his guests looked too impressed by the virtually brand-new Merc. What had they expected?

Peake got them on their way, traveling steadily, as though sudden turning or braking might harm his passengers or their belongings.

'So you're not just a driver,' the man said. A question or a statement?

'Sorry?'

'You said you're Harry's guy.'

'Yeah. You know Harry?'

'Not yet. But you're not Irish like the Laffertys. At least, you don't sound it. I've spent time there.'

'No. I'm not part of the family. But then they don't sound Irish either. They're all Americans, really.'

He looked a little confused by that.

'This is your first visit to America?' Peake asked, catching the man's eye in the rearview mirror. The woman hadn't been off her phone since they'd stepped in the car. Was she listening?

'No,' the man said. 'Not for me. For my wife, yes.'

'That's a beautiful ring,' Peake said, looking at the huge diamond on her wedding finger. She caught Peake's eye and smiled before quickly looking away, and Khalid leaned over and whispered something in her ear. Chastising her, he thought.

'Sorry,' Peake said. 'I wasn't trying to offend either of you, by talking to your wife. You probably have customs I don't understand—'

'You're sure you don't understand?' Khalid asked, kind of challenging in his tone. 'But... I'm not offended. She just... Don't worry about it.'

'So you're newly married?'

Khalid smiled, though it wasn't particularly friendly.

'A few months,' he said.

'And you're visiting your family here?' Peake said.

'No. My wife's family.'

Interesting. Given the guy's arrogance and everything, Peake had just assumed he was the son, or at least direct relation, of Harry's new business partner, the sheikh. But it was the daughter who had the wealth. So who was this guy really?

'Sorry,' Peake said. 'I'm not meaning to pry. Just interested to meet you. I've heard a lot about your family recently. Your wife's family.'

'Have you really?'

Peake shrugged.

'But you haven't heard of me?'

'No.'

'I work for my wife's father.'

'That must get awkward sometimes.'

'Not for me.'

Something about his tone...

'We're kind of in the same position then, right?' Peake said.

'Excuse me?'

'I work for Harry, but I'm not Irish. You work for your wife's family, but you're not Saudi.'

'How do you know—'

'I saw your passport when you came out. You were still holding on to it.'

Peake held the guy's eye for a moment.

'No. I'm not from Saudi Arabia. Have you ever been?'

'A long time ago. A lifetime ago, really.'

'You'll have to tell me about it some time.'

'Yeah, maybe.'

They reached the hotel. An ultra swanky and newly opened place near Times Square. No sooner had Peake parked as a bellboy rushed up to open the doors. Peake got out of his own accord and pulled the luggage out of the trunk.

Khalid took out a huge wad of money and started thumbing through it and gave two hundreds to the bellboy. Then he looked up from the money still in his hand and at Peake.

'It was good to meet you,' he said. He smiled. More like smirked. 'You think we're the same? Not quite, I think. You should see your eyes.'

'I guess we're not all married into a billionaire family, right?' Peake said with a wink.

Khalid laughed. 'No, that's true. I know it's etiquette, and I'd give you a tip but... like you said, you're not really a driver, are you? You're one of Harry's guys.'

He turned then walked away.

'See you around, Peake,' he called out without looking back.

23

OPERATION ZEUS – DAY 44

'Is this thing even working?' Hera said, tapping the old-school thermometer that was strapped to the doorframe of the Jeep.

'It only goes up to 50 degrees Celsius,' Ares said, sitting behind the wheel. 'That's over 120 if you're old-school like me.'

'It's obscene, is what it is,' Talos said from the Jeep in front.

Peake, sitting behind Hera, for once agreed with Talos, though he wouldn't admit to his discomfort. Over 50 degrees Celsius inside their Jeep? Even with all windows down and air blasting in as they moved, it remained like a furnace, the air temperature outside well over forty.

'You ought to see this place on a really hot day,' Minos said, sitting next to Peake and with a sly grin on his face.

Despite his words, sweat covered his forehead too and as they'd entered the car Peake had noticed the thick, wet patches under his arms. However much of a 'local' Minos thought he was, there was no escaping that these temperatures were inhumane.

'OK, Hermes, you have the drop site in view?' Ares asked.

'Yes. All good. The street is empty.'

'Good. We're stopping here,' Ares said, pulling to the side of the road, and Talos's vehicle headed on into the distance before turning left.

Peake and Minos got out of the car. Peake had expected – hoped – for a bit of relief from the heat of the oven-like Jeep, but moving into direct sunlight the little exposed skin he had on his face and neck and hands stung immediately.

They started their walk. Talos would take the Jeep with the goods to the drop site – an alley a couple of streets away. Kind of like the alley where a few days ago Peake had escaped the ambush by those four men. As he thought back to that his side ached. Not that he'd let the quickly healing injury hinder him today.

'Everyone happy?' Ares asked.

'We're good,' Hermes said.

'Nice and easy, Talos,' Ares added.

Peake and Minos reached the doorway to the abandoned button workshop. Minos stood watch as Peake worked the lock of the door. Seconds later they both stepped into the dusty interior. Without saying another word Minos moved off to the eastern side of the building, close to the dead-end of the alley at the back. Peake carried on directly through into an airy space that reminded him of old Victorian factories back home, with steel girders spaced around the room, propping up the floors above. He moved to the grimy windows and spotted the Jeep out in the alley, all of ten yards from him.

Talos stepped out of the car and looked around the alley, but there was no one else in sight. He seemed to take a moment as he stared through the back window – looking at the goods stashed in there?

'Let's hope we see these things again soon,' Talos said.

'In one piece,' Minos added.

Talos walked away from the Jeep and out of sight – he'd soon be back with Ares and Hera. Peake kept his eyes busy, working over the buildings that surrounded the alley. Not apartments but plain-looking commercial buildings. Offices, workshops.

No signs of life.

'Do you see anyone approaching?' Peake asked to no one in particular.

'Not yet,' Hermes said.

'Nothing,' Ares confirmed.

Peake looked at his watch. Five minutes to go.

'Do you think they had eyes on him?' Minos asked.

Peake looked out of the window and at the building opposite. The question reminded him of the comments made about the ambush four days ago, when he'd killed those two men. A very similar location. Had they been watching then? Were they now?

'I see a vehicle approaching from the south side,' Hermes said.

The opposite side to Ares's Jeep.

Peake heard the engine but couldn't see the vehicle.

'This is it,' Hermes said. 'They're coming to a stop at the edge of the alley... One man out... Now another... The vehicle is moving.'

'ID?' Ares asked.

'Can't tell yet.'

'Hades. Minos?'

'I see them,' Peake said, doing his best to watch while staying discreet behind the dirty pane. 'It's not Zeta. Nor Delta.'

'Then who the hell are they?'

'Don't know,' Peake said.

'What about the vehicle?' Minos asked.

'It's heading toward you, Ares.'

'Land Cruiser?'

'Yeah.'

Pause.

'Don't recognize the driver.'

'Should we follow?' Hera asked.

'No,' Ares said. 'For all we know, he's a taxi driver. We stay with the goods.'

'They're inspecting the goods right now,' Peake said as he watched the men open the back of the Jeep then peer inside together.

'That was quick,' Hermes said a moment later, when the taller and thinner of the two men closed up and moved to the driver's side. 'Very trusting.'

No one responded to that.

'Only one of them got in,' Peake said. 'The other's... walking down the alley.'

'To the lock-up at the back,' Minos said.

'What lock-up?' Ares asked.

'I told you, when we did the recce,' Hermes said. 'There were two properties here that we—'

'Yeah, OK,' Ares said. 'But that lock-up—'

'The guy on foot has opened the garage door,' Peake said. 'I can't see much inside. Minos?'

'It's just a storage space. Pretty much empty.'

'But it connects to that building,' Ares said.

'It's a simple office block,' Hermes said. 'I'm looking on thermal now. Six, seven signatures max across the whole space.'

'Office? Hideout?'

Ares sounded pissed off, though Peake couldn't understand why. They'd all been privy to the same info before coming here today. Had they expected the detonators to be taken all of ten yards from the drop site? No. But in a way, it could make their lives easier.

'Maybe we don't even need to follow our targets today,' Peake said. 'They've already arrived at their location.'

He didn't get any response to that.

The driver took the Jeep into the garage and moments later the door crashed down with a thud and both men and the vehicle were out of sight. The alley returned to some sort of superheated serenity.

'They're inside,' Minos said after a few moments of strange silence.

'Hermes, what do you see?' Ares asked.

'These buildings... There's a lot of thick concrete. I didn't see anyone else on the ground floor but...'

'I'm not asking for excuses,' Ares said. 'Just answers.'

'I count seven total.'

'Including the two that just went in?'

'Yes. Three on the ground. The rest at the east side of the third floor.'

'That's less than before, then.'

'I'm just saying what I'm seeing.'

'There's five of us,' Talos said. 'Why—'

'There's no benefit in turning this into an assault,' Peake said. 'If we've found a hideout, we need to set up watch over this place.'

'We need to stick to the original plan,' Minos said. 'Follow the goods.'

'Except the goods aren't moving now, are they?' Talos said.

'Wait,' Ares said.

Everyone went silent. Peake held his breath as though channeling whatever Ares had seen or heard.

'Police,' Ares said.

'Shit,' Hera added. 'Two vehicles. Fast approaching.'

'I see them,' Hermes said. 'Another from the far side.'

'We need to go,' Minos said.

'No,' Peake said. 'Let's see how this plays out.'

Silence again – at least from the crew – though Peake could now hear the sirens.

'At least eight men inside the vehicles,' Ares said. 'Just gone right past us.' Which was a relief at least. The Zeus team weren't the targets. 'This is an assault. Stand by.'

The sound of screeching tires filled Peake's ears a moment before he saw the first of the militarized vehicles. It skidded to a stop right where the Jeep had earlier been parked. Four men jumped out. Full combat gear. Carbine rifles in their hands. Police? These were soldiers in all but name.

Another vehicle slammed to a stop next to the first and the assault team spread out around the alley and quickly closed in toward the garage door. Peake held back from the window, wary of the wandering eyes of the police. He didn't even twitch at the explosion a moment later as the assault team breached the entrance to the adjacent block.

'They're in,' Peake said, before shouting and gun blasts erupted. 'Hermes, what do you see?'

'Chaos,' he said.

Peake waited for more.

'Hermes, give us something useful!' Ares shouted.

'I... The police are swarming. I can't tell. Three, maybe four apprehended. Others are... They're at the southeast end of the building. A stairwell. Three of them. Let me swing the drone around that side.'

'Make sure the sky is clear,' Hera added.

'What the hell are we doing just sitting here?' Talos asked, sounding grumpy as ever, as though he'd much rather be part of the ruckus.

'Are the police following the runners?' Peake asked.

'No,' Hermes said. 'They're going to get away.'

'We need IDs on them,' Ares said.

'I'm going after them,' Peake said. He half expected Ares to tell him otherwise. '...If they're our targets, we need to follow.'

'Minos, stay with Hades,' Ares said instead.

Peake spun on his heel and headed for the door. He stepped back out into the heat and, hands in pockets, head down, strode away down the street. After ten yards a door further ahead opened and out walked Minos. No acknowledgement. The two of them set off, five yards apart.

'Which way?' Peake said as they both took the next left.

'They're forty yards ahead of you,' Hermes said.

Forty yards. A big gap to close.

'They're walking now,' Hermes said. 'Three of them.'

'I don't see them,' Peake said. 'Can you get a visual ID?'

'I don't recognize any of them.'

'Shit, police,' Minos said, a moment before a cruiser swung into the street.

'They're running again,' Hermes said.

'Abort,' Ares confirmed. 'That's not our race. Hermes, give me an update on the drop site.'

Peake grumbled in frustration but both he and Minos stopped. Peake looked up at the metal fire escape next to them.

'That's where they came out of,' he said to Minos.

'The police are pulling out,' Hermes said. 'Four apprehended. Including... It's Zeta. There's a scuffle. Zeta is fighting. Shit... he's taking a beating.'

'What do we do?' Minos asked. To Peake?

'We wait,' Peake said, trying to hide his frustration.

'One of the police cars is leaving,' Hermes said. 'With our guy.'

'I'll follow,' Ares said. 'Hades, Minos, Hermes, keep watch on the drop site. Look out for our goods.'

'Confirmed,' Peake said.

He and Minos returned to the button workshop though they stuck together this time.

'What are we even doing here still?' Minos asked, sounding disgruntled.

'Where else should we be?' Peake asked.

Minos didn't answer. In fact, they stood in silence for a good few minutes as they watched the police preparing to clear out.

But then they become more animated, more frantic.

'What the hell is going on?' Peake said.

'What do you mean?' Ares asked.

'The police,' Hermes said. 'They're running for their lives.'

'Oh shit,' Peake said, a moment before the explosion.

He and Minos threw themselves to the floor as the windows in front of them shattered, throwing shards all over. The ground shuddered, the whole structure of the factory shook and groaned and creaked. A blast of heated air swept over them before a deeper rumble a moment later, and a second wave of dust and debris-filled air pulverized them.

'Guys, tell me what's happening!' Ares shouted over the comms.

'An explosion,' Hermes said. 'A booby trap or what, I don't know.'

'Is everyone accounted for?'

'We're fine,' Peake said, still on the floor as he pulled an inch-long piece of glass from his shoulder. Any more? Possibly, but now wasn't the time for a thorough check. He could move, that was the main thing. He rose to his feet and held out his hand to pull Minos up.

Peake glanced outside. A better view now that the windows were blown. Fires crept out of window frames here and there but the building where the blast had come from remained standing at least. Minos groaned next to him as he pulled glass from his side and thigh.

'This guy's in a shitload of trouble now,' Talos said.

'Excuse me?' Peake said.

'We were on embassy row,' Ares said. 'Now we're on the service road at the back.'

'And the police have stopped,' Hera said. 'Right outside the Saudi embassy.'

'Looks like Zeta's for the chop,' Talos added.

'That makes no sense,' Peake said. 'Why would the police take Zeta to the Saudi embassy?'

'I don't know,' came Ares's voice. 'But that's exactly what they've done. Dragged him out the car, dragged him to a door in the wall. He's inside, out of sight now.'

'The last we'll see of him in one piece,' Talos said.

Peake and Minos exchanged a look. Minos looked as confused as Peake felt.

'We need to get inside that building before any more police or anyone else at all arrives.'

'Agreed,' Minos said.

'Talos will stay and watch the embassy, but we're coming back to you,' Ares said. 'Fuck knows what's going on here.'

'I've watch on the drop site still,' Hermes said. 'Hades, Minos, you're good to go, if you can find a way in, and if you're quick before the police send another response to that explosion.'

Peake didn't hesitate. Pushing the uneasy feeling aside, he and Minos headed out through the window and up to what remained of the garage door, the metal all twisted – though he didn't know if that was from the police's initial breach, or the more recent explosion.

'I don't like this,' Minos said.

'I see nothing on thermal,' Hermes said.

Peake and Minos shared a dubious look regardless. Peake bent down and hauled the warped metal door upward.

'Still there,' Peake said, staring at the Jeep that was covered in grit and rubble. He only took a half step forward before he saw inside. '...Fuck.'

'What?' Minos said.

'The goods are gone.'

Peake opened the back... Empty inside.

'What do you mean, the goods are gone?' Ares asked.

'The detonators... they're all gone.'

'How is that even possible?' He sounded even more agitated than before.

'The police?' Minos suggested.

'The police didn't leave with anything but prisoners,' Hermes said.

'Then where the hell are our fucking detonators!' Ares blasted, the strength of his shout enough to cause Peake to wince.

Despite the force of the question, no one offered an answer.

'Wait, what's that?' Peake said, wiping dust away from a patch on the floor to reveal the network of scratches on the pockmarked concrete floor beneath them.

The two of them fell to their haunches in unison. They had just enough light spilling from outside to follow the neat line of scuffs to the darkness underneath the Jeep.

'There's a manhole here,' Peake said.

'A manhole?' Ares asked.

'Manhole, hatch for a cellar, whatever,' Minos said. 'There's a fucking door in the floor, that's what there is.'

'You're telling me our targets slipped under the Jeep and out? With the goods?'

'No way the men could fit with the Jeep in place,' Minos said.

Peake agreed, and there was no way the Jeep could be moved out of the way when the garage door was closed. But the goods would have fitted.

'Someone was already waiting below,' Peake said. 'All they had to do was slide the boxes under the Jeep and—'

'Just tell me where the detonators are,' Ares said. A little more calmly, surprisingly.

'I don't know,' Peake said. 'But if you give me permission, I can try and find out.'

A pause.

'Do what you need to do,' Ares said.

'OK,' Peake said to Minos with a smile. 'Let's get this Jeep moved. We're going underground.'

24

The vibrating phone on the bedside table roused Peake from his sleep. He opened his eyes and found himself staring into Katie's. Not a bad sight first thing in the morning. And he was glad to be waking up with her without a hangover for a change.

Perhaps he was capable of something resembling a functional relationship after all.

But he was just glad to be waking up with her at all. After the hastily cut-short date at the steakhouse three nights ago, he'd worked hard to get back into her good books, and last night she'd finally relented and suggested she come over to his place. He'd have preferred hers, but had taken up the offer without resistance.

'Morning,' Peake said.

'Hey.'

He kissed her on the lips but she squirmed and covered her mouth. 'Morning breath.'

'Me or you?'

'Both.'

He smiled and turned over and tilted his phone screen toward him without picking it up from the bedside table.

'Let me guess,' Katie said. 'One of my cousins giving you an order.'

'Just some information.'

'Information about what?'

'It's... nothing.'

She shuffled up in the bed. 'People only ever say it's nothing when it really is something.'

'OK. Yeah, it's something. But... it's... nothing for you to worry about.'

She sat up further. 'Now I'm really worried.'

He chuckled and moved over and kissed her on the cheek, but her face remained deadpan.

'You sound more and more like them every day,' she said. 'Act like it, too. And just like with them, I'm always on the outside, looking in. Silly little Katie. Not one of the boys. Not big enough, strong enough, clever enough.'

'You'd really want to be part of it?'

'No. But that's not the point.' She huffed, looked exasperated as she folded her arms, her brow creasing. 'I just... I hate that you're always ready to jump for them.'

'It is what it is.'

'But it shouldn't be. You're better than them. Better than this.'

'It's a job. I need the money.'

'But I don't.'

'Don't what?'

'I don't need the money.'

Well, yeah, because aside from the nice apartment, she received a twenty-thousand-dollar monthly allowance from her dad. She benefitted massively from the family business even if she wasn't a firsthand part of it. Perhaps that only added to her turmoil though, a sense of self-loathing because she was taking the money, even knowing where it came from, even knowing it tied her to the family.

'You want me to be your kept man?' Peake said, trying to keep the mood light despite his morose thoughts.

She held his eye but didn't say anything for a few moments. 'I just don't want you to... be like them.'

He didn't know what to say to that. Was he like them? Not at all. Was he a better person than the Laffertys? No. He really didn't believe so...

'You want something to eat?' he asked.

'No, I'm good.'

Peake grabbed some shorts and his phone and headed off to the kitchen. He put some coffee on and set an omelet on the go before calling Sean back.

'You got a pen and paper?' Sean said when he answered the call.

'Just tell me, I'll remember.'

Sean rattled off the address.

'So are you gonna tell me what this is about?' Sean asked.

'I can't. But it won't come back to you.'

'It had better not,' Sean said. 'But you need to be careful with this. Alessi told me the guy's NYPD. They don't know each other, but still.'

'I'll be careful. Thanks, Sean.'

'But seriously, Peake. This is me doing you a favor, and—'

'I get it. I owe you one.'

'Yeah. You do.'

Peake ended the call when he sensed Katie coming into the room behind him. She was showered and dressed already.

'I take it that was the nothing that I don't need to worry about.'

'Yeah.'

'So who do you owe a favor to?'

He held her eye. What had started as a bit of playfulness in bed was starting to grate, though he'd try not to show it.

'You don't want to tell me?' she said.

'Not really.'

She stood staring a moment.

'I'm going to see my dad later today. I'd... It'd be nice to have some company. It's not always easy.'

'You want me to meet your dad?' Peake said, feeling pathetic for some reason.

'I'd like you to, yes.'

'Yeah,' he said. 'I will.'

She smiled. 'I guess I'll see you later then. Pick me up at three?'

She moved up to him and he pecked her lips before she turned and walked out. Peake heard the front door bang shut a few moments later. He sighed and flipped his omelet over, poured his coffee and was about to dig in to the food when he heard giggling out in the corridor.

He stood and listened for a moment before heading for the door where the voices became louder and more distinct, though by the time he put his face to the peephole Katie was already walking away to the stairs. Peake waited a moment then opened his door just as Jelena was about to close hers.

'Morning,' she said.

'Morning.'

'So that's who you've been spending all your time with?'

'Katie.'

'Yeah, I know. We met that other time too, remember?'

'Coincidence.'

'I was just coming back from the store. I... like her.'

'Yeah.'

An awkward silence followed.

'You OK?' Peake asked.

She paused. 'I'm fine.' She smiled, but he could tell it was forced. The next moment she disappeared into her apartment.

* * *

Peake had a couple of hours to spare. In short time he'd become quite used to the regularly scheduled collection rounds, so unless he had a call from one of the Laffertys, needing him for an ad hoc errand, then he wouldn't need to start 'work' until at least midday.

So he went to the address Sean had given him earlier. Not far at all actually from where Peake lived. The small apartment building took up a corner spot on West 60th Street and Peake found parking a couple of hundred yards away and began a slow recce of the area. He wouldn't bother going into the building. Not today, anyway.

Did he expect to see his mark straight off? No, not really. So he felt his luck was in as he sat drinking coffee in a cafe across the road from the building and spotted Wyatt coming out of the apartment block. On his own. Casual clothes. Day off work, perhaps.

Wyatt set off west. Peake quickly finished his coffee and set off after him. He stayed a comfortable distance behind; it was quite easy on ever-busy Manhattan streets to remain discreet. Wyatt walked a couple of blocks to an electronics store. Peake waited outside. Then Wyatt went to a clothes store, a jewelers, and finally a grocery store – the latter the first time he came out with a bag in his hand. A single bag. Not particularly full. A morning of simple errands. To everyone passing by this guy appeared as normal as any other. But what was Peake even expecting to see?

After nearly an hour of traipsing, Wyatt came to a stop outside a chic-looking cafe with an abundance of greenery – mostly fake – cluttering the outside, both the indoor and outdoor tables nearly entirely filled with New Yorkers enjoying brunch.

Peake carried on past, almost brushing shoulders with the guy, before he turned and headed back along the other side of the road. As he did so he spotted a young woman approaching Wyatt. Dark brown hair, jeans, leather jacket. Casual, pretty. The two of them embraced then moved into the cafe. Date, or girlfriend? Either way, Peake had no doubt even from that brief interaction that Wyatt saw himself as a charmer.

Peake could have left it there. But instead he walked across the road and into the cafe and asked for a table for one, and suggested to the waitress that he take the spot by the window, if that was OK.

It was. Peake took his seat, facing the window, facing Wyatt who sat at the next table. Peake ordered coffee and pancakes. The same order as Wyatt, it turned out. He subtly listened in on their conversation for a few minutes. Nothing too exciting. A catch-up on work, her parents who were visiting in a couple of weeks. Peake got the impression she worked in advertising of some sort, and her parents were traveling from Washington though he didn't know if that meant DC or the state. Wyatt talked little about his job, other than the toll of lengthy shifts. No mention of his nighttime activities with Jelena. Did this woman know anything at all about that side of him? Had she suffered at his hands like Peake was sure Jelena had? This woman certainly seemed relaxed enough around him.

She stood up and walked off to the restroom. Peake sensed Wyatt staring at him, so he met his eye.

Dead Reckoning

'Why are you following me, you piece of shit?' Wyatt said, voice slightly raised, his anger clear.

'Excuse me?'

'You've been following me all morning.'

Peake looked about him as though confused and realized a few other customers had taken notice too. 'Sorry, buddy, I'm just enjoying some food.'

'Bullshit. I know you.'

'You know me? I can't possibly think from where,' Peake said, trying his best to sound dumb.

'No. I know exactly where from.'

'You do? Are you going to explain that to your girlfriend then?'

Wyatt didn't answer that, but he was raging. Peake could tell by the way he gripped his coffee so tightly his knuckles had turned white, and a vein throbbed at the side of his head.

'What do you want?' Wyatt asked.

'To eat in peace.'

'Don't play games with me. Do you know who I am?'

'You're a nobody.'

'You think? You leave me alone, or you'll regret it. I'll make your life hell.'

Peake shrugged nonchalantly, which only seemed to add to Wyatt's anger.

'Don't forget, I know where you live,' Wyatt said.

'Yeah,' Peake responded. 'I know where you live too. How do you think I found you here?'

Peake winked at him. Wyatt looked about ready to explode but then noticed his girlfriend coming back to the table. Peake saw the effort it took the guy to try to relax again.

The two were soon back in conversation, though Wyatt had lost his voice, answering in short, sharp and quiet bursts.

Peake's phone rang. Sean.

'Yeah?'

'You busy?' Sean asked.

'Not really. Just eating pancakes with a friend.'

He caught Wyatt's eye in that moment and was sure his girlfriend had heard too, the way she shuffled awkwardly – probably thinking Peake was a weirdo.

'Then finish up. Come and collect me at home. I've found something.'

He ended the call. Peake didn't bother to finish his pancakes. He wiped his mouth and left some money on the table and when he stood up, he did so in such a way as to nearly brush against Wyatt's table, catching the attention of them both.

'Have a good day, Officer,' Peake said with a salute before walking away.

'Who was that?' he heard the woman ask.

'I have no idea,' Wyatt replied.

Peake smiled to himself as he moved outside. Would the interaction stop Wyatt abusing Jelena? Probably not. But perhaps it'd at least cause the guy to think, and Peake would be ready if he messed up and hurt Jelena again.

Hopefully this more subtle approach would help Jelena more than just turfing the bad guys out every time. If not... He'd definitely enjoy it when it came to giving Wyatt a dose of his own medicine.

It didn't take long to head across to Soho. Peake waited in the car for only a minute or so before Sean came out, looking strangely subdued.

'Everything OK?' Peake asked.

'Why wouldn't it be?'

Peake shrugged. 'So what are we doing?'

'Our dead guy showed up.'

'From the Bronx?'

'Yeah. The police found the body last night out on Long Island. It's not public yet but they identified him from his fingerprints. I spoke to Hector. He says they deliberately dumped the body so it'd be found, so it could be identified.'

'Helps us, I guess.'

'Creates risks too, but yeah.'

'Risks for them, more than you,' Peake said.

'Maybe.'

'So who is he?'

'Was. David Beck. Never heard of him, but Alessi's given me his last known address.'

Sean handed Peake the piece of paper. Centre Street. Not far from where they were, down toward Chinatown. Sean probably could have walked there in the time it'd taken Peake to drive over, but clearly he wanted the extra pair of hands. Or just for Peake to do the dirty work for him.

Peake got the car moving.

'He's a good contact,' he said. 'Alessi, I mean.'

'He's a she.' Sean gave him a strange look. 'And before you ask, yeah, I know her like that.'

'I'm not judging.' And he hadn't been about to ask, either.

'But I knew her a long time before I knew Ell. Maybe I should have stuck with her.'

Problems with Ell? Peake had sensed a certain tension between them the other night, and knew she'd gone away for a few days on a photoshoot or catwalk somewhere. He decided not to probe.

'You go find your NYPD guy yet?' Sean asked.

'Maybe.'

'Am I gonna read about a dead cop sometime soon?'

'Hopefully not.'

'Good. Like I said before, I won't ask about it, as long as it doesn't come back to involve me.'

'It won't.'

They carried on in silence for a few moments.

'You seen any more of the Arabs?' Sean asked.

'No,' Peake said.

Sean sighed and looked away.

'Are you going to tell me what's up?' Peake asked.

'Nothing's up.'

'Fair enough.'

'You know, it just feels like... they're cutting me out.'

Ah, so that was the issue.

'Harry gave you the Cubans to run.'

'The Cubans are bottom-feeders. This sheikh... Joey reckons we stand to make tens of millions, maybe more. And I'm not even invited to say hello to them. It's like... Harry's made a choice to keep me as far away as he can.'

'I don't think that's true.'

'You're saying you know better?' Sean asked, his irritation clear in his tone. Peake also got the sense he might already have had a drink or two.

'Not at all,' Peake said.

'Good, because you don't. I'm Harry's son. I know him. I know all of them. You're just the errand boy. And that's all you'll ever be to us.'

Peake said nothing. Sean was looking to vent. Something, or someone had got his back up. Ell, Harry, Joey, perhaps all of them. Peake would take the flak.

'I'm sorry,' Sean said.

'It's fine.'

Sean huffed and then sighed, and despite his apology moments before, it seemed his agitation was on the rise once more.

'You know what really bothers me about you?' he said.

'I sense you're about to tell me.'

'You're so fucking calm and cool all the time. Like nothing at all bothers you. But then when you need to be, like up in the Bronx, you suddenly explode into this kick-ass action guy. I've never seen anything like it.'

Peake said nothing.

'I know Chops did everything he could to find out about your past. From before you were inside. He found nothing. Nothing interesting, anyway.'

'Maybe there's nothing to find.'

'No. You've got a past. A dark past, I think. The kind of past that maybe torments you, day after day, that you struggle to keep locked inside, that you try to pretend isn't there, until those moments when you need to rely on that man.'

Peake glanced over. Sean had a satisfied look on his face.

'So do you want to tell me about that side of you?'

'No.'

'Didn't think so. My grandad... He wasn't a wise man, really. He was a drunk and a gambler and a horribly violent bastard to my grandma. But sometimes... He had a way with words. Perhaps just copying what he'd overheard drinking in bars, maybe even mixing it up. But he said to me once... sometimes people do bad things for good reasons. And sometimes people do good things for bad reasons.'

Peake frowned. 'I got the first one, but good things for bad reasons?'

Sean laughed. 'Yeah, and he followed up with the example of a pedo doctor working on a children's cancer ward.'

Peake tried to shake that thought away.

'But I think the point goes deeper than that.'

'The point being?'

'I've done some bad things,' Sean said. 'I always felt I knew why, that I was justified... What about you?'

'What about me?'

'You've done some bad things too, right?'

'Yeah.'

'Really bad things. I can tell. You see it in people. And you have to live with that. It eats at you.'

'I guess it does.'

'You religious?'

'Not really.'

'I used to be. Now? You think heaven lets people like us in?'

People like us. Peake didn't really think he was anything like Sean, and he didn't really believe in heaven either, but he thought about the question anyway. 'If I were let into heaven, they'd probably just exile me somewhere, keep me away from everyone else. The other people there would be horrified to see me.'

Sean laughed. 'Destined to die alone in heaven. You and me both, if we get in at all.'

'Something like that.'

'More likely we'll both burn anyway.'

Peake said nothing.

The building on Centre Street where David Beck had lived sat in the middle of a row of aging four and five-story tenements, shops and cafes at street level, rusting fire escapes dominating the front facades. Rundown would be the one word Peake would use to describe the overall appearance.

'Put these on,' Sean said, handing Peake a pair of clear latex gloves as they moved toward the entrance.

The outer door to the building wasn't locked and Peake and

Sean made their way to the second floor and to the door of apartment 2b. Peake tried the handle. Locked.

'He lived here alone?' Peake asked.

'As far as I know.'

The door, the lock, didn't look particularly sturdy. Little signs of life inside here so Peake took the simplest option and lifted his foot and hammered his heel against the wood, right above the handle. The door splintered, the lock failed.

'You decided against subtle,' Sean said.

Peake shrugged. 'The guy's dead. I don't think he'll mind too much.'

They headed into the cramped studio. Basic. Shabby, really. Messy. It looked like the home of a down and out.

'There's nothing much personal here,' Peake said, rummaging through a shelf behind the worn sofa.

'What are you expecting? Family photos from Disneyland?'

Peake smiled and moved to the kitchen area. He found a jar in one of the cupboards with a hoard of coins and a few dollar bills.

'This all he got, do you think?' Peake asked.

'You get the impression we're the first people to come here?'

'There was no police tape outside. But then it's not a crime scene.'

'I'm not talking about the police.'

'The people he was working for?'

'No electronics, no ID, no mail, bills.'

'Sanitized,' Peake said.

But then something caught his eye in the jar. A piece of card, rather than money. He opened the jar, rummaged inside and then pulled it out.

'What is it?' Sean asked.

'Business card. For a health food store. Chinatown. Could be nothing.'

'Could be something.'

Sean took the card and stared at it for a few moments before pocketing it. He opened his mouth to say something, but Peake's phone rang.

Joey.

'Hey,' Peake said, turning away from Sean.

'You got a nice suit?'

'Not really.'

'You got some cash in your shitty apartment?'

'Some.'

'Then go and buy yourself something decent. Something smart. Then come and pick me and the gang up, 7 p.m. at the bar.'

'What's it for?'

'To impress our new buddies.'

The call ended. Peake turned back to Sean whose face had soured. Neither said a word. Sean took out his phone. Didn't look at the screen. After a while he held the device in the air and shrugged.

'Let me guess,' he said. 'You're off to meet the Arabs again.'

'Yeah.'

'Joey?'

'Yeah.'

'Just Joey?'

'Don't think so.'

'Still waiting for my phone call. My invite.'

He waved his phone about. Peake didn't know what to say. Eventually Sean put his still-silent phone away.

'Yeah, just as I thought,' he said. 'Off you go, then.'

'I've got plenty of time—'
'I told you to go.'
So Peake did.

25

'There's a few things you should know,' Katie said as Peake drove them across George Washington Bridge into New Jersey. 'He normally recognizes me, but today he might not. And if he does or he doesn't he'll not be able to hold a conversation for more than a couple of minutes at a time. He drifts off. Sometimes falls asleep just like that. A lot of the time he just can't remember what we're talking about, and he'll ask the same things over and over. He forgets where he is. Forgets the time of day. You—'

'Katie, it's OK, I get it,' Peake said, reaching across to put his hand on hers.

He'd not seen her so nervous, fidgety before. She gave him a meek smile.

'It means a lot to me that you're coming.'

'I'm glad you asked me to,' he said.

'I can't remember the last time any of my cousins came with me. It's almost like... they're embarrassed by him.'

'Or embarrassed of themselves, so they don't want to show their faces.'

She gave him a curious look, as though she'd not thought of it that way, and actually liked the idea.

'It's not even… He wasn't ever even that good a dad. I mean, he wasn't the worst, he never abused me or anything like that, but he was just so… controlling. And his views… Fuck, you'd think he was living two centuries ago, and with his mind going now it's only getting worse and worse, more extreme. It's just… such a shame to see him… kinda disappear.'

He squeezed her hand and she sighed as though releasing some of her obvious tension.

'If he asks you about yourself… don't tell him where you're from. Or about the army.'

Peake raised an eyebrow in response. 'He doesn't like the English?'

'You know how it is?'

'I guess.'

'I'm too young, but that generation… I mean my da and Harry were still over there when the Troubles started in the seventies in the north. They were never part of it, but they've told me all the stories about how when they came to New York nearly every person of Irish descent here supported the IRA. You'd walk into bars and see the signs and the flags and everything.'

'It's fine. I get it. I won't mention I'm English. And I won't mention I was in the British army.'

She squirmed as though unsure of his tone but what she was asking really didn't trouble him. He was sure there was nothing a man like her father could say to him that would offend him. And he had no desire to impress the man anyway. Only to keep Katie happy.

They arrived at Oakhampton Retirement Home not long after, a sweeping drive leading up through nicely manicured gardens to a huge building that looked like a British stately home. Clearly not a retirement home for your everyday retiree.

They parked up and headed into the reception and waited a couple of minutes before a chaperone arrived to take them through into the north wing. As soon as they headed through the security-locked doors it became clear that this side of the building was quite different to the glossy outside. Much more clinical. This part was a hospice in all but name, the residents confined to their quarters unless under supervision, likely for their protection as well as for others. Katie appeared all the more nervous as they reached the door to 11a which had a sign with 'Patrick Lafferty' in fancy lettering screwed in place.

The chaperone – nurse – knocked and poked her head in for a second before addressing Katie.

'He's still got some of his lunch left. He said he wasn't hungry, but you could try and get him to have another go if you want. But he's probably quite tired. He was up all night thinking the Nazis were coming.'

She laughed at that. Peake wasn't sure he got the joke, and Katie didn't look too amused either. She turned to Peake.

'The idiot wasn't even alive during the war, but he's started having these dreams that it's 1945 or something,' she said.

She rolled her eyes as if it was nothing, but Peake could sense the distress behind her words.

Peake followed her inside. Patrick Lafferty was in an armchair in the bay window, a blanket over him as he stared at the greenery outside. He hadn't taken any notice of them until Katie kneeled down to his side and took his withered-looking hand.

'Hey, Da, it's me, Katie.'

Peake stood over her shoulder. Patrick looked at his daughter blankly for a couple of seconds before a smile creeped up his face.

'Katie... My Katie.'

He lifted her hand up and pecked the back of it, his movements strained. From what Peake understood, Patrick was only a couple of years older than his brother Harry, but he looked two decades older.

'I didn't know you were coming. I would have...' He looked behind him and trailed off.

'It's OK. Don't worry. The room looks great. You look good too.'

Patrick's smile widened a little as he turned back around, but then he finally seemed to realize that Katie wasn't alone and he locked eyes on Peake's midriff before his gaze rose up to meet Peake's.

'Da, this is my friend, Simon.'

'Pleased to meet you, Mr Lafferty,' Peake said, holding his hand out.

Patrick didn't take it. His smile faded.

'Friend, huh?'

'Yeah.'

'I've not seen this one before, have I? You know how forgetful I am.'

'No. You haven't.'

'So you two only just met?'

'Recently, yeah.'

'At least he's the right color this time.'

Katie pulled her hand away. From frail and disorientated, Patrick had taken on a cold, hard edge.

'Where you from, Simon?' Patrick asked.

He glanced at Katie before answering. 'New York.'

'Yeah? You have any Irish blood in you?'

'Don't think so.'

'And what do you do?'

'I'm... I'm actually working for Harry now.'

Peake thought perhaps that was a good thing to say, but Patrick's face only twisted in distaste.

'Harry and his little litter of fucking runts.'

'Da!' Katie said.

'What? When'd any of those little bastards ever bother coming to see me? But they still take my fucking money, don't they?'

Katie straightened up. She looked more mad than anything now.

'I'm right though, aren't I?' Patrick said. 'So, Simon, you like working for my brother?'

'It pays.'

'Yeah, I bet it fucking does.'

Patrick faced the window again and the room fell silent. Peake reached across and brushed his fingers across Katie's hand to offer some sort of comfort, but she moved away from his touch.

'Do you want any more of your lunch?' she asked.

'I ate already.'

'But you left most of it. Are you not hungry?'

'I don't want to eat.'

Katie flinched when Patrick jolted in his chair and sat forward, sending daggers at two people on the outside who'd stopped to take a seat on a bench in the garden.

'There they are again! That's the one I was talking to you about. I know she's stealing the flowers.'

He glanced up at Katie and his hardness faltered.

'Oh. Katie. It's you,' he said. 'I... I didn't... When'd you get here?'

He looked further behind him as though expecting to see someone else, perhaps the nurse.

'That woman,' he said, nodding to the outside. 'She's a thief. I've been telling Esme all about it, but she doesn't do anything.'

'I'll let her know, if you like.'

Patrick didn't answer, just set his gaze on Peake once more. 'And who's this?'

'This is Simon. My friend.'

'Boyfriend, you mean?'

'Yeah. I guess.'

Patrick rolled his eyes. 'At least this one's not Black,' he said. 'You're not a banker too, are you? Scheming, cheating bastards, the lot of ya.'

'No. I'm not a banker. I work with Harry.'

His face brightened. 'Yeah? Glad to hear it. Not enough men these days understand hard graft. But you stick around the Laffertys... You'll see what it is, and how it pays off.'

He nodded at his own triumphant words, then looked back at Katie. 'It'd be nice to see my nephews here every now and then though. The little shites.'

Silence again as Patrick stared outside. After a few moments he jolted in his chair, almost exactly as before.

'Jesus fucking Christ. There she is again! That dirty rotten flower thief!'

* * *

They were nearly back in Manhattan before either of them spoke. He could sense Katie's dejection.

'I'm sorry,' she said.

'You've nothing to be sorry for.'

'I told you it'd be hard.'

'That's why I wanted to be there for you.'

'Are you not going to ask me?' she said.

'About?'

'Come on, Simon, you know.'

'About your Black ex-boyfriend? The banker?'

His upbeat tone showed he'd misread the situation.

'I'm sorry,' he said. 'I'd like to hear it, if you want to talk about it.'

'His name was Aaron. And he was... he was great.'

'But your dad didn't think so?'

'What you saw today was only a tiny part of who he used to be. But... growing up under powerful, arrogant men like Harry and him... A girl like me never stood a chance. I just wanted to do something with my life.'

She broke off and he gave her the chance to compose herself. She pulled up the sleeves of her blouse a little, revealing the lumpy flesh on her wrists.

'I said to you before this was teenager-crying-out-for-help. And you know what?'

'What?'

'I guess it kinda worked. It made my dad sit up and listen. Realize that if he kept me caged my whole life... under his watch and control... it wouldn't be a life for me. In a strange way I think this helped make him finally understand I needed more than just his money and his protection and his idea that one day I'd shack up with some carbon copy of himself. So I persuaded him to let me go to college. Columbia, so I'd at least still be in the same city. But it was a big, big win for me.'

'You met Aaron there?'

'He was a senior my freshman year. But... the whole experience opened my eyes and made me realize just how much I wanted a life away from every single goddamn Lafferty. But my da, Harry, hated Aaron from the start. Never gave him a chance, despite how polite, charming he was, despite how he'd got the best education, a ridiculously good career path at a leading investment bank in the city after he graduated, which was when I first introduced him to everyone.'

'So what happened with you two? Patrick forced you apart?'

'He tried his best. Even down to cutting off the money. But it was never about the money to me. And anyway, Aaron made more than enough, and I had plans of my own once my master's was finished. But... Aaron got a job offer in California...'

'He went without you?'

'No. He would never have done. And I wanted to go, but when I told my da... I really don't know how far he would have gone to stop me. But that one thing... was like an irritating... itch that just got bigger and bigger and bigger. Tension that I couldn't face... and that was driving Aaron away from me and...'

'And?'

'We had a fight. We'd fought too much by that point. Aaron went off in the night. I was sleeping on the sofa, waiting for him to come home when I got the call. A drunk driver had crashed head-on into him near the Lincoln Tunnel. He had no chance.'

She wiped at the tears in her eyes.

'I'm sorry,' he said.

'Yeah.'

He said nothing more, just gave her the time to settle.

But then he realized she was glaring at him.

'Damn, Simon, that look in your eyes?'

'What look?'

'Harry and my da had nothing to do with it.'

'I wasn't...'

'It was just pure shitty luck.'

He really hadn't been about to suggest the accident was in any way planned by her family. But it was interesting that she'd gone there.

She turned over her wrist again and her index finger lightly traced across the lines of raised flesh.

'So yeah, all these little ones are the cries of help from a disgruntled teenager. But this one...' The longest, most jagged scar, nearly three inches, lengthways on her wrist rather than across like the smaller ones. She touched the almost mirror image spot on the other arm. 'And this one... That was me really trying to end it all. And a lot of the time I'm angry at myself for not having done a better job.'

He wrapped his fingers around the scars. 'Don't say that. Don't ever think like that. Whatever your family has ever said or done to you, whatever pain they've caused you... you've got so much to live for still.'

'You're a good man, Simon. And meeting you has been... a tonic. I just wish you realized that every life my family touches... eventually turns to shit. And I'm afraid. For you, more than I am for me.'

Peake said nothing more, just gently caressed her wrist as they headed on.

26

Peake arrived outside the bar fifteen minutes early, the conversation with Katie replaying uncomfortably in his head. The visit to Patrick Lafferty had been awkward, but really not all that surprising to Peake. But the dismay he sensed in Katie in the aftermath... It tore at his heart. He'd been ready to call Joey and tell him where to shove his job, so he could spend the night with her, so he could pull her away from her family totally, finally... but she'd insisted she wanted to be alone.

He'd give her the space she asked for, but he despised the Laffertys – Harry and Patrick in particular – a little bit more now than before. Sean included, even if his wrongs to Katie were perhaps only by means of his apathy toward her situation. Although that was only Peake's take, as Katie had never badmouthed him specifically.

At 7 p.m. on the dot the doors to the bar opened and out walked the gang: Joey at the front, then Dolan, Chops, finally Harry at the rear. All wore suits. The first time Peake had seen them like that and for some reason he imagined them heading off for a funeral. Harry's attire was the most formal: black suit, shiny black shoes, white shirt and a neat, striped tie. The youngsters had gone for a more hip look with tight-fitting suits and a combination of contrasting brown shoes and pinstripes and snazzy open-necked shirts.

Harry got into the front, the other three into the back. Peake sensed Joey staring at him – mocking because of Peake's own choice of clothing? A simple gray suit, white shirt.

'He's looking more and more like a chauffeur every day,' Joey said, nudging his brother in the side.

'Just needs a cap and some gloves,' Dolan suggested.

'The Sapphire Hotel,' Harry said, face a little sullen.

Peake got them on their way.

'So what is it?' Peake said after a few moments. 'Party?'

'Yeah, that's right, driver,' Dolan said. 'The Arabs traveled halfway across the world for a bit of a disco.'

'Fucking clown,' Joey said.

'It's not a party,' Harry said. 'It's a social gathering. A very important social gathering from our perspective.'

'The great and the good of New York,' Chops added.

'Which of those are we then?' Joey asked.

Harry glanced back at him as though reprimanding him for that question.

'We're invited because we're the ones pulling the strings for them in this city,' Harry said. 'And we'll continue to do that as much and for as long as we can.'

'Oh yes,' Joey said, rubbing his hands together in glee.

Everyone went silent for a few moments. Peake had the question on the tip of his tongue but it took him an age to get it out.

'Sean's not coming?' he asked.

Silence followed but somehow it screamed loudly at him.

'No, Sean's not coming,' Harry eventually said.

'But I am?' Peake said.

The look Harry gave him was far from friendly, but the old man was beaten to answering by Dolan.

'Don't go getting silly ideas,' he said. 'You're coming for one reason only.'

'And that is?' Peake asked.

'You were asked for.'

'By who?'

'By the sheikh's son-in-law,' Harry said. 'Apparently you made an impression the other night. Whether or not that's a good thing...'

'We'll soon find out,' Dolan finished for him.

* * *

Peake had only ever seen the Sapphire Hotel from the outside. The inside looked as glitzy and fashionable as he expected. The highly trained staff showed Peake and the Laffertys to the gold-trimmed express elevator which took them up at speed to the forty-fifth floor, the button for which was marked simply as private events. The doors opened to a huge open space and soft mood music and a swathe of servers in white-tie uniforms. Trays of champagne and orange juice were held out toward them as they stepped out. All four of the Irishmen took the alcoholic option so Peake decided to as well.

'Not too many for you, Driver,' Joey said with his usual snide grin.

'Cheers,' Peake said, raising his glass. 'Here's to a good party.'

He downed half the glass. Harry raised an eyebrow at him a moment before Khalid spotted them and strode over, champagne in hand.

'Gentlemen, welcome,' he said, beaming a smile, shaking

each of their hands in turn before he paused to take in Peake. 'Ah, I'm glad you came too.'

A more hesitant handshake for him.

'What a place this is,' Harry said, which drew a smile from the host.

'Yeah, never seen palm trees inside a hotel before,' Joey said.

Peake didn't think he had either, nor could he understand the point.

Khalid turned back to Harry. 'Please, there's someone I'd really like you to meet.'

The two of them headed off to mingle. Joey finished his drink and grabbed another.

'Start as you mean to go on,' he said to no one in particular.

'Steady,' Chops said to him. 'We're here to impress, remember.'

'Oh, don't worry about me, I'm in full charm mode today.'

They moved through the clusters of people. Fifty, sixty guests in total. One end of the room, by the tall windows, was taken over by a long buffet stand, the far-reaching views of the city an impressive backdrop behind. At least two-thirds of the guests in the room were men, all smartly dressed, most in suits but a few in traditional Arab dress. All of the women looked Western – no sign of Khalid's wife today.

Within a few minutes Chops was mingling with a group of four men while Dolan and Joey stood drinking, looking a little bit out of their depth. Peake hung close to the brothers though wasn't interested in chatting with them – he instead looked across the room, scoping out the people. He recognized a few of the faces from online news pages and TV reports: the deputy mayor, a governor, senator, a few prominent businessmen. The great and the good? Certainly a room full of power and influence. What on earth were the Laffertys doing among these people?

More to the point, what on earth was Peake doing there...

Joey and Dolan headed away when Chops beckoned them to chat to some people Peake didn't recognize. He noticed a few wary glances toward the trio now and then. Perhaps some of the guests knew of the Laffertys and their reputation.

Peake took out his phone for a distraction. Nothing from Katie. He began to type out a message to her.

'You're looking a little lost,' said a woman to Peake's right, before he'd finished the text.

He looked over at her. Mid-fifties, blonde and gray hair, a smart blue dress. He'd seen her earlier with the deputy mayor and his wife though he couldn't place her relatively familiar face. Familiar, or did she just look like everyone else here? Stuffy, rich.

'I'm good,' he said, holding his glass up to her before taking a swig.

'Making the most of the free food and champagne, right?'

'Right.'

She hovered a moment.

'I'm Abigail Middleton,' she said, holding out her hand. Peake took it. Middleton. The Manhattan district attorney, he realized.

'Simon Peake.'

'You know who I am?' she asked. Not a power trip, he didn't think, more curious as to his answer.

'Yeah.'

'And you know Sheikh Al-Bishi?' she asked.

'His family,' Peake said. 'A little. What about you?'

'I'm still waiting to meet him,' she said, sounding a little irritated by that fact. 'You came in with Harry Lafferty.'

Was that a question? 'Yeah.'

'You're related to him?'

'I work with him.'

'And what exactly do you do for him?'

He wondered how she knew of the family and their activities. Obviously not enough given Harry and his boys were free men in her city.

'Pretty much whatever he asks,' Peake said.

She kind of chuckled even though Peake remained stony-faced.

'Yeah. That sounds about right for Harry.'

'You know him?'

She shrugged. 'I know he doesn't belong in a place like this. Which makes me all the more curious really as to why he's here.'

She pulled away from Peake a little as Khalid made a beeline in their direction. The way she edged toward him suggested that she thought Khalid was coming over for her, but after a brief acknowledgment he instead turned his attention to Peake.

'Would you like to meet the sheikh?' he asked.

Peake glanced at Abigail then back to Khalid. 'Yeah. Why not.'

'Please, follow me,' he said, beckoning Peake away.

'It was nice to meet you, Simon Peake,' Abigail said, her face not hiding her suspicion.

Peake walked away with Khalid. He noted dubious glances from Dolan and Joey too. Chops was too busy charming his newfound friends to notice.

'You're enjoying yourself?' Khalid asked.

'Every minute,' Peake said.

Khalid smiled. 'You're probably wondering why I asked you to come here today.'

'Yeah,' Peake said, then left it there.

'You're very intriguing,' Khalid said as he opened a set of double doors which led into a much plainer and quieter room. Two bouncer-types stood guard at an identical set of doors at the far end.

'Thanks,' Peake said.

'That wasn't necessarily a compliment.'

Khalid moved over to a table in the corner of the room.

'What's this?' Peake said looking over the kit on the table which he was sure was for taking fingerprints.

'Do you know much about the sheikh?' Khalid asked.

'A little,' Peake said with a nonchalant shrug. Not entirely true. He'd spent a good couple of hours researching the guy on the internet – Khalid too – since the airport pick-up a few nights ago.

'Aren't you curious about this?' Khalid said, indicating the table.

Peake looked from the table to Khalid. 'What do you want me to say?'

'Do you want to meet the sheikh or not?'

'I'd be happy to.'

'Perhaps you should show a little more enthusiasm. There are a lot of very powerful people in that room behind us. They're all clamoring to get into here. Not all of them will tonight.'

'So why me?' Peake asked.

The question elicited a wide smile from Khalid. 'Finally, I piqued your interest. Even if a little. Just a few formalities first. Fingerprints. Headshot, for our records.'

'So you want to check up on me? You don't believe I am who I say I am?'

'The question is irrelevant. These are our protocols. Let's say it's based on experience. So?'

On the outside Peake knew he remained as calm and nonchalant as ever, but inside his mind whirred with questions. Was this really normal protocol or had they – Khalid – singled Peake out? Of course, he could hardly refuse the request without inviting more questions.

'Come on then,' Peake said.

They spent a few minutes doing the formalities. Khalid uploaded the results to his phone and spent a few minutes tapping away on his screen.

'That's all submitted,' Khalid said.

'To who?'

'That's for me to know,' Khalid answered with a wink.

'You're happy now?'

'Not yet, no. Now we wait.'

'For how long?'

'As long as it takes. Would you like another drink?'

'Sure.'

'I'll be back.'

Khalid walked off, back to the masses, leaving Peake alone in the room with the two guards. Both of them stared directly across the room, not paying him any attention at all. Kind of like the uniformed guards outside the palaces in London that always got the tourists all excited.

Somewhere deep inside, Peake's nerves ramped up ever so slightly as his mind played out different reasons for Khalid's actions, and different scenarios for what would come next.

He took his phone out once more and finished the message to Katie.

> Missing you. This party sucks as much as I thought it would. I'll drop by after if you want me to? xx

He stared at the screen, waiting for a response. None came.

He tensed when the doors reopened again – not nervous tension, just readying himself.

Khalid. Alone. Two filled champagne flutes. He moved over and handed one to Peake and took a sip from his, then stared expectantly as though waiting for Peake to do the same. He didn't.

'You're not thirsty now?' Khalid said.

'Just being careful,' Peake said. 'I'm driving later.'

'Of course you are. I should have brought you a juice.'

'This is fine.'

They stood again in silence.

'So who's in with the sheikh right now?' Peake said, indicating the guards and the closed doors.

'Who says the sheikh's through there?'

A bluff? If not the sheikh, then who or what?

'You're very calm, aren't you?' Khalid said.

'Is there a reason I shouldn't be?'

Khalid drained his glass dry. Peake still hadn't touched his. Khalid's phone vibrated. He took it from his pocket and stared at the screen a moment. Peake couldn't read anything from the guy's face, but he liked the situation less and less.

'OK,' Khalid said. 'Let's go.'

He turned and moved toward the guards who remained sullen and statuesque. Peake walked behind, still primed. Khalid muttered something in Arabic to the guards. They both nodded and edged ever so slightly to the side so Khalid could reach the handles...

Noise behind them. Out in the main room. Rowdy shouting, together with murmurs of discontent. Smashing glass.

The guards quickly stepped back in front of the doors. No fuss, no words, Peake's invitation withdrawn in that instant.

'What the hell is that?' Khalid said, his usual smile faltering as he turned and stormed off. Peake kept up a step behind.

Khalid pushed open the doors to the main room and the noise levels ramped up and Peake locked on to the source.

Sean. Swaggering about. Smartly dressed? Kind of. Except his shirt was untucked, one sleeve up over his elbow, the other down. He had a drink in his hand and downed the champagne, then tossed the flute and the group it headed for cowered before the glass smashed against a wall. Some people gasped in horror. Sean grabbed a whole tray from a bewildered waitress and took another glass from it.

'So where's this sheikh?' Sean slurred before he downed his next glass. He locked eyes with Khalid. 'Thanks for the fucking invite.'

He toasted before dropping the glass and picking up another. Across the room Dolan peeled away from Joey and Chops and made a beeline for Sean. Peake set off at pace to get there first. But a suited man even closer by broke away from his own group, looking ready for a confrontation.

'No!' Peake shouted out. A few eyes turned his way. The man reached out to take the tray from Sean but took a kick to the stomach instead before he stumbled and fell to the floor.

'Don't touch me, you piece of shit!' Sean hollered as he tossed the tray and the filled glasses over the man, then bounced on his toes, ready to take on the world.

Ready to take on Dolan?

'I've got this,' Peake said, darting in front of Dolan and grabbing Sean and pulling him away.

Sean threw a flurry of expletives at Peake, tried to punch him but Peake took hold of his wrist and twisted and dug his fingers into the bundle of nerves there and Sean creased over.

Movement behind him. Peake spun both him and Sean around, keeping the Laffertys behind him.

Dolan had backed off, looking lost. But Khalid was there, a group of men – guards? – standing around him.

'What is this?' Khalid practically spat.

'It's nothing,' Peake said. 'He's had too much to drink. I'll take him out.'

Peake caught Dolan's eye. He looked so sheepish. Embarrassed, or perhaps just worried about the repercussions. Maybe he hoped the people here wouldn't realize the drunk maniac was related to him.

'I'm not going anywhere,' Sean said, trying to wrestle out of Peake's grip.

Peake turned and grabbed him around the shoulder and nearly took him off his feet as he pushed him back toward the elevator doors. Sean writhed and tried to fight him off but Peake slammed him up against the metal. 'You need to stop,' Peake said, still holding on strong. 'Stop, or I'll—'

'I just want to see the sheikh!' Sean screamed at Peake. Then to the room. 'Where's Harry? Where's my dad?'

A good question. Where the fuck was Harry?

Peake hit the elevator button with his foot. The doors opened and he tossed Sean inside. Sean hit the wall at the back and tried to bounce forward again but Peake jumped in and held him back and pushed the close button. The doors slid shut in super slo-mo as Peake tried his best not to look at the myriad staring and shocked faces.

The set of eyes his gaze rested on? Khalid. Rage on his face.

Finally the doors closed. Peake hit the button for the ground floor and shoved Sean away again and this time he finally decided not to fight back.

'Bastard,' Sean said.

Peake didn't bother to ask who that was directed at.

Silence for a few moments. Sean was wasted. Could barely stand.

'So?' Peake said.

Sean said nothing.

'You know what?' Peake said. 'I'm glad for the chance to leave that place. Full of arrogant assholes.'

Sean still didn't speak.

'Want to hit a bar, so you can tell me what that was all about?' Peake asked.

Sean opened his mouth to respond but then stopped himself, confusion taking over. He fixed a stare Peake's way but still said nothing.

'After being in there with those stuck-up pricks, I really need another drink,' Peake said just as the elevator touched down. 'Join me if you want.'

Finally Sean smiled. 'Yeah. But you're buying.'

Peake drove them back to O'Hare's. A safe bet, he decided, given Sean's state. Of course he could have – perhaps should have – taken Sean home instead, but he didn't feel he had the authority to insist on that and would rather try to get Sean to calm if he could. Plus, he was kind of intrigued as to how and why Sean had got into this state in the first place in the few hours since he'd last seen him.

The bar was near empty – a good result. Peake took Sean to a booth in the corner then went back to the bar and ordered two beers. Sean had his head in his hands as Peake headed over with the drinks.

'So?' Peake asked after he took a long sip from his glass.

'What?' Sean said, looking up and glaring at him.

'You think Harry's going to be more likely to get you involved with the Arabs now?'

'Who asked for your opinion?' Sean said. He downed half his beer. 'You water this down?'

'No. Who asked for my opinion? No one. I'll take you back there if you want so you can see what happens?'

Sean held his eye but didn't say anything to that.

'This isn't just about your dad, is it?' Peake said after a couple of minutes of silence, during which Sean managed to finish most of his beer as he gently swayed back and forth.

'What are you, a shrink now?'

'Just someone who knows what it's like to feel trodden on.'

'You don't know anything about me. Or my family.'

He had a flashing thought about Katie, and how she'd been so badly treated by the family. He decided not to bring that up.

'And you know nothing about what I've been through either,' Peake said. 'But I'm the one sitting here with you now, willing to listen.'

Sean nodded, as though that comment had struck a chord.

'Ell left,' he said, before finishing his drink off. He slammed the glass down.

Peake didn't say anything.

'She packed a bag and fucked off to Paris. I thought it was for a job, but she called to say that's it. She's not coming back. Not to me, anyway.'

'I'm sorry.'

'Nah, you couldn't care less. You're only sitting there because you want to stay in Harry's good books.'

'You really think I still am, given—'

'Oh, poor little Peake. Did I spoil things for you back there?'

'You want another drink?' Peake asked, finishing his beer.

Again he received the confused look from Sean. And perhaps filling him with more booze really wasn't the best idea. But, quite simply, Peake felt like getting wasted too. That interaction with Khalid had left him unsettled. Had they really done those checks on everyone who went in to see the sheikh?

'Yeah,' Sean said. 'Another beer. But get me a whiskey too.'

Peake headed back to the bar.

'You think he needs any more?' the barman – Al, was it? –

asked. Peake glanced back to see Sean with his head slumped on the table.

'Just get me the drinks,' Peake said.

So the guy did. But Peake hadn't managed to move from that spot before the door to the bar burst open behind him.

'You...' Dolan shouted, seeming to lose whatever expletive rant Peake had expected to follow as he stared over at Sean.

Dolan stormed toward his cousin. Joey walked in behind. Chops and Harry? Still at the party perhaps.

Sean sat up and leaned back in the booth. A cheeky smirk crept across his face as Dolan grabbed him by the scruff of his neck and pulled him up and dragged him out into the open.

'What the hell is wrong with you?'

Sean said nothing, just laughed in Dolan's face. Dolan slapped him. Peake went to intervene, but Joey pounced toward him.

'Stay there,' he said. 'We'll get to you after.'

Dolan turned and yanked on Sean's arm to send him scuttling toward Joey who grabbed him. Sean wrestled free and stood there, chest heaving as he squared off to the two brothers.

But Dolan turned his attention to Peake instead.

'Seriously?' he said. 'You think he needed more drink in him?'

'I took him away from the party,' Peake said. 'Damage limitation.'

'You're an idiot,' Joey said, shaking his head.

'You're going home,' Dolan said to Sean, jabbing a finger toward his face.

'Like hell I am,' Sean replied, making a mad swing for Dolan.

Bad idea. Dolan ducked and sent a punishing punch into Sean's side. He winced and stumbled and then fell to one knee.

'No more!' Dolan shouted before he grabbed Sean and dragged him out of there.

'Go back to the hotel,' Joey said to Peake. 'Wait for Harry and Chops. But if you take one step inside that place...'

He left without adding to the threat.

Peake paused a moment before turning back to the barman.

'Cash or card?' he asked, indicating the four drinks, looking as calm as anything as though such problems with the Laffertys were everyday occurrences.

Peake shook his head and walked to the door. Dolan and Joey had just bundled Sean into a waiting cab when Peake stepped onto the sidewalk. The taxi pulled away with the three of them inside. Peake stood there a few moments, deliberating.

Then, without a better idea, he got back in the car and set off for the hotel.

27

OPERATION ZEUS – DAY 44

'This should help us,' Minos said, flicking on the flashlight that he'd taken from the Jeep.

He shone the light down the hole in the ground to the slushy bottom five yards below.

'Maybe this will too?' Peake said with a wry smile as he held aloft the crowbar. The closest thing to a weapon that he could find. 'Let's go.'

Minos took the lead. Peake soon landed down below next to him, in the inch-deep murky water.

'Sewer?' Minos asked.

Peake followed the beam as Minos twisted the flashlight up and down the tunnel.

'Perhaps at one time,' Peake said, 'though it doesn't smell much like it's in use anymore.'

'Something to be glad about.' Minos stamped down on the water. 'Storm drain?'

'If it is, I don't think we'll be getting washed away any time soon, given the weather up there. In fact, I wouldn't mind staying down here for some time.'

Minos shone the flashlight in Peake's face, and he had to hold up his hand to shield from the light.

'Oh,' Minos said. 'I thought you were joking.'

'Must be 20 degrees cooler down here,' Peake said.

'Maybe. But... let's just say I'm not a fan of enclosed spaces.'

Peake waited for more, hoped there was more. As before with Minos, his words suggested there was a story behind the statement, but the story wasn't forthcoming.

'Come on then, sewer rat,' Minos said. 'Which way?'

Peake looked around. No indication in which direction whoever had taken the detonators had gone. 'The runners headed north,' he said. 'Let's assume whoever was down here did the same.'

'Good enough for me.'

'You get that, Hermes?' Peake said.

No answer.

'Ares?'

Nothing.

'Looks like we're on our own,' Minos said.

They moved off, Peake close behind his colleague. They traveled only a short distance before they came to a junction. As when they'd first entered, Peake saw no indication of recent use in any direction, but then, what were they expecting to see?

'Keep going straight,' he said.

Within a few more steps Peake touched Minos's shoulder to get him to stop.

'You hear that?'

Minos scrunched his face. 'Water?'

'Up ahead.'

They moved a bit more cautiously until the tunnel opened out into a chamber where little more than a trickle of water fell from a crumbling pipe into a crevice that went down and out of sight.

'What is this place?' Minos said, sounding more unnerved now.

'There's a ladder there,' Peake said, nodding to the far corner.

'We haven't moved far,' Minos said. 'I reckon that's only a block or two from where we started.'

'Let me take a look.'

Peake started up the rusted rungs. A manhole cover sat above his head. He heard street noise beyond. He pushed up but the cover didn't budge – welded or rusted shut?

'They didn't go this way.'

'This is pointless,' Minos said. 'We're wasting time down here.'

Peake didn't respond but he unfortunately was beginning to come to that conclusion too.

'Wait,' Minos said as Peake touched back down on the ground.

'What?'

'I heard something. Not the water.' Minos shone the flashlight along the tunnel off to the left of where they'd come from. 'Shit, did you see that?' he said, almost a whisper as he flicked the beam off.

Both of them stood in absolute silence – darkness too – for a few moments.

'What?' Peake asked.

'A light. It's gone now.'

Neither of them said a word.

'We could try to figure out where we are,' Minos said. 'Go and take a look at street level.'

'Or we could act while we still have the upper hand.'

'You call this the upper hand?'

Peake didn't answer but slowly set off in the direction Minos had indicated, treading lightly so his feet made next to no sound at all as they landed in the ever-present water.

Pitch black now, he couldn't see Minos at all but heard the man's soft breaths behind him.

A shaft of light shot across in front. It took Peake's brain a few beats to correlate the distance. Five yards. He and Minos both froze.

'A door?' Minos asked when they were in darkness once more.

Peake moved off again without answering. He used his hands on the cold stone walls to guide him forward.

Then the wall ended. Or at least it veered off at a right angle and as Peake put his foot down onto hard ground the soft noise echoed differently to before.

'Another chamber.'

No sound of water this time though.

Peake carried on around the corner, his hands moving all over the wall, searching for—

Behind them. A clunk. A door opened in the blackness and light burst out.

Peake pressed up against the wall. Minos did the same. Both held their breath. A man stood in the doorway, flashlight in his hand which he wafted about.

The beam of light crept closer and closer to Peake and Minos and for a fraction of a second the light jumped over Peake's foot before a voice from beyond tore the man's attention back that way.

Conversation over, the man clipped the flashlight to his side and stepped forward, his body nearly fully in shadow as he bent down to pick up a crate which he dragged back toward the door.

He took the crate – their detonators? – into the room beyond. Moments later the door closed once more.

'We should go,' Minos said. 'We can map where this place is.'

Peake thought a moment. They could. And they hadn't come down here for confrontation. He saw no point in selling the detonators to these people only to then ambush them before they'd even figured the plan for their use.

'OK,' Peake said.

Except as they both straightened up, the door burst back open and this time, flashlights blaring, three men stood there, shouting, pointing guns at Peake and Minos.

Rumbled.

'And now?' Minos said. He put his hands in the air.

'Walk forward,' Peake said to him quietly.

'What are you—'

'Walk forward, slowly.'

Minos, between the men and Peake, did so as the three continued to shout out instructions. They were on edge. Worried. Often, with people not used to close combat, that meant erratic. A twitchy finger was a very dangerous thing. Were these guys trained at all? Peake had no clue.

He stepped in unison with Minos, the crowbar behind his back.

'They're telling you to move into view,' Minos said. 'With your hands up.'

But Peake didn't. Not enough to satisfy the men anyway.

'Hades, you bastard,' Minos said. 'I'm not your fucking human shield.'

'Tell them we're not the enemy,' Peake said.

Minos didn't say anything.

'Tell them!' Peake said, nudging his colleague in the back.

Minos rattled off in Arabic. His words did nothing to calm the men.

'Tell them we were in the next building. The police stormed that one too. Started shooting. We came down here to get away after the explosion. We just want to go.'

Minos relayed it all only a couple of words behind Peake, like a professional translator, but the men clearly didn't buy it.

One of them stepped forward and pointed his gun at the ceiling and fired a shot.

The blast echoed. Everyone ducked at the sound, at the reverberation, at the cloud of dust and grit that cascaded down.

Everyone except for Peake who stepped around Minos, crowbar held out. He tossed the tool which arced in the air and struck the shooter in the head. Peake leaped forward. He grabbed the next man around his neck and slammed him against the wall behind him. Minos made a lunge for the third man. Another gunshot boomed. Then another. Minos roared in pain. Peake snatched the gun from the weakened grip of the man he held but as he twisted the barrel around a fourth man stepped out from the doorway. Automatic weapon this time.

Peake had to retreat. He fired off his gun as he ducked and dove for cover along the tunnel, a moment before a volley of fire raked along the walls, the whole area lighting up in strobe from the rapid fire.

'Hades!' Minos shouted.

Peake, gun in hand, bounced back to his feet, ready to counter...

Slam.

The door closed and he was plunged into darkness – and silence. He waited a moment.

Minos had gone. He was on his own.

No. Not alone. He heard movement.

He stooped down and fired first. The flash of light revealed the man's position, but Peake's shot missed and the next moment more bullets sailed his way. He threw himself to the puddled ground. Fired off the handgun's remaining bullets. Enough to give him some breathing space at least.

Then he scrambled to his feet and sprinted back the way he'd come. He skidded around the next corner just as another hail of bullets smacked into the ground and wall right next to him.

None of them hit, but Peake simply had no other choice but to go. He couldn't stand and fight on his own.

He couldn't help Minos.

His only choice was to keep on running. Save himself, find the others.

And pray that they found a way to get back to Minos before it was too late.

28

OPERATION ZEUS – DAY 44

Peake heard voices as he re-approached the manhole at the drop site. Police? Paramedics? He didn't know, but he felt he couldn't risk traipsing further through the tunnels looking for another exit – especially with gunmen potentially hot on his tail.

He climbed up the ladder and peeked into the garage. No one inside but plenty of people outside – mostly pedestrians by the looks of it, perhaps concerned about the earlier blast and formulating a rescue plan for searching the bomb site.

'Anyone hear me?' Peake said quietly into his chest.

No response, and he only then realized both his mic and earpiece had come loose somewhere in the scuffle in the tunnel.

He reached his hand up to the concrete floor above and wiped his hand over the surface, then smeared the dusty soot onto his face and clothes. He felt under his shirt and dug a finger in between his stitches, clenching his teeth shut at the pain but not making a noise. Then he wiped the fresh blood over his face and climbed up into the garage and pulled to the side wall to stare out. No one had seen him.

After a silent count of three he stumbled out into the open.

A few people gasped. A policeman and a paramedic rushed up to him, barking something he didn't understand. He said nothing in return.

Despite the policeman's suspicious look, the paramedic won out and moments later he was tending to Peake's face as he sat on the back ledge of an aging ambulance. The medic looked a little surprised when he found no wounds. As the paramedic turned his back and delved into his medical supplies, Peake slipped away.

It took him nearly an hour to retrace his steps to the safe house. He held back on the street outside for a few moments, thinking. Perhaps the safe house was already compromised. Perhaps others on his team been captured too.

He moved away from his spot and made a beeline across the street for the doors and nearly made it before he heard the engine behind him. He crouched and spun and only partly relaxed when he recognized the Jeep.

'Get in!' Ares said as the vehicle rocked to a stop.

Peake jumped in and they shot off.

'Just you?' Peake asked after Ares had taken the next corner to leave the safe house behind and slowed to a steady speed on the busier street.

'Hera and Hermes are waiting for us,' Ares said.

'And Talos?'

'Still spying on the Saudi embassy. Where's Minos?'

Peake glanced over, hoping the look on his face would say it all.

* * *

The warehouse was big and decrepit and empty except for Hera,

Hermes and Talos sitting on the floor in the corner, a few bags and boxes of belongings near them.

'Where's Minos?' Hera asked, getting to her feet, the concern already evident on her face.

Ares had already explained to Peake that having seen the gathering crowd at the drop site, he and Hera had headed to the safe house and made the snap decision to clear the place out. Having arrived at the warehouse – a location Ares had always known about, apparently – he'd ditched his comms, thinking it safer that way, given the unfolding mess, and had gone looking for Peake and Minos, with Talos and Hermes apparently arriving not long after.

'They took him,' Ares said.

Hera and Hermes both looked to Peake for confirmation. He simply nodded.

'You left him out there,' Talos said, glaring at Peake. 'You never leave a man behind.'

'We'll get him back,' Peake said.

'Yeah? And what if he's already been sliced up? Because you ran away.'

'What if both me and him had already been sliced up?' Peake said. 'And you lot had no idea where we were or who'd done it.'

Talos grumbled and plonked himself down.

'But you know?' Hera asked. 'Where he is?'

'Give me a map of the city,' Peake said to Hermes. The guy rummaged for a tablet.

Peake had already mentally walked the above-ground route a few times but wanted to see the map to make sure.

Hermes handed him the tablet and he, Ares and Hera gathered closer. Talos remained on the floor, scowling.

'This is the drop site,' Peake said, pointing. 'We headed northeast. Then turned about here. And we ended up... here.'

He looked up. Hera, Ares and Hermes all glanced at each other.

'You're sure?' Ares asked.

'About as sure as I can be.'

'Where'd you say you lost Zeta?' Hera said to Talos.

'You lost him?' Peake said. 'I thought he went into the Saudi embassy?'

'He did,' Talos said. 'And I honestly thought he'd never walk out of there, given form. But not long after he strolled out of the front entrance a free man. I followed him, but...'

'But you lost him near the old palace building?' Hera said.

'Yeah, why?'

'Because right around the corner you have the gardens. And right around the other side of the gardens you have the Pearl Mansion.'

'As in—'

'As in the home of Alpha.'

'Home? Prison, more like,' Hermes said. 'He has half the army outside his walls making sure he never leaves.'

Which was the main reason why they'd never made any inroads in getting close surveillance of the guy – a superrich businessman who'd propped up the previous government. The only reason he remained alive and in the city following the coup was because of his enduring popularity with the public and because his business interests – and his connections in other countries – remained crucial to the new regime in ensuring the economy didn't collapse overnight.

'You're suggesting Zeta, our low-level mark, is in cahoots with Alpha?' Talos said. 'That one of the most prominent men in this country has just helped secure a shipment of detonators to help... help what?'

'That mansion is also where Minos is,' Peake added.

Silence, though Peake felt he knew what everyone else was thinking.

'We go in,' Talos said. 'We go in tonight.'

No one objected, but no one confirmed either.

'I don't get the involvement of the Saudis,' Hermes said. 'That police raid earlier... then they took Zeta, handed him to the Saudis. Then the guy walks straight back into the hands of Alpha?'

'I get it,' Peake said. All eyes turned to him. 'We came here to help prevent another war. For whatever reason, the Saudis want one. Zeta is their asset. So too a handful of police. The raid today? Faked. To heap pressure on the people Zeta is working with.'

'You mean Alpha?'

'Alpha, whoever.'

'That explains why the police cleared out so quickly,' Hera said. 'And the explosion there? They did that. Covering their tracks.'

'Whatever plans these guys had... those plans are going to be ramped now. They'll strike as soon as they can.'

'They'll be even more edgy given the run in with you and Minos,' Ares said. 'These guys are going to act soon.'

'And we just gave them exactly the equipment they needed to wreak havoc,' Hera added.

'The Saudis want a war... and if we don't act, they're going to get it,' Ares said.

'We go in,' Talos said. 'We go in tonight. We get Minos back, and we stop these bastards in their tracks.'

Everyone turned to Ares whose brow was creased with him deep in thought.

'We have no weapons,' Ares noted.

'But the guards outside the Pearl Mansion do,' Hera said.

'Then we take them,' Talos replied.

Ares seemed to consider that, then turned to Hermes. 'We'll never get the drone over there.'

'I'm more than just a drone operator,' Hermes responded.

'We'll have no thermal, no night vision...'

'We have no other choice,' Hera said. 'We need to do it now. For Minos, if nothing else.'

'We're in this together,' Talos said. 'Whatever Chief's rules, we're a team.'

'You all agree?' Ares said, looking over each of them.

Nods all around.

'Then I'd better get Chief on the line. Do what you can to prepare. I have a feeling this is going to be a long night.'

29

Peake waited outside the hotel for several hours, checked his phone over and over. He'd had a message in reply from Katie to say she was fine, she'd see him tomorrow, but he felt less than satisfied at leaving her alone all evening after seeing her so low earlier.

He'd make it up to her, as soon as he got the chance.

Harry and Chops didn't show their faces until gone 1 a.m. By that point Peake had caught perhaps a couple of hours sleep – boredom mostly, helping him to drift off. At least the sleep and the time helped him flush some of the alcohol out of his system for the late-night drive home.

A very tense late-night drive. Neither Harry nor Chops said anything as they got in and Peake set off.

'Everything OK?' Peake asked.

'Is that a serious question?' Harry responded, though he didn't sound angry. More deflated.

'I think Sean—'

'Whatever you're about to say about my son, don't bother,' Harry said. 'I'll deal with him myself.'

'I'm sorry if I made it worse,' Peake said. 'That wasn't my intention.'

He didn't get any response to that and no one said another word until Harry and Chops were out of the car and Peake received a somewhat perfunctory good night from Harry.

Peake headed home and straight to bed. But he couldn't sleep as his mind replayed the key moments from the night again and again. He was sure there'd be more said about the night, about Sean and his own actions, at some point.

Was there anything he could do to make the situation better?

His brain remained active – dragging real-world thoughts into dreamland and vice versa – and he wasn't sure if he was asleep or awake when his phone vibrated on the bedside table. He shook his head to help properly wake up. He checked the time. Gone three.

A message from Sean.

Call me.

Peake did so.

'You OK?' Peake asked when Sean picked up. He didn't get an immediate response to the question. 'Sean?'

'I... Are you busy?' Sean asked. He didn't sound drunk anymore, the words clear, just... quiet.

'It's 3 a.m. What do you think?'

'Can you come over to my place?'

'Because?'

'Just come over. I need... to talk to you.'

Sean ended the call.

Peake made it to Soho in only a few minutes. He didn't know if Sean had seen the car approaching or had been waiting but he opened the door to the building as Peake walked up and ushered him inside, glancing along the street as he did so as though worried about onlookers.

'What happened to your face?' Peake asked.

Sean's right eye was swollen. He had a cut there and his bulbous nose had dried black blood caked around the nostrils. Blood speckled his shirt. The same one he'd worn earlier though it looked even more scruffy now, even without the blood.

'Dolan's got a hell of a punch,' Sean said as they headed to his apartment.

They moved through into the airy living room. The apartment was a classic loft conversion with tall ceilings and windows, plenty of exposed brick on display. Pipes and wires too. Sean seemed to hover over by two closed doors in the corner – bedrooms? – before moving to the dining table and sitting down there.

He definitely didn't seem drunk anymore. High? His pupils were huge and he was jittery. Either hyper nervous or he'd taken something.

'You've had a long night,' Peake said.

Sean fixed him a look. 'You know what they said to me?'

'Dolan and Joey?'

He nodded. 'They brought me back here. Told me to go to bed and not leave this place until I was told what to do. You can see what Dolan did to my face to make his point. But do you know what he said to me before he left?'

'What?'

'If I've messed up this deal with the Arabs... I'm out. That's what Dolan said.'

'Dolan's not in charge. Harry is.'

'No. This came from Harry. I know it did.'

'You're his son.'

'So what? Remember what I told you before? He's not a

father, really. He cares more about money and his reputation than he does about me.'

'I don't believe that.'

'But that's your problem. You have no idea.'

Sean shook his head. Peake glanced around the room. Something about the place, about Sean…

'That was hours ago,' Peake said. 'You've been up all night chewing on a comment Dolan made to you in anger?'

Sean stared and smiled. 'Have I?'

'Then what?'

'I'm not as useless as they think I am. So I decided to prove it.'

Peake really didn't like the way he said that.

'What have you done, Sean?'

Peake looked around the room again. Scratch marks on the wooden floor. Nothing to suggest they were recent, but they… all led in the same direction, toward one of the closed doors. A smudge of red on the wall. Droplets on the dark floor – Peake had thought at first they were knots in the wood.

'Sean? What have you done?' Peake asked.

Sean's foot tapped the floor furiously. His face went from manic to smiling to morose.

'Just tell me what's going on.'

'What's going on is I've been working hard while you lot were drinking free wine. I followed that lead. David Beck. Chinatown. I found one of his accomplices.'

'Shit,' Peake said. The bad feeling grew even bigger.

He turned and Sean jumped up out of his seat.

'Wait,' Sean said.

Peake did.

'Ask me why I called you.'

Peake didn't.

'Ask me.'

'Why'd you call me?'

'Because I trust you, Peake. More than any of the others.'

Peake didn't say anything.

'I trust you,' Sean said again. 'And I know you'll help me.'

His confidence had drained. He sounded... desperate.

Peake strode for the bedroom door. He flung it open. Wished he hadn't. His eyes rested on the bloodied heap on the carpet. The unmoving, bloodied heap.

A man.

At least he had been.

'I know you'll help me,' Sean said, sounding even more desperate. 'Please, you have to.'

30

First step: confirm the inevitable.

'You have any more of those plastic gloves?' Peake asked.

Sean nodded and rushed off. He came back and threw a pair toward Peake, as though not wanting to get too close to the man, to the damage he'd done. Sean stood in the doorway looking lost while Peake moved over and crouched down next to the body. He gently tugged on the man's shoulder to pull him out of his balled position and Sean murmured and jolted as the body flopped over and an arm splayed out. Peake looked at the beaten-up face. Bruising, lacerations to the lips, eyebrows. Even with the damage done, he was pretty sure he didn't recognize the guy, though could definitely make out his East Asian features. Chinese? Peake wondered.

Peake looked across the man's bloodied body and clothes. Certainly one arm was broken, a few fingers. What had killed him? He reached his fingers toward the neck. Checked for a pulse.

Definitely dead. And he now saw the marks there.

'You choked him,' Peake said.

Nothing from Sean.

Peake sighed and rose to his feet.

'What are we going to do?' Sean asked.

We? Peake thought. What he could do was to walk out of there and call the police and leave the Laffertys for good.

Why didn't he?

'Where did you pick him up from?'

'An apartment. Chinatown.'

'Anyone else live there?'

'I didn't see anyone else.'

'And no one else saw you? How'd you get him here?'

'He was outside—'

'So he wasn't in the apartment.'

'No, but—'

'Were you?'

'What?'

'Were you in his apartment?'

'Yeah. I wore gloves, but—'

'Doesn't matter,' Peake said. 'It's possible you left traces there. You need to come up with a good story for why. And out on the street, what happened?'

'I was waiting for him. I saw him. I hit him. I pushed him into the car.'

'What car?'

'It's... it's outside. I stole it, changed the plates. It's not going to come back to me—'

'Sean, stop.' He did. 'And when you got here?'

'I'd tied him up in the car. He was conscious again, but I dragged him into here—'

'And you're sure no one saw? It's a pretty busy street.'

'It was late. But...'

'But what?'

'Like you said, it's a busy street.'

Peake closed his eyes and shook his head and thought. 'No one called the cops,' he said. 'Otherwise they'd be here already. Which is a good sign. But that doesn't mean there weren't witnesses, someone who saw something. Here, or in Chinatown. And you've got the inside of his apartment to consider too. You've got the car.'

'Fuck the car. I'll go out and dump it and burn it. What I need is to get this fucking corpse out of my home!'

He said that as though he'd been wronged somehow. As though it wasn't a huge mess of his own making.

'What happened in here?' Peake asked.

'The bastard wouldn't talk. So I made him.'

'You killed him.'

'He tried to fight back! He had a knife in his fucking shoe.' Sean indicated the nightstand where said pocketknife lay, blood on the blade. 'He slashed at me.' He lifted his shirt to show the small cut. 'Look what he did to my face!'

'You said Dolan hit you.'

'Dolan did hit me. But he did this.' Genuine anger, bitterness, toward the man who'd lost his life.

'Who is he?' Peake asked.

'His name is Ji Wang. He was Beck's buddy. He was there that night in the Bronx. The asshole who had a gun to my head.'

'So who did he work for?'

Sean looked a little less sure of himself at that question.

'I don't know for sure.'

'What do you mean?'

'He told me a name... but...'

'But what, Sean?' Peake said, sounding as irritated as he felt.

'But it was pretty fucking hard for him to speak properly with my hands around his throat!'

Peake held Sean's eye, waiting for more. Eventually Sean huffed and shook his head. 'We've found two of the guys now. It's enough to work with. The big problem is the fucking dead body in my apartment.'

Peake didn't say anything but looked back at the deceased.

'I mean... I've seen a body before,' Sean started, sounding more subdued, 'but I've never killed anyone. I've never had to deal with this. But... don't take this the wrong way. I think you probably have.'

Peake didn't bother to confirm.

'And you owe me, Peake. Right?'

'We don't have long until daylight,' Peake said, deliberately ignoring the last comment. 'Best to get this done as quickly as possible.'

'What do we need?'

'Black garbage bags. A saw. Pliers. We'll take him into the bathroom. It'll be easier to clean up the mess.'

Sean didn't say anything and didn't move. Peake turned to him. 'Sean, wake the fuck up. I'm helping you here, but you need to help me.'

Sean nodded and scuttled off. Peake got the body into the bathtub. Sean rushed back with the tools.

Then they got to work...

Identifiable features first: teeth, fingers, tattoos. They'd be dumped separately. Then it was time for the hard, messy work.

Sean threw up within the first few minutes. And again soon after. Peake retched and felt queasy and dizzy and his brain swam with ominous, hellish thoughts and memories.

Operation goddamn Zeus among them.

He also thought about Katie. Jelena. Their disgust...

'We're going to need bleach,' Sean said when they were down to the final few pieces. 'A lot of bleach.'

'Yeah,' Peake said, out of breath from effort and running on empty mentally too. 'But it depends what type.' He thought as he sawed, and knew the distraction of talking would help too. 'A normal chlorine bleach will clean up the mess, but it'll leave behind traces. Hemoglobin in blood enables the cells to absorb oxygen. You've heard of luminol, right?'

'Yeah, the police use it to find blood traces.'

'Luminol contains hydrogen peroxide. It reacts with the blood. The cells take on the oxygen molecules from the luminol, but the chemical reaction produces energy, basically light. It glows blue.'

'You've been watching too many true crimes shows.'

'Something like that.'

'So if not bleach, then what?'

'We can use bleach. But it's better to use an oxygen bleach, like you get in a stain remover. It creates oxygen bubbles to lift stains from fabrics. But with blood, that action causes the blood to degrade, basically destroying the hemoglobin so the cells can't take up any more oxygen. Which means no positive test with luminol.'

Sean was silent.

'You got anything like that?'

'Ell probably did,' Sean said before moving off.

He brought back two different bottles.

'Both'll work,' Peake said, scanning the labels. 'Let's get the bags in the car, then we'll start the clean.'

After which point both of them were exhausted, only another hour or so before sunrise.

Sean stood in the bathroom, shaking his head.

'I can't... I can't believe... It looks better than ever.' He somehow managed to find a smile.

'There're no guarantees,' Peake said. 'But we've done what we can. Come on, we need to go.'

Sean headed out first while Peake did a final wipe down. He locked the apartment door behind him, took off his gloves and tied up the bag with all the cloths and cleaning gear. He pocketed the keys and turned and walked to Sean, sitting in the driver's seat of the stolen car.

'I'll see you there,' Peake said.

Sean nodded. 'Thanks, Peake. Consider this a debt repaid.'

He drove off leaving Peake in his thoughts. A debt repaid? Sean had provided Peake with an address of one guy. Peake had just helped to chop up a dead guy and clear up a murder scene.

Were they only square?

His brain too worn out to find an answer, he parked the question and walked over to his car.

31

OPERATION ZEUS – DAY 45

Peake had never liked much about this city. He particularly didn't like it at nighttime, which surprised him a little as he welcomed quietness as a general rule. But this place... With no active social scene, no bars or restaurants or clubs or tourists, residents simply had no need to be out at night. The only people on the streets were small groups of bored male youths and patrolling police crews, giving the place an overall unnerving feeling as though perpetually on the brink of something bad.

Initially the crew traveled together in the Jeep, but a half mile out Ares pulled to the side of the road. They'd make the rest of the way on foot.

'Everyone happy?' Ares said as he shut the engine down.

He received a series of nods and 'yeahs' in response.

'Then let's get to it.'

They all stepped out into the night and within a few yards had split into three groups: Hermes on his own – he'd take a position in the gardens which overlooked the mansion; Ares and Talos would enter the east wing; Peake and Hera would enter the west.

'You know why they call it the Pearl Mansion?' Hera asked as she and Peake casually walked along a deserted side road. No sounds around them, not even distant traffic noise. No nighttime creatures around here either. Just... nothing.

Unsettling.

'Something to do with pearls,' Peake said.

Hera hit his arm playfully. 'Genius. Alpha started life as a jeweler. He became one of the biggest exporters of pearls in Asia. He had the mansion built for himself twenty years ago – the plushest private residence in the country. And he very deliberately chose this site, directly across the gardens from the royal palace. Two fingers up to the royal family, showing his own power and control over the country.'

'Was this before or after the royals were rounded up and lost their heads?'

'That's not how it happened,' Hera said a little defensively. Yet another reaction from one of the team which raised questions as to their past lives and allegiances. Although it had already been made very clear that they all looked at him with suspicion too.

The fact was, the country had been at war in various guises for decades. A monarchy then a republic, then a monarchy then a republic. The fighting spurred on all the while by both religious and political differences, but mainly promoted by one group of rich men wanting power from another group of rich men.

At least that's what Peake saw.

'Rumor has it that there's a vault in the west wing with the single largest pearl in the world,' Hera said.

'Rumor,' Peake replied, 'being the key word there.'

'You don't believe it?'

'We could ask him tonight?'

'I might just do that.'

'You know why he has an east wing and a west wing?' Peake

asked. To be precise, two carbon-copy mansions – at the least on the outside – next to one another on the multi-acre plot.

'Wife and mistress?' Hera suggested.

'The west wing is his home. The east wing was used for business, originally, but was then commandeered by special forces during the last rebellion. They called it the Butcher's Shop. That's where they took their political prisoners.'

'And most of them never came out alive,' Talos said on comms. 'Yeah, yeah. We all heard that one.'

'Enough of the chit-chat,' Ares remarked. 'You're not on a date.'

Peake looked over at Hera and she smirked. He liked it when she did that. It showed off her... playful side. He shook his head.

'Remember,' Ares said, 'expect this place to be well-guarded. Arm yourselves as quickly as you can.'

Peake and Hera turned a corner and the seven-foot-high walls to the mansion came into view in front of them, a glimpse of the west wing beyond. No police or military or any other guards in sight.

'Quiet night,' Hera said.

Peake didn't say anything though for some reason felt even more unsettled.

'I'm in position,' Hermes said a moment later. No drone in the sky tonight, but he would still use the equipment from his perch to get a glimpse of the mansion on the thermal camera.

Peake and Hera carried on and moved around the outer wall toward the front.

'We have two vehicles this side,' Peake said. 'Four guards, I think.'

'Nothing at the back,' Talos said.

'Maybe Alpha's in the good books with the rebels now,' Hera said.

'OK, if we can get in without confrontation, do it,' Ares said.

'What about arming—'

'Keep things simple. And quiet.'

A couple of minutes later, and Peake was straddling the top of the wall on the northwest side. He held out his hands and Hera scrambled up to the top. They dropped down on the inside, landing in shrubs.

'How the hell do they get this stuff to grow here?' Hera whispered.

'Money gets you whatever you want, anywhere you want,' Peake said.

He looked over the grounds in front of them. A couple of vehicles parked up. A couple of lights shone around the outside of the front of the property, but he saw no one in sight.

'No guards here,' Peake said.

'Like we said earlier, this place isn't a fortress, and the guards are only to keep Alpha inside.'

'Looks like someone's home,' Peake said, indicating several windows where lights could be seen beyond curtains.

'Remember,' Ares said, 'find Minos. Find Alpha. Disrupt their plans.'

'Hermes, what do you see?' Talos asked.

'West wing... I've got three bodies. All on the second floor. Two together. East wing... at least eight. More movement there too.'

'Looks like we're going to have some fun,' Talos said.

'He's finally getting the action he really needs,' Peake said to Hera with a wink.

She looked like she didn't know how to take the comment.

'I heard that,' Talos said and Hera tried her best to stifle a laugh.

'Come on,' Peake said to Hera, and the two of them moved toward the side door a few yards away.

'Easy enough,' Hera said, looking at the two simple locks.

'We're in position,' Peake said.

'Confirmed,' Ares remarked. 'You're good to go.'

Hera did the business with the locks using the tools she'd brought for the purpose – the only tools of any kind they had. No guns, no knives. Yet.

'I'm in,' Hera said.

'Same,' Talos said.

Hera stepped back and Peake tried the door. Slowly. Quietly. It opened into a dark corridor.

'I see you, Hades and Hera,' Hermes said. 'But I don't see Ares and Talos from this spot.'

'You'll see us soon,' Ares said.

Peake tried his best to ignore the voices. He wanted to concentrate on only him and Hera and what lay in front of them.

'Lights on in there,' Hera whispered, indicating the closed first door they came to.

'But Hermes said everyone he saw in the west wing was up,' Peake responded.

And they soon found the stairs and went that way.

'Hades, two new signatures in the west wing. I didn't pick them up before. Five in total now. When you reach the top, the new ones are in the room on your left.'

Neither Peake nor Hera said anything to that. They stopped at the door. Peake glanced into Hera's eyes. No hint of nerves or fear. He liked that.

He held up his hand and counted down with his fingers.

Then he pulled down the handle and kicked open the door and he and Hera rushed inside.

32

OPERATION ZEUS – DAY 45

Two men inside the room. Both wore combat clothes. Not official army, or police. These were Alpha's people. Home guards? One had a handgun on a holster on his side. The other had a carbine rifle on a strap on his shoulder.

Neither had expected the interruption as they enjoyed a bit of downtime in the room, which looked like a mini apartment.

Peake went for the guy with the rifle. He hadn't even managed to put both hands to the weapon before Peake darted up behind, took him around the neck and wrestled him to the ground in a sleeper hold.

Hera swiped the other guard from his feet. She crashed her elbow into his face as she slammed down onto the floor next to him. She smacked him twice more. His nose erupted, his jaw crunched.

She jumped up then took his weapon and searched his pockets.

'Handy,' she said, pulling out some cable ties.

Peake finally released the hold on the now unconscious man.

Hera tossed Peake a set of ties and soon they had both men

gagged and secured and locked in a cupboard which they jammed shut with a dining chair.

Peake only fully took stock then that Ares and Talos were similarly involved in a fight. Shouting. Banging.

Gunshots.

Although the reception had become grainy and poor.

'Shit,' Hera said.

'Ares, Talos, you OK?' Peake asked.

But the crackling only got worse.

'I heard the shots on the comms, but... not out here,' Hera said.

She was right. He'd not noticed the gunshots at all except through his earpiece. Odd.

'Hermes, you hear us?' Peake said.

'I got you.'

'Where're Ares and Talos?'

'I can't see them. Can't hear them.'

'We need to help them,' Peake said to Hera.

She nodded, no hesitation.

They set off the way they'd come in and were soon standing in the warm nighttime air once more. Warm and... quiet and calm.

'What the hell is going on?' Hera said, for the first time sounding other than her usual confident self. 'Those gunshots...'

'It might just be the thick walls,' Peake said.

'Thick enough to hide the sound of gunshots a few yards away?' Hera said. 'Thick enough to hide screams?'

'The Butcher's Shop.'

They marched across the plot to the east wing, the quietness more and more unsettling. They found the open door where Ares and Talos had entered.

'Hermes, what do you see inside now?' Peake asked.

'Seven signatures. Four ground floor. Three above, but faint because I think they're at the far side of the building to me.'

'And Ares and Talos? Where'd you lose them?'

'Ground floor.'

'OK. Let me know what you see, we're going in now.'

Peake and Hera moved inside. All quiet to start with, but within a few yards Peake heard distant voices. Thudding.

'Hermes?' Peake said.

No response.

'Hermes,' Hera hissed, a little too loudly.

'Interference,' Peake said. 'This whole wing is a blackout.'

'Then what the hell do we do?' Hera asked, sounding ever more rattled.

'We find the others,' Peake said, setting off toward the noise.

They reached a closed door. The intermittent voices on the other side grew more distinct. Not Ares or Talos.

'Same as before,' Peake whispered. 'Don't use the guns if we don't need to. Just in case.'

Hera nodded. He gave her the countdown then flung the door open and both burst into the room – at least this time with weapons in their hands.

Four men. All armed. Clustered at the far end of the room, hunkering to shield themselves from a closed door there.

They hadn't expected Peake or Hera at all.

Peake leaped through the air and swiped the butt of the rifle against the head of the first man he came to. He side-stepped and stamped his heel down against the knee of the next man whose leg buckled. Hera wrestled with the third guy. The fourth... He lifted his gun and fired and the bullet thwacked into Hera's shoulder, knocking her away from the man she was holding.

Peake had no choice. He lifted his weapon and fired and the bullet hit the man in his ear and he collapsed to the ground.

Hera went to retrieve her fallen gun but the man she'd held spun around, knife in hand.

'Watch out!' Peake said, twisting his gun that way.

Hera could do nothing. The blade swooshed across her belly and a gaping wound opened up. Peake fired again – at the knifeman. Another headshot. He heard movement behind him and turned and smacked the man on the ground there in the face with his boot, nearly taking his head off.

But the first man he'd felled was up again and readying his aim...

Peake pulled the trigger again. Chest shot this time – into the man's Kevlar. Enough to knock him back but not to kill him. Peaked zigzagged forward. The man tried to aim again but Peake launched himself and clattered into him, then jumped back to his feet and stomped down on the man's head.

Out for the count.

'Hera!' Peake shouted.

He turned and raced to her. She'd slipped down onto the floor. Blood poured from her belly, but she'd taken two bullets too – shoulder and side.

The door at the end of the room opened. Peake twisted his gun that way.

'Hera!' Talos shouted. He rushed over, Ares a couple of steps behind.

Talos slid down to Hera and wrapped his arms around her.

'Hera, stay with me!' Talos shouted and Peake heard the agony in his voice.

She didn't say a word in return. Just gargled her last breaths as she locked eyes with Talos. She reached up with a bloody hand to his face...

She never made contact. Her eyes slid back and her hand flopped down and her head lolled to the side.

'What the fuck did you do?' Talos screamed, grabbing Peake by the scruff of his neck as both men rose to their feet. Talos lifted Peake from the floor and slammed him up against the wall. 'What did you do!'

'Talos!' Ares shouted. 'Let him go.'

Talos snarled and bared his teeth and Peake did absolutely nothing in return. He felt... numb.

After a few seconds Talos finally let go and Peake slumped back down.

'What the hell are you doing here?' Ares said.

'We came to help.'

'That wasn't the plan.'

'She's dead because of you!' Talos said, before slamming his fist into the wall right by Peake's head.

'Enough!' Ares said. He grabbed Talos by the shoulder and pulled him away.

'What happened over on west?' Ares said.

'We armed ourselves. Two down. We lost you on comms, so we came to help.'

'You should have stuck to the plan.'

'First Minos, now Hera... You're a fucking deathtrap,' Talos said, pure hatred in his voice and his eyes. 'Hades, right?'

'Where's Minos?' Peake asked. Neither answered. 'Tell me what's happening!'

Both remained silent still but Ares turned and walked to the door they'd come from in the corner. Peake followed him into the next room. A plain room. Concrete walls. Nothing in it except a strip light and an open trapdoor in the floor.

'Go on,' Talos said from behind. 'Go down. See what you've caused.'

Peake headed down the steps. The room below looked identical to the one above, except this one wasn't empty. In the middle of the room stood a metal gurney. Next to it an array of surgical tools on a workbench.

In a heap on the floor by the bench lay Minos. What was left of him, at least.

'Shit,' Peake said.

'Is that it?' Talos said, coming around and kneeling down next to the dead man. 'They fucking took pieces of him. Sliced him open.'

And he wasn't wrong. Fingers missing. Toes. Chunks of skin and flesh sliced off. Broken bones. Blood everywhere from countless lacerations.

'He was still alive when we found him,' Ares said. 'He told us what he could. Zeta is here. Alpha too. But the detonators aren't. They've already taken them across the city. Twenty bombs. Twenty sites. They taunted him as they tortured him.'

'Did Minos talk?' Peake said.

'That's really what you care about most right now?' Talos said.

'He said not,' Ares said. 'And I believe him. Not that it makes much difference now. We have to end this tonight.'

'After we found Minos, they cornered us in here,' Talos said.

So Peake and Hera had helped them after all. He decided not to argue that.

'We need to get moving now,' Ares said. 'We have to find Zeta and Alpha. We have to stop them.'

'They used the tunnels,' Peake said. 'That's how they distributed the bombs.'

'And we know where the entrance is,' Ares said. 'Come on.'

They moved quickly back up to ground level and grabbed whatever weapons they could from the dead and wounded. Peake took one last look at Hera. Talos caught him doing so.

He slapped Peake on the back. Hard.

'The fact we have to leave them both here... When this is all over, you and me—'

'Save it,' Ares said.

The three of them rushed out and Peake followed Ares along the corridor to the far end.

'Hermes, you there?' Ares asked.

No response.

'I could still reach him on the west wing,' Peake said. He got no response to that.

'Down here,' Ares said, moving into what looked like an interview room of sorts, except at the end of it lay another unfitted, concrete anteroom, trapdoor once again in the middle.

The Butcher's Shop. Once again, the nickname spun in Peake's mind. A name born of brutal reality rather than rumors. Was this whole wing nothing but torture chamber after torture chamber?

Ares went down first. Next Talos. Peake took three steps down. Spotted the manhole below to take them into the sewers.

Then heard a noise further away, back where they'd come from. He focused that way, ready for an ambush, ready to fire.

'Guys,' Peake said as he glanced back around. Ares had already gone down. Talos was just about to disappear from view...

Two small red dots blinked either side of the open manhole cover.

'Get down!' Peake said a moment before the explosion.

33

OPERATION ZEUS – DAY 45

The explosion lifted Peake into the air and unceremoniously dumped him on the hard concrete floor above. He lay there and groaned and tried to regain his focus and to ignore the ringing in his ears.

He rolled over and looked down at the basement room below. A pile of rubble lay where the manhole had been moments before.

A booby trap.

No way for Peake to get down to the sewers now.

He heard banging. The other side of the plugged entrance.

'Hades?' came a distant shout.

'I'm here,' Peake said.

'Find Alpha,' he was sure he heard Ares say.

Did that mean he and Talos were OK?

Movement in the corner of his eye. Peake crouched low and swung the rifle around and let rip toward the doorway. Shards of concrete burst into the air. The men the other side of the door shouted out. To each other? To Peake?

He darted forward just as one of them reappeared in the space, rifle held out. He didn't get a chance to use it before Peake slammed the butt of his weapon into the man's throat, the blow accompanied by a sickening crunch. The man collapsed, gasping for air.

Peake fell to his knees just as the second man, to his left, pulled on the trigger of his handgun. Peake took aim. A single shot to the groin.

Peake took the man's weapon and ran.

He made it back out into the open. Expecting sirens or shouting or... something...

Serenity.

Confusing, except... it made sense. These people were planning attacks on the very people standing guard beyond the gates. They wanted to be quiet and as discreet as possible so as to not set anyone on alert.

Peake, on the other hand... Would it help or hinder to get the police and the army involved?

'Hermes?'

'Hades. Is that you just coming out of the east wing?'

'Yeah. I lost Ares and Talos. They've gone down into the sewers. They're chasing after Zeta and the explosives, the detonators. Twenty sites across the city.'

'Shit.'

'What can we do? The two of them will never get to twenty sites in time.'

'Alpha... Most likely his people will be planning remote detonations. They could be individually programmed, or they could be running together off one command.'

'So we're looking for between one and twenty trigger pullers somewhere within about a three-mile radius. Great.'

'Trigger pullers? It's not quite like that. It's a wireless

programmable system. But yeah, between one and twenty people have the access to stop these things.'

'Can you hack it?'

'It's... possible.'

'What do you need?'

'I need to know more about how they've set it up. I—'

'Hermes, these are the detonators you sourced. You know the system.'

Hermes didn't say anything in response.

'Come down here,' Peake said. 'Into the west wing. I'm going to find Alpha.'

'But Ares—'

'Ares isn't here. Do it now.'

Peake rushed back in through the still-open door of the west wing. He moved up the stairs and into the room where he and Hera had earlier attacked the two men. The chair remained propped in front of the door.

Three more people on this floor? Hadn't Hermes said that earlier?

Peake walked further along the corridor. The house was dark and quiet, despite the chaos happening somewhere outside.

Footsteps behind him. Peake turned...

'Hermes.'

'There're still three up here,' he said, out of breath. 'Two in the room at the far end there. One in the left here.'

They reached that door. Peake put a finger to his lips. Hermes nodded before Peake slowly opened the door. A bedroom. Even in the darkness he could tell it was a bedroom. A kid's room? He heard soft breathing and as he stared, the thin light creeping in from the hall gave away the single bed, a small curled up bundle under the sheets.

'Hades?'

Peake took delicate steps toward the bed.

'Shit,' Hermes whispered. 'We can't—'

Peake again put a finger to his lips. Can't what? What they couldn't do was let those bombs go off. And they couldn't let this kid scream out either.

Peake moved in closer. With the light from the hall he could just make out the face. A boy. Seven, eight, perhaps.

Doubts blared but Peake closed his eyes a moment then reached into the bed and scooped the boy up. For a couple of seconds the kid didn't move at all. Then he murmured and his eyes sprang open, and he bucked and writhed and opened his mouth to scream until Peake smothered it.

'Don't,' Peake said, squeezing as tightly as he could as he moved quickly for the door.

The boy kicked and scratched but Peake took no notice. He stormed toward the end of the corridor. Noticed the edges of the door at the far end suddenly glow – the light turning on in the room beyond because of the noise? The door handle turned. He kicked the door open and it smacked into the face of the man standing behind it, sending him reeling back.

A woman screamed. Peake tossed the boy across the room toward her. Hermes stepped in and Peake kicked the door shut behind them.

'You're Faisal Al-Qarni,' Peake said to the bearded man on the floor, his nose bleeding all over his white pajamas.

The man glanced at his wife and son, huddled in the corner of the room, the mom sobbing. The boy looked terrified. The man, Faisal Al-Qarni – aka Alpha – nodded.

'Then listen to me very carefully,' Peake said, 'or you're going to watch your family die.'

34

Peake woke at gone 11 a.m. He'd slept better than expected, but perhaps only through utter exhaustion. He and Sean had dumped the weighed-down bags in the river. Nothing they could do if anything broke free and floated to the surface and washed up along the coast. They left the car and set it alight in wasteland across the water in New Jersey. The fire wouldn't destroy everything, but it'd be enough to remove any trace of Sean – and hopefully Ji Wang – from the vehicle.

Peake checked his phone, trying to erase the grim thoughts. A message from Dolan giving Peake his instruction for the day. One from Katie too. Asking him to go for a walk with her in Central Park later, grab some brunch. Such an ordinary request, an everyday thing that people – couples – did together. Today the idea of strolling, eating, seemed all the more surreal, with the bloody, gory images still so vivid in his mind – even if he really needed the distraction of doing something.

But he couldn't see her anyway. Not given Dolan's request.

He took a long shower. A hot shower. As hot as he could manage without pain, and he scrubbed his skin over and over until it was red raw. Still, he couldn't get rid of the thought of the blood on his hands – both literal, and metaphorical.

He headed out into the lounge where Sean remained fast asleep. Sleeping like a baby, as some might say. A clear conscience? Or just utter relief?

Peake put some coffee on, and the noise eventually caused Sean to stir.

'Shit,' he said, sitting up and putting a hand to his head.

'Hangover?' Peake asked.

'I dunno,' Sean said.

Peake had no idea what that meant.

'You want anything?' he asked.

'Just water.'

Peake poured him a glass.

'You know when you wake up and... you just wish you were still in your dream because reality is too shit?' Sean said.

'Yeah,' Peake said, handing him the water. 'What are you going to do?'

'How do you mean?'

'You should tell Harry what happened.'

Sean glowered but didn't respond.

'Better than getting into a mess again like last night,' Peake said.

'You think my cousins would have done a better job than we did?' Sean asked. 'They think they're tough guys, but... they're just brawlers. Thugs.'

'Still, Harry—'

'Would you shut up about Harry,' Sean said. 'I'll tell him what he needs to know, when he needs to know it. Got it?'

Fighting talk given the state he'd been in last night when Peake had arrived in Soho.

'Yeah,' Peake said.

'We'll go back down to Chinatown together—'

'You think that's a good idea right now?'

'We need to find out who this guy was working for,' Sean said. We.

'Okay. But it needs to wait.'

'Let me guess – the Arabs?'

Peake held his phone up as if that was enough explanation. 'I'm needed again.'

'I'm surprised, given last night.'

'Me too.'

'You know what for?'

'No. Dolan only said to get to the hotel for twelve-thirty.'

'Ominous.' Sean smiled, looking far more relaxed than at any point over the last few hours. 'Like that scene in Goodfellas where the guy thinks he's about to become a made man.'

'Yeah, thanks,' Peake said, knowing full well how that scene ended. 'I'll come and pick you up at your place later, and we'll go down Chinatown.'

'My place?' Sean said. 'I'm not sure I ever want to go back there now.'

'Then crash here for a few hours. Rest up.'

Sean didn't say anything, just nodded.

* * *

He reached the Sapphire Hotel ten minutes early, a little surprised to see Khalid already standing outside. He moved over to the car as Peake pulled up and opened his window.

'I heard you wanted to see me again,' Peake said.

'Wait there, they'll be down any minute.'

They turned out to be Khalid's wife and some guy Peake had never seen before. The sheikh's daughter looked much smarter than at the airport pick-up, wearing a skirt and blouse combo – obviously expensive gear – with high heels, a leather handbag, and jewelry galore. The man accompanying her had on a plain black suit, big sunglasses. A stiffness to him like a wannabe Secret Service agent or something.

He got into the front. Khalid and his wife sat in the back.

'Peake, this is Salman.'

The guy nodded to Peake but didn't say anything, so Peake decided not to say anything to him either.

'So what can I do for you today?' Peake asked, deciding to keep things simple even though his brain screamed at him about what the hell he was doing in the car with these people, and why they'd asked for him.

'We're going shopping,' Khalid said. 'My wife would like something to show for her visit to America. Something expensive.'

Peake waited for more. Did he look like the type to know all the high-end stores in the city?

'Is there a problem?' Khalid asked.

'No, but is there somewhere in particular?'

'You choose.'

'Let's start at Fifth Avenue then,' Peake said.

It was where tourists tended to head to at least, and he knew there was a Tiffany store there, near the corner of Central Park, among a load of other stores way too expensive for him.

He set off in that direction. There was silence in the car for a few moments.

'I hope you enjoyed the rest of the evening?' Peake said. 'After the... distraction.'

'We managed to rectify it.'

No further explanation than that.

'Sean was just... He's having a bad time.'

Khalid said nothing.

'I'm sure you understand,' Peake added.

'And why would you think that?' Khalid let the question hang. 'The man acted like a crazed idiot. He embarrassed me, and the sheikh, in front of a lot of very influential people.'

'I'm sorry, anyway,' Peake said.

No response from Khalid, and no more chat until Peake had parked on East 57th Street.

'Whatever you want,' Khalid said to his wife before kissing her on the cheek. She and Salman got out.

'You're not going?' Peake said.

'I trust her to make a good decision.'

'What is he? Security guard?'

'No, he's an astronaut.'

Sarcasm, Peake assumed, but it was hard to tell given Khalid's expressionless face.

'I'm surprised you asked for me today,' Peake said.

'Are you? Why?'

'Because of—'

'Like you said. That was down to Sean Lafferty, not you.'

'It was a shame to miss meeting Sheikh Al-Bishi.'

'I'm not sure you would have anyway.'

No further explanation on that.

'Tell me, Simon Peake, why do you work for Harry Lafferty?'

'I'm not sure I understand.'

'The sheikh came here, I came here, to make money. To strengthen the global standing not just of our business ventures but of the family, the whole Saudi nation in turn. You saw for yourself the pedigree of person we had at last night's event, and that's just a start.'

'The great and the good.'

Khalid looked a little confused by that as though not familiar with the expression.

'And then there's Harry Lafferty,' Khalid added.

A strange thing to say. Given he'd invited Harry to the event. Hadn't he?

'The thing is, when you're looking to make headway in a new country, it's very important to make acquaintances with the right type of people. Politicians. Policymakers. Financiers. Competitors and allies alike. And when you have money like we do, those connections soon get you on the right track. But I find sometimes... you need to see the other side of the coin too.'

'I'm not sure what you mean.'

'Oh, I think you do. Harry Lafferty is a successful businessman here, but don't insult me by telling me his activities are wholly legitimate.'

Peake didn't.

'But in many ways, I like men like Harry. Because they see all the politics around them, the barriers and the red tape and often the pompous corruption of the elite, and they... find ways to make things work for them anyway. And that's what we need here. And that's why Harry is... necessary.'

'I appreciate the explanation,' Peake said. 'Though I'm not sure why you bothered with it.'

'My point is that I believe Harry's a good business partner for me, and for Sheikh Al-Bishi. But what I don't like is some of the people around him.'

Peake held Khalid's eye in the mirror.

'You mean me?' Peake said.

'Tell me about your past,' Khalid said.

'Nothing much to tell,' Peake said.

'I don't think that's true.'

That comment led to a long, drawn-out silence. How much did Khalid know?

'You were in the British army?'

'A long time ago. And since then... I've not done much. Honestly? I've struggled.'

'You were in prison. Here in New York.'

'Yes.'

'Assault.'

'Yes.'

'You beat up two teenagers, very badly.'

'I did. To save a girl.'

'So you thought you were doing a noble deed?'

'At the time.'

'You didn't explain that to the judge?'

'Sometimes when you can't afford a good lawyer, the system doesn't give you much of a chance to explain anything. Or at least, no one really listens.'

'And since you were in prison?'

'I've tried hard to pull my life back on track. Now I'm working with Harry Lafferty.'

'You consider that being back on track.'

'For me? Yeah.'

'I have to say, even knowing who Harry Lafferty is... at least there's a certain... conformity to him. But you... Are you anything more than a lowlife thug?'

What the hell was this? Was the guy just trying to rile Peake? Why?

'I'm a guy who's made some poor choices. And I've suffered because of them.'

'Tell me about your time in the army.'

Peake caught Khalid's eye again. He looked so... smug.

'There's nothing much to tell,' Peake said. 'I did a couple of tours. Saw some pretty nasty shit, as most active soldiers do.' Which really was about as bland an explanation of his time serving that he could give. 'In the end I got thrown out.'

'Why?'

'Fighting. Specifically, I hit one of the higher ranks.'

A light way of putting it.

'Violence. A common theme for you.'

'It was a long time ago.'

'Yes. Except... I don't believe you.'

Peake channeled his inner tension down into the pit of his gut. He'd do anything to not let it show now.

'Don't believe what?' he said.

'Did you ever spend time in the Middle East?'

'Yeah,' Peake said with a shrug. 'Like I told you. I did a couple of tours. Iraq and Afghanistan. So is this what yesterday was all about? You taking my headshot and fingerprints so you could run some background checks on me?' Khalid didn't say anything to that, but Peake hadn't really expected him to. 'Well, go ahead. Do whatever checks you want. I've nothing to hide. And you know what? If you don't want me in front of the sheikh because you don't trust me? Fine. I've no idea why he'd want to see me anyway.'

Khalid smiled, but it was far from friendly.

'Have I touched a nerve?' he asked.

'Yeah,' Peake said, 'you have.'

'What will you do if I annoy you too much? Will you snap like you have done before?'

The guy was so calm, cocky.

'You know what?' Peake said.

But before he could answer, Salman and Khalid's wife came out of the shop across the road and strode over. They jumped back into the car.

'You got something?' Khalid said with a wide smile.

His wife opened her shopping bag a little to show off whatever was inside.

'Wow,' was all Khalid said.

'Anywhere else?' Peake asked.

'Actually, I think we've done what we needed to do.'

His wife didn't look like she agreed but she didn't protest.

Peake drove them back to the hotel, not a word said by anyone on the way there. Khalid hung back a little as his wife and Salman got out.

'Thanks for the ride,' Khalid said. 'And for the discussion. I think I got from it what I needed.'

'I'm glad.'

'Maybe you won't be. I'm going to suggest to Harry that he shouldn't be associating with ex-convicts like you. It's not a good look for me or Sheikh Al-Bishi. Good day.'

Khalid stepped out and slammed the door. He moved up to Salman and Peake remained frozen a few moments as rage bubbled away inside him. The two men entered into a quiet conversation, leaning into each other's ear as they took turns to speak, all the while with an eye in Peake's direction.

Then they turned and moved toward the hotel entrance.

Only when they were inside did Peake finally release his death grip on the steering wheel.

35

No sign of Sean back at Peake's apartment, though the guy hadn't gone to his own place as Peake had realized earlier that he still had the keys to the Soho apartment in his car from the night before.

Most likely Sean was off causing a stir in Chinatown. Which had the potential to really screw things up.

He tried to call. Sent a message.

> Let me know if you need anything

He got no response. He sent a message to Katie but she'd already headed out for brunch with a friend. He didn't sense that she was angry that he'd blown her off earlier, but he really didn't know.

As he sat in quietness in his living room, all seemed quiet next door in Jelena's apartment too, altogether making him feel unusually isolated and alone. No, that wasn't unusual really. He'd lived like that for years – it was only in recent days that things had changed.

Two choices. Stay in and take the edge off with drink, or head out.

He found the strength to choose the latter, though as he closed his apartment door he stood there a moment and thought about knocking on Jelena's. Just for some company. And to check she was OK.

A ping on his phone.

Dolan.

> We're meeting at the bar. Come now

He wondered if that meant Khalid had already passed the message on to Harry...

Just like the night before in Sean's apartment, Peake thought about packing up and leaving there and then. Once again, he didn't.

Instead, minutes later he completed the now-familiar route to the Lower East Side. The bar officially wasn't open, but the doors weren't locked and Peake walked in to see the whole gang already there, Sean included. No one looked particularly happy.

'Help yourself to a beer,' Joey said. 'Heard that's what you did last night anyway.'

He himself had a beer in his hand as he stood propped by the bar. Chops did too, sat in a booth with Harry and Sean – a coffee for the old man, no drink for the latter. Dolan was sitting on a table, arms folded.

'This is a family meeting,' Harry started. 'And usually you wouldn't be invited. You're only here because I need to better understand just what the hell you and my son have been up to.'

Peake looked at Sean who had his head down.

'OK,' Peake said. 'What do you want to know?'

'Didn't I just say?' Harry responded. He was angry. Very angry. As angry as Peake had seen him.

He wondered if this was only to do with Sean and if the 'news' from Khalid was yet to come...

'What's Sean told you so far?' Peake asked.

Harry screwed up his face, looking like he'd just swallowed a piece of shit. Dolan stood up from his perch and took a couple of steps toward Peake. Joey did the same, as though his brother's shadow.

'Are you deaf as well as stupid?' Dolan said. 'Harry asked you to talk. So fucking talk.'

'OK,' Peake said, holding his hands up. 'This started yesterday morning. Sean told me he had a lead from Alessi about a body that'd washed up. Sean thought it was the dead guy from the Bronx. His name was David Beck. We went over to his place.'

Peake carried on, telling the story as fully and succinctly as he could. Right up to the point about chopping up the dead body of Ji Wang, at which point Harry's face turned even more sour than before.

'OK, OK,' Harry said. 'Save us the gore. No one's impressed.'

'Sure,' Peake said. So he skipped most of that part and finished off with the dumping.

'And that's all I know. Sean stayed with me last night. Well, this morning. I don't know what else he's found today.'

Eyes turned to Sean. All except Harry who remained staring at Peake.

'There's been a hell of a lot of shit happening since you arrived,' he said.

'Damn right,' Dolan said.

'I can't figure out if you're causing it, if you're cursed, or if actually you're making a bad situation better somehow.'

Joey raised an eyebrow as though he couldn't believe the old man had just said the latter.

'I know Khalid doesn't like you,' Harry said. 'But from what I gather it's only because he doesn't like your criminal past. I can live with that part of you at least. The rest? I'm just not sure.'

Did that at least confirm that Khalid had been in Harry's ear since the shopping trip?

'This has gone too far,' Dolan said. 'I don't even know why we took this clown on.'

'We took him on because he has something we don't,' Sean said. 'You think we're in a mess because of him? I'm alive because of him.'

'Yeah, he's saved the fuck-up's ass a couple of times and—'

Dolan didn't get to finish his sentence because Sean bounced up from his seat and launched himself for his cousin and sent a hook for his face. Dolan didn't quite manage to duck out of it before returning with an uppercut. Not a great connection but enough to push Sean away a split second before Joey joined the melee, although it wasn't clear if it was to help one of the others or to break them apart.

'Stop!' Harry bellowed and the room went silent and still. He glared at each of them in turn. 'Look at you all, you bunch of self-righteous, entitled little pricks. I worked my backside off for decades building a future for you all and this is how you behave?'

His words had the desired effect. Dolan and Joey and Sean each brushed themselves down. Chops hadn't moved from his seat as though the antics of the others was simply beneath him.

Harry got up and moved around and right up to Dolan's face.

'And I don't care whose son you are. I hear you call my boy a fuck-up again and I'll feed you your tongue. You understand me?'

'Yeah,' Dolan said, sounding anything but regretful. 'I understand.'

'Peake, go wait outside,' Harry said.

He didn't hesitate.

He pushed the door open and stepped out and sucked in fresh air and his brain swam as he reached for his cigarettes. He pulled out a smoke and lit up and took the biggest drag he could. He leaned against the wall and looked up to the sky as he exhaled and listened to the voices drifting from within the bar. Still raised, still bickering despite Harry's intervention.

He'd finished his first cigarette and was partway through another when Sean came out. A neutral look on his face.

'I'll take one,' he said, indicating the cigarette.

After that the two of them stood in silence a few moments, smoking in unison.

'You think it's true?' Peake asked.

'What?'

'You think I've brought shit onto your family?'

'Are you kidding? This is the way it's always been. We're not office workers. Joey and Dolan just don't like you. Maybe because they see you have more talent than they do.'

Talent for what, exactly?

'You know what?' Sean said.

'What?'

'He didn't say it... but I actually think Harry is impressed with what I found, what I did yesterday.'

Peake presumed he meant what he'd done about Beck and Wang, and not the drunken escapade at the Sapphire Hotel. Sean too seemed to have forgotten about that, about how down and paranoid he'd been. Had it only been the drink and drugs talking?

'The thing is—'

'Wait,' Peake said.

Sean raised an eyebrow, then followed Peake's line of sight

down the road. A black SUV. It'd been parked up fifty yards away when he'd stepped out. Had pulled away a few seconds ago. Now its engine revved as it shot forward toward them at speed.

The windows slid down.

Two gun barrels poked out.

'Move!' Peake screamed, already fearing it was too little, too late.

36

Peake dove for Sean and grabbed him and tugged him toward the ground as the gunmen opened fire. Bullets zinged and thwacked all around. Peake could do little else except brace himself before he and Sean hit the deck. Peake unintentionally landed on top, crunching down on Sean's shoulder and Peake heard a pop. Sean moaned in pain. One second, two passed as Peake cowered and covered the man beneath him.

Then the gunfire stopped just as quickly as it'd started, and the SUV shot off down the street as the door to the bar burst open and Dolan then Joey raced into the open.

'What the—'

Joey made a mad attempt to sprint after the SUV but stopped after a few strides. Peake pulled himself off Sean.

'Hey,' he said pulling on Sean's jacket.

His face was creased with pain. Not from his popped shoulder.

'He's hit,' Dolan said. 'For fuck's sake, he's hit!'

And more than once. Four bloody holes in his jacket. Chest,

two in the gut, one in his shoulder. He was breathing, squirming in pain, and it didn't look good.

Peake reacted. No pre-meditation. He bounced to his feet and raced for the Merc.

'Where the hell are you going?' Dolan shouted to Peake before reaching out and gently shaking his cousin. 'Sean, stay with me!'

Peake jumped into the driver's seat, engine on, and he floored it. Tires screeched, the back end swung out before the Mercedes accelerated away. He glanced in the rearview mirror. Behind him Joey glared, phone pressed to his ear. Dolan continued to try to keep Sean awake. Peake focused on the road ahead. He pushed all other thoughts away. One aim: he had to get to the SUV. It'd already taken a right, momentarily out of sight. Peake followed...

There it was. Two hundred yards ahead. Struggling to push through a cluster of cars at a red light. The driver eventually managed it but not without a couple of shunts, and horns blared everywhere. By the time Peake reached the melee, the lights had turned green and the confusion somehow helped him to speed through the junction and close the distance to the shooters to less than fifty yards. Peake needed more. He couldn't afford a drawn-out race around Manhattan in the middle of the day. The police would descend within seconds.

He pushed his foot to the floor. Rapidly closed the gap. The SUV driver must have realized he was under attack because he increased his speed too. Sixty. Seventy, heading for another junction and another red light. It looked like the SUV would blast right through but at the last moment red brake lights flicked on.

Peake had a choice. He could slam right into them...

No time. The SUV had already turned and was pulling away, past a truck which had slammed to a stop almost blocking Peake's path.

He yanked on the wheel and spun around the corner, and within a few seconds his lighter and more agile Mercedes had closed the gap some more. Five yards. Four. The SUV swerved erratically, as though the driver hoped it'd lead to Peake making a fatal mistake.

He didn't. Instead he waited for the driver to straighten up as they approached another junction, then he accelerated again, coming up alongside. As soon as the nose of his car had passed the back end of the SUV, Peake tugged on the steering wheel. The contact was minimal – probably a scratch at most – but simple physics won out. The shunt was enough to cause the back end of the SUV to swing out, and at speed, momentum took over from there. Peake lifted his foot off the accelerator. The driver of the SUV battled for control, but it was no use. The SUV fishtailed...

Peake expected it to spin to a stop, but the high-sided, unstable vehicle rocked, two wheels lifted from the ground and then it toppled, rolled over and over, metal crunching, glass shattering, until it slammed into a row of parked cars.

Peake thumped his brakes. He darted from the car. Pedestrians shouted and cowered from the near impact. Peake rushed to the steaming, hissing, upside-down wreckage. Two bleary eyes stared at him from within the back as he approached.

'Oh God, someone help them!' a woman cried out, gasping in horror and turning around, hand over her mouth.

'It's OK, I'm a doctor,' Peake shouted. 'Call an ambulance. Everyone stand back.'

The gathering onlookers, in their confusion, listened to him and Peake turned and crouched down. The two eyes that had been staring at him from the back... That guy was dead. A huge shard of metal from the door pillar had pierced his chest. The passenger in front of him, the other gunner? Still alive. Or at least bloody spittle bubbled out of his mouth and nostrils, but he wasn't otherwise moving and his body was compressed up against the crumpled dashboard. He didn't have long to live.

They'd got what they deserved, as far as Peake was concerned. But who were they? He didn't recognize the bloody faces.

'Do something,' a man behind Peake said.

'We can't move them until the emergency services get here.'

He quickly moved around to the driver's side. Pushed past the people there.

'Please, let me see,' Peake said.

Once again, the bystanders were happy to oblige to the authoritative voice.

'Motherfucker,' Peake whispered under his breath as he locked eyes with the man behind the wheel.

Christine. Chan's minion. His oversized shape, the crumpled roof of the SUV above him, meant his head was pinned to his shoulder at a crazy looking angle. But he was still breathing, or at least rasping.

'Get back!' Peake shouted to the crowd, pushing out his hand to signal them to move away. The closest few took notice and shuffled back, but more still joined behind them.

'You piece of shit,' Peake whispered to Christine, locking on to his panicked eyes.

No response. Perhaps he couldn't speak, or just understood his predicament.

Peake reached in and pushed his wrist onto the guy's throat. His eyes bulged. With his other hand he pushed his fingers into the wound in the man's shoulder and he moaned and writhed as much as he could in the constrained space.

'We need that ambulance now!' Peake shouted out without turning.

'The police,' someone said. 'The police are here.'

And Peake could hear the siren. Still a distance away.

'They can't save you now,' Peake said. 'You're not leaving this vehicle alive. And I'm going to fucking tear Chan to pieces when I find him.'

'F-fuck y-y-you.'

'Not today,' Peake said. He pushed as hard as he could with his wrist. A sudden, sharp move.

Crunch.

Spine? Windpipe? He didn't know which. He didn't care. Christine was dead.

The police car pulled up to a chorus of shouts and cries.

Peake straightened up and ignored the bystanders and strode to the police officers.

'What happened?' one of them asked him as though they sensed he was in charge.

'They were speeding, lost control,' Peake said. 'Three occupants. The one on the driver's side... He's really bad.'

Peake feigned emotion and the officer – Lopez, his badge read – put a hand to his shoulder.

His partner looked along the street. 'We got this. The paramedics are here.' Then he turned to the masses. 'Alright, I need everyone to stay back! Give us some room.'

'You need to wait right here,' Lopez said before turning and rushing around to the driver's side.

Peake stayed on the spot for only a moment before quietly retreating to his car. He didn't know if anyone followed his moves because he kept his head down, but seconds later he'd swung the Mercedes around and was traveling steadily back toward O'Hare's.

He only realized a couple of streets later that his body was shaking from adrenaline. Shock too, and the apprehension as to what came next.

Perhaps shame, for what he'd just done... No, he could bury that one easy enough. He was well used to it by now.

Peake took the car into a quiet alley and spent a couple of minutes swapping the plates on the Mercedes with one of the sets from the hidden compartment in the trunk. He checked his phone. Nothing from Harry or the boys.

He got moving again and soon turned onto the street by the bar and pulled over. In front of him an array of flashing lights. Three police cars, an ambulance. Police tape cordoned off the street all around O'Hare's. He spotted Harry talking to a policeman. Joey sitting on the ground. Chops and Dolan standing, looking forlorn.

Peake called Joey. No answer. He didn't have a number for Chops. He bit the bullet and called Dolan.

'Where are you?' Dolan asked when he answered, turning around to scan the street.

'How's Sean?'

Pause. 'He's dead.' No particular emotion in his voice, though Peake felt a stab in his chest. Guilt, rather than sorrow. But also extreme anger, even if he'd already dealt a dose of revenge. 'No thanks to you, running off like a—'

'I caught them,' Peake said.

Dolan seemed to become even more alert at that, and he stared right over to where Peake was parked.

'You have them?' he asked.

'No. I caught up with them. They crashed. They're all dead.'

No response to that.

'But I know who did this,' Peake said. 'I know who they worked for. Who ordered this.'

'Go on.'

'His name's Chan. He's...' He held back from saying he's my landlord. The words sounded so surreal even to him. He'd always known the guy wasn't above board, but this? 'I know where he lives.'

Silence for a few moments.

'We're going to be tied up for some time here,' Dolan said. 'But you stay close. I'll call you when we need you.'

Dolan ended the call. Peake thought for a few moments. He could go to Chan's place on his own...

No, another realization struck him instead. Most likely, Chan was behind the previous robbery attempt up in the Bronx too. Beck and Wang were his men. Chan had organized the drive-by that killed Sean as revenge for their deaths. Sean was a clear target in that attack. But so too was Peake.

What would Chan do now that he knew Christine and the others were dead too?

Adrenaline surged once more. Peake needed to get home, and fast.

37

Peake called Katie as he drove. She didn't answer. He had no idea where she'd gone with her friend. He'd go to her place soon enough, hopefully find her there. If Chan was intent on punishing Peake, the Laffertys, then he had to believe she was in danger too. He tensed a little with every cop car he passed, always on the lookout for anyone on his tail, ready to attack, yet he made it back to the Upper West Side without incident – just the constant internal battle going on in his mind.

He took the steps to the sixth floor two at a time, his chest heaving with deep breaths by the time he made it. He banged on Jelena's door. No answer straightaway so he banged again, looking over his shoulder every other heartbeat.

She opened the door, on the chain.

'Peake, what are—'

'We need to go.'

'What?'

'Jelena, open the door, we need to go.'

'Go where? What—'

'Jelena, open the goddamn door!'

She pulled back and he thought she was about to shut the door on him but then he heard her release the chain and she edged the door open again.

When he noticed her face a swathe of his anxiety disappeared, but he couldn't explain what it was replaced with.

'Jelena,' he said, reaching tentatively toward the gash above her swollen left eye. Her lip, too, was bulbous and cracked. She ducked her head away from his touch. 'Who did this?'

'Peake, please—'

He grabbed her by the arms, as if to shake some sense into her.

'Who did this!'

She yanked away from his grip. 'Why do you even care?'

She turned away from him, hobbling off into the apartment and Peake stood a moment, desperately trying to contain himself before he exploded. He followed her in.

'Wyatt?' he asked. 'Chan?'

She faced him, she looked so... desperate and broken.

'Yes, it was Wyatt!' she said, looking as though she might break down any second. 'Happy now?'

'No,' Peake said. 'Not at all. I'll explain later, but you need to pack a bag. We're leaving. It's not safe here.'

'What are you talking about?'

'We're leaving.'

'Because of Wyatt? He's just a—'

'No, Jelena, not Wyatt. Chan.'

She looked broken in that moment, as though she hadn't realized he'd known and it made her feel so much worse.

'I know you work for him,' he said.

'How do you think I afford this place?' she said with a wry smile.

'Chan is going to come here. He and his guys could be on the way right now. And he's going to try and kill me. And if he thinks hurting you will hurt me? He'll do that too.'

'I don't know what you're saying.'

'All you need to do is pack a bag. I'll keep you safe.'

She shook her head as tears rolled.

'Please,' Peake said. 'Trust me.'

She didn't say anything.

'You've got two minutes.'

He turned and rushed out and into his own apartment and packed the few belongings he thought he'd need. Jelena met him at the door.

'Where are we even going?'

'Anywhere but here.'

They made their way down, Peake rushing forward, but Jelena moved so gingerly.

'What is it?' he asked her.

She simply tensed her face and shook her head. She was in pain. What had that bastard cop done to her? Seeing her like that only made it harder for Peake to control himself.

They reached the doors to the street. Peake hesitated a moment, scanning as best he could, the prospect of yet another drive-by all too real. He saw nothing, but he couldn't get a full view until they stepped outside. He put his arm around Jelena – both to help her along and to shield her. They walked out into the open...

All clear.

He ushered Jelena to the Mercedes. She winced in pain as she sat down in the passenger seat. Peake rushed to the driver's side and got them on their way.

'You really need to tell me what's happening,' Jelena said.

But Peake's brain was too scrambled for him to process the words. He glanced over at her.

'What did he do to you?' he asked.

'This isn't about Wyatt,' she said, sounding angry. With him? 'You said so yourself.'

But in that moment, with all the other turmoil sloshing in his mind, Peake didn't agree. Not at all.

He thought and thought and thought about it...

Then took a sharp left at the last second and pulled the car to the side of the road.

'What are you doing?' Jelena asked, but Peake said nothing as he stared out of the window at the building opposite.

'Peake, talk to me.'

He was silent for a few seconds, then, 'He can't get away with this.'

'Who? Wyatt? Screw him.'

'No,' Peake said.

'Wait... Does he live here? Peake, he's NYPD, have you any idea—'

'Someone needs to stop him!' Peake shouted and his voice bounced around the cabin and Jelena reeled back in shock from the force of it.

'Yes... but not like this.'

Peake didn't agree. He put his fingers around the door handle, but Jelena grasped his arm.

'You said you wanted to help me,' she said, sounding calm and composed now.

Peake didn't move.

'More violence isn't what I need.'

Peake let the handle go and grasped the steering wheel. He crushed it under his hands. Felt like he could tear the thing off if he tried.

'That isn't the way,' Jelena said.

The pleading in her voice allowed him to reach for just a little bit of clarity.

'If you want to help me... take me away from this, not further into it.'

He thought for only a moment more before pulling into the road.

He wrenched his thoughts away from Wyatt, from the anger that consumed him thinking about what he'd done to Jelena. Yet Peake remained far from relaxed, constantly wary as they headed downtown, expecting the police or Chan and his cronies to pounce any moment.

They didn't. After parking up, he took the keys from the cupholder before getting out. He moved around to help Jelena who clearly struggled going from sitting to standing and vice versa.

'I'm OK,' she said to him once she was upright, but she only half-heartedly brushed him off. He left his arm around her shoulder as he helped her to the door of the Soho apartment.

'Where are we?'

'It's a... friend's place.'

She looked a little dubious but didn't say anything more before they walked into the converted loft.

'Wow.'

'Yeah.'

'Your friend must have some money.'

'My friend...' is dead, he nearly said. 'Yeah, he does. We'll be safe here. At least while we figure things out.'

But safe for how long?

Jelena settled down on the sofa and Peake checked out of the windows. He saw no threats on the street. He took out his phone. Nothing more from any of the Laffertys. Perhaps they were still tied up with the police. And he didn't even know if he would take the flak from the family for Sean's death, or be hailed the hero for finding the culprits. Very soon he could have both sides of a newly started gang war after him.

He tried to call Katie again. No answer. He messaged her. No response. He really didn't like that at all.

The longer the silence from her went on...

He'd go to her apartment. Jelena was safe enough here for a while... Wasn't she?

'You're really scaring me,' Jelena said.

'Sorry,' Peake said, taking his fingers from the slats of the blind and turning to face her.

'Talk to me, please,' she said.

He moved over and sat down next to her on the sofa.

'This is so messed up,' she said. 'Why is Chan even after you? Me?'

'It's all my fault,' Peake said.

'What is? How?'

'That money,' he said. 'The money you hid for me.'

'I never told Chan about that.'

'I know, you didn't need to. He knew I had it. He knew because I turned up at his door one day with several thousand dollars. He didn't trust me. He must have had someone follow me to find out what I was doing, where it came from.'

'And then?'

'I was collecting for the Laffertys. Chan's guys tried to rob us. I didn't know it was him then, but one of them was killed. Then Sean—'

'The guy who was at yours the other day?'

'Yeah. He went on a mission to find who made the hit. He found another guy. He... killed him.'

Peake struggled to look over to the closed bedroom door as bloody thoughts resurfaced.

'We thought we'd done enough to cover it up,' Peake said. 'To make sure no one found out. But Chan must have. I don't know how. And then earlier... They hit us again. A drive-by. Revenge. They shot Sean. He's dead.'

Peake hung his head.

'You think it was Chan?'

'I know it was his people. That big guy, Chris, was the driver. But everyone in that car is dead.'

'You... killed them?'

He shook his head, didn't want to think about what he'd done. 'It was... a crash. But Chan will be even more set on revenge now. Anyone close to me is in danger.'

Katie...

But how would Chan even know about her?

Jelena didn't say anything, but he realized she was staring, though surprisingly she had the slightest smile on her face.

'Your life is even more messed up than mine,' she said. 'I'm kinda impressed.'

'You don't know the half of it.'

'I know I've been angry with you...' She sighed and looked away but then edged closer to him and nuzzled into his shoulder. 'But it's only because I'm... ashamed.'

'You've nothing to be ashamed of.'

'I'm not so sure. But my point is... thank you. Thank you for helping me, for thinking of me. Nobody else does. Nobody else keeps me safe like you do.'

'Maybe it's the opposite.'

'I don't understand.'

He thought for a moment. 'A long time ago... I was given a nickname. More of a snide insult, I think. Hades.'

'Hades? Like the Greek god?'

'God of the underworld. You know why they chose that name for me?'

She shook her head.

'Because everyone around me, everyone I try to help... It's like getting close to me is a death sentence.'

Jelena shook her head again, smiled. 'Then you don't know the story of Hades at all.'

He raised an eyebrow.

'To the Greeks, the underworld wasn't hell,' Jelena said. 'Hades wasn't evil or bad and he wasn't Death, walking around waving a scythe. He was strong and just, the god of the afterlife, a gatekeeper, there to help keep balance between the world of the living and the world of the dead.'

'Still... I don't even know.' He sighed and thought then opened his mouth to speak when his phone rang.

He hoped it was Katie...

Joey.

'Yeah,' Peake said answering.

'Where are you?'

'At Sean's.'

'What the fuck are you doing at my cousin's place?'

'I'll explain.'

'Yeah, you will. You told Dolan you know where this guy is?'

'I do.'

'OK. We're coming over. Don't go anywhere.'

38

He heard the cars pulling up outside only a few minutes later. Jelena sat up on the sofa, lifting off him, and he moved to the window to check. Two vehicles. Harry and Dolan got out of the first. Joey and Chops the second. But all were passengers, so who was driving?

He turned back around and noted the fearful look on Jelena's face.

'I shouldn't be here,' she said.

Perhaps she was right, but where else could she go now?

Moments later a knock came at the door. Peake walked over and opened up and moved aside. A sullen-faced Dolan stepped in first. The others filed in after him before Peake closed the door, but they all just hung there in the entranceway, staring over at Jelena.

'And who the fuck is she?' Dolan said, glowering at Jelena.

'She's my neighbor,' Peake said. 'My friend.'

'Oh, yeah,' Joey said. 'A friend. She's here with you, but not Katie. Interesting.'

Harry slapped Joey on the back of his head as Jelena stood from the sofa, face creased in pain.

'I should go,' she said.

'No,' Harry said. 'You're not going anywhere.'

'That means sit your ass back down,' Dolan said to her, and Jelena did.

Peake gritted his teeth, trying to stay calm.

'Sean is dead,' Harry said. 'You need to talk. Tell me why my son is on the way to the morgue.'

Peake kept it as short as he could, not wanting to dwell on any of the mess. The same story he'd told Jelena earlier, except he didn't mention the stolen money at the start, just that Chan had figured out about Peake's new job, had followed Peake at some point before setting up the first attempted robbery.

'You're actually telling me this guy is your damn landlord?' Dolan said when Peake had finished.

'Clearly he's a bit more than that,' Peake said. 'But yes, that's how I know him.'

'You brought this mess to our family,' Chops said, jabbing a finger at Peake. 'You've jeopardized our relationship with the Arabs. You're the reason Sean is dead.'

'And look at him,' Joey said. 'Swanning around in here like he's on the rise, while the blood in Sean's body is still warm.'

'OK, I get the point,' Harry said. 'But Peake still found the people who shot my son. And he made them pay.'

'Or maybe it was pure luck,' Dolan said.

'We'll make the call on that later. Right now... we find this Chan guy. We punish him and anyone else who had a hand in Sean's death.'

No one said anything to that, as though the trio couldn't quite believe Peake was getting off so lightly.

'You said you know where this guy lives?' Harry asked.

'Yeah,' Peake said. He gave the address.

'Then let's go.'

Everyone turned to the door. Everyone except Harry, who remained facing Jelena. 'And you stay here. Understood?'

She nodded but didn't say a word.

'I'll be back,' Peake said.

'Come on, lover boy,' Dolan said, shoving Peake toward the door.

They moved outside in a line.

'You go up front in the first car,' Harry said. 'Given you're the one who knows this place.'

Peake didn't say anything but made his way for the door. Dolan moved alongside to go into the back. Peaked opened up and slipped into the seat and looked across at the driver.

Salman?

'Hi, Simon,' came the voice of Khalid from the back, a split second before the needle jabbed into Peake's neck. A strong arm from behind held him in place – Dolan? – while the sedative took effect, spreading out through his bloodstream like wildfire.

Peake fought and fought, did what he could... but it wasn't enough.

'Thank you, Harry,' Khalid said, his voice soft and distant as Peake struggled to keep awake, his body heavy and unmoving as the arm moved away from his neck. 'We'll be in touch very soon.'

Peake was only vaguely aware of the sound of the car door closing, the gentle rumble of the engine turning over, before his eyelids slid closed.

39

OPERATION ZEUS – DAY 45

Alpha's wife and son remained huddled as they sat on the bed. The man himself lay in a heap on the floor in front of Peake, his nose pouring blood, to go with the gash somewhere in his hairline. The last punch he'd taken to the chest had broken at least two ribs, Peake thought.

'How do we get access?' Peake asked again, trying to control his building rage.

Hermes sat at the desk across the way with a laptop Alpha had directed him to. Hermes had unlocked the device, but Alpha was now playing dumb, despite the threat to him and his family.

'Access to what?' Alpha shouted.

English. The whole conversation had been in English. The guy spoke it perfectly, posh accent and everything. Peake hadn't expected that.

Peake crouched down and grabbed the man by the scruff of his neck and got right into his terrified face.

'The bombs, you piece of shit! How do we shut them down?'

'I... I... don't know what that means!'

Peake launched his fist into the man's stomach then leaned

back and clattered his forehead onto the bridge of Alpha's nose, opening up another gash there and eliciting yet another horrified murmur from the man's wife and son.

Peake took two big breaths to try to keep his cool.

'There are twenty bombs covering this city,' he said. 'They're going off tonight. Hundreds, possibly even thousands will die. You have a simple choice. You let that happen? I'm taking your family's lives too. This is your chance to save them.'

'I don't know about any bombs!' Alpha said.

'Hassan Al-Dawsari!' Peake shouted, giving Zeta's real name. 'He works for you.'

'Hassan? Yes... he... he does.'

'He bought detonators from us. Those detonators came here. East wing.'

'I don't go over there! This is my home!'

'This is going nowhere,' Hermes said. 'I need to know more. I'm onto his private network but there's nothing else I can do unless I know where the program is running.'

'You hear that?' Peake said. 'Give us what we need.'

'I don't know!'

Peake let go of him and stomped on Alpha's gut and the guy creased over clutching his stomach. He marched over to the bed where Alpha's wife and son squirmed away from him. He reached out to them but then stopped when he heard a voice in his ear.

'Hades, Hermes, you there?' Ares said.

'In the west wing still,' Peake said. 'We have Alpha. He's not talking.'

'Not talking? For fuck's sake, Hades, make him talk.'

'Did you find Zeta? The bombs?'

'We've had a few scuffles, but we only made it as far as the drop site. We've come above ground. We can't chase shadows down there all night.'

'So that's a no,' Peake said.

'It's a fucking no. We'll try and get back to you. But I don't know how much time we have. Do what you have to do. It's all down to you now.'

Peake grabbed Alpha's wife and pulled her to her feet. She resisted until he placed the trigger of the handgun against her skull.

'This is your last chance,' Peake said to Alpha. 'Tell me how to stop it or her brains'll soon be covering your face.'

'Please!' Alpha said, moving to a kneeling position and clasping his hands together as though in prayer.

'Tell me!' Peake screamed, so hard that the last word sounded choked and he was sure he could taste his own blood at the back of his throat, the lining scratched raw from the force of the instruction.

His finger twitched on the trigger, but the small gesture of pulling, firing came with not so small repercussions.

A line crossed. Mental turmoil.

Again.

'Tell me, or you know what happens!'

But Alpha said nothing.

'Come on, do it.' Talos. 'We don't have time. Do it now.'

'Tell me or she's dead,' Peake said, not sounding as angry or even as urgent now. More... pleading. 'Just tell me.'

'You have no choice! You have to do it.'

He pushed the barrel of the gun more firmly against the woman's skull.

'Please!' screeched the bleeding man.

But it was too little, too late.

Peake pulled the trigger.

Alpha screamed. So too his son. Peake winced – a reaction to the piercing boom so close to his ear. Not as close as it was to Alpha's wife's ear. Peake had pulled the barrel away from her head ever so slightly. The bullet missed her by a fraction of an inch. Burst eardrum? Judging by her screams, very likely.

Peake kicked her away.

'Hermes, come on,' Peake said.

He strode over to Alpha and grabbed him by his hair and dragged him to the door.

Hermes didn't move.

'Come the fuck on!' Peake shouted before hauling Alpha up and shoving him along the corridor. Down the stairs. Into the open.

'Call for help,' Peake said. 'See what happens.'

Alpha didn't.

'Hades, what's happening?' Ares asked.

Peake reached into his ear and pulled out the receiver and tossed it. Then he propelled Alpha forward, and he only just managed to pull up his hands to protect his face before he crashed into the open door at the side of the east wing.

Peake took hold of the man's hair again and dragged him into the room where several bodies lay broken and twisted. Hera among them. Looking at her lifeless eyes, her blood-soaked clothes, only further dredged up feelings in Peake that he usually tried so hard to keep down.

Not tonight.

'What the fuck...' Hermes said.

'Yep,' Peake said, before he kicked Alpha down the stairs into the torture chamber below.

Peake chased down after him and Alpha rolled into a heap right next to Minos's mutilated body. He propped himself onto his elbow before he took in the sight, and then shouted in horror and tried to scrabble back. Peake grabbed him once more to pull him to his feet.

'See what you've done,' Peake snarled.

'What are you talking about!'

Peake grabbed Alpha's wrist and slammed it down onto the gurney. He took a hammer from the tools and smashed it down onto the upside of Alpha's hand.

'Tell me how to stop it!' Peake boomed.

'I don't know!' Alpha yelled, his face twisted in agony.

Peake hammered down again. Again, again, until Alpha's screams had turned to animalistic shrieks and his hand had turned to a pulpy mush, his body hanging limply from the edge of the table.

'If we don't stop those bombs... I'm going to do to you exactly what you did to my friend.'

'It wasn't me!'

'Hermes, give me something,' Peake said turning to his colleague who still had the open laptop in his hand, but he looked dumbfounded.

'I'm... I'm... Give me time.'

'We don't have time!' Peake shouted, before turning back to Alpha and lifting the hammer up again. 'How do we stop it?'

'I don't know! This wasn't me!' he said again.

'It was you. Your man, Al-Dawsari. He bought detonators from us,' Peake said. 'You're using them to blow up this city, to restart the war. Al-Dawsari was operating from here.'

'I already told you!' Alpha said. 'I don't come here anymore. We have... an arrangement.'

'I don't believe you,' Peake said.

He slammed the hammer down one more time then tossed it and picked up a scalpel from the side. He pulled Alpha's hair back and placed the tip of the blade against Alpha's eyeball.

'Don't make me do this,' Peake said.

'Wait,' Hermes said. 'There's another network. Hidden. I think I've... This is it.'

He turned the screen to Peake who twisted Alpha's head that way. Peake stared.

'A timer,' Peake said.

'We have less than ten minutes,' Hermes said as Peake's eyes focused on the steadily reducing numbers.

'How do we stop it?' Peake asked.

'I need the code,' Hermes said. 'That's all.'

'What's the code?' Peake said to Alpha.

'I don't know.'

'What's the goddamn fucking code!' Peake screamed.

'I don't know!'

'Wrong answer.'

Peake slashed the scalpel across Alpha's face...

After that... his inner beast finally won out...

* * *

Peake slumped against the wall, panting, his clothes and face and arms covered in blood. Across the room Hermes looked shell-shocked, the laptop on his knee as he stared at the barely breathing Alpha. There was nothing more Peake could do. No more pieces he could take without killing the man.

'How long?' Peake asked Hermes.

'Less than two minutes.'

Peake smacked the back of his head against the wall.

'Where are the others?' Peake asked.

'I've not heard from them,' Hermes said.

Were Ares and Talos already dead?

'There's no way you can hack the code?'

'No.'

Peake inhaled until his lungs felt ready to explode and his brain ached from the sudden surge of oxygen. He released the air and moved toward Alpha. His one good eye watched the movement, but he had so little strength remaining that he didn't even cower or squirm as Peake took hold of him and turned him over onto his back.

'Hades, please,' Hermes said. 'I really don't think he knows.'

'He has to,' Peake said. *After what I've done to him. He has to.*

Disgust at his own actions and an agonizing regret churned away, threatening to overflow.

Somehow, he forced it all away even though he knew, when this was done, whether they stopped those bombs or not, those feelings would never leave him, would consume him.

Two minutes. Only two minutes. And thousands of lives depended on him.

Peake reached across and took the bone saw in his hand. Alpha didn't say anything as Peake wafted it in front of his face.

'You can still stop this,' Peake said, sounding dejected. 'You can still save lives.'

He got nothing in return from Alpha now – was he already too far gone?

'Less than sixty seconds,' Hermes said. 'We should go.'

Peake placed the blade against Alpha's wrist. He held it there as the counter in his head wound down. He pulled back once and the metal tore into the skin beneath and Alpha's body writhed in agony, but he didn't let out a sound.

'Hades,' Hermes said, sounding on the verge of breaking down. 'Stop. Please. It's too late.'

Peake dropped the blade and dropped to his knees, head hung low, unable to contain his revulsion, his despair, not just at his own actions, but at what was now an inevitable outcome.

He'd counted down to two when he heard the distant rumble.

Then another. Another. Another. Closer. Surrounding them. The ground shook.

Peake locked eyes with Hermes. Neither said a word, but both knew what it meant.

Everything they'd done... it'd made no difference at all.

Peake slumped against the wall.

He'd failed.

The blood of a city would stain his hands forever.

And he'd never forgive himself for what he'd become.

40

OPERATION ZEUS – DAY 47

The military base was a very different place to when Peake had first arrived in the country. The bombings, less than forty-eight hours ago, had set in motion a chain of events including a hard-line crackdown across the city, across the whole country. Martial law was now official, even if the police patrols had made it feel like that was the position for some time. Tit-for-tat retaliations had taken place all over, and unless one side was willing to compromise, all-out civil war would soon be inevitable once again.

The door in front of Peake opened and Chief stood there, a strangely relaxed look on his face.

'Come in,' he said, and Peake stood from his chair and walked into the makeshift office.

'Good result for you, then,' Peake said. Both men remained standing.

'What is?'

'War. Keeps you in a job here.'

'You think I wanted this?'

Peake said nothing.

'Have you any idea the problems I've had to—'

'Problems?' Peake said. 'How about the nearly one thousand people who lost their lives in those blasts? The lives we lost.'

They'd had no contact with Ares or Talos at all since the bombs had gone off, the only conclusion being that they'd either been killed by one of the blasts or were being held by the perpetrators. Having seen the state of Minos, Peake only hoped they'd died quickly.

The state of Minos? What about Alpha?

Peake swallowed hard and buried the thoughts as far down as he could, even though he knew it was a pointless task now.

'We've had further intel the last few hours...' Chief began. 'Alpha... It definitely wasn't him.'

'Why are you telling me this?'

'I thought you'd want to know.'

Peake clenched his teeth.

'You tried, Peake. I know that. You came here for a job, and you did what needed to be done. It's only—'

'You sent us on a fucking suicide mission.'

Chief glowered but didn't respond.

'Did you know?' Peake asked. 'Did you know about their plans? Were we there all along as a catalyst for this?'

Peake didn't know why but he'd long been dubious of the true motives of the operation from those up high. Another civil war meant keeping a stranglehold on the country, from afar. The fact Chief didn't answer the question straightaway only added to Peake's suspicion.

'The op is closed down as of now,' Chief said after a while. 'You can go home, Peake. Go home and forget about this place. No one needs to know what you did here.'

'What I did?'

Peake tried his best. He really did. He wanted to walk away.

He wanted to turn and walk and never look back on this op, on this country.

But the demons in his head wouldn't let him.

Peake leaped forward and grabbed Chief's neck, and he swiped his feet and slammed his head down onto the desk. He grabbed Chief's wrist with one hand and a paperweight with the other.

'You want to know what I did?' he shouted.

He slammed the weight down onto Chief's hand and the boss yelled in pain.

'You really want to know what I did... for you?'

Peake hit down again. Got ready for a third strike. His whole body trembled with rage.

'You fucking animal!' Chief screamed.

Peake let him go and Chief cradled his smashed hand.

'You're finished!' Chief said. 'I'll see you behind bars.'

After what he'd done... perhaps it was the best place for him...

Peake threw the paperweight and it smacked off Chief's shoulder and onto the floor.

Neither man said another word as Peake turned and walked away.

41

Even as he dreamed, he knew it wasn't real, though that didn't deter from the feeling of uselessness, the pain. He was back in the Middle East. Back in the crew of Operation Zeus. A desperate, last-ditch effort to prevent a massacre. Except this time it wasn't Peake who had a captive at his mercy, him able to find an inner demon to assist in what needed to be done... This time, he was the captive. Tied up, his tormentors brutalizing him, taunting him...

He woke with a jump and even in his confusion he dwelled for a few moments on just how much of the dream had actually been a premonition, how much had been his subconscious, somehow aware of what was happening around him even with him comatose.

'And he's back,' Khalid said. Peake's focus rested on Khalid as his scrambled brain took a renewed look at the scene. Khalid was standing. Peake was in a chair. Wrists tied behind him, ankles clasped together.

What else? Peake blinked several times as he did his best to look around the room. A big room. Concrete floor. High ceiling.

Dirty, scratched-up walls. An industrial space. Not decrepit, just unused. Windowless? Nothing in front of him except a door and the only illumination was from the lightbulb above. A window behind him, perhaps, or did the lack of natural light mean it was nighttime?

'You have nothing to say?' Khalid asked.

Peake didn't. He didn't know this man well, but he knew enough to realize that if he wanted to talk, to rub Peake's face in the mess he was in, he would.

'I feel like I should explain why we're here,' Khalid said, looking around the room. 'Because it might seem like an unexpected turn for you. And honestly? It's unexpected for us all, even if it is in many ways welcome.'

Peake rolled his eyes and looked away, showing his disinterest in the explanation.

'Let's get the introductions out of the way.'

Khalid banged on the door behind him and a moment later it opened and two more men stepped inside. Salman, still smartly dressed, but his sunglasses off for the first time that Peake had seen to reveal one deep-set eye and another that was missing, the skin where it'd been folded over with scars.

'Should have kept the sunglasses on,' Peake slurred.

He looked to the other man who walked in – similarly smartly dressed like Salman, except... Peake kind of recognized him.

'Of course, you've met Salman,' Khalid said. 'And if you're lucky, perhaps he'll tell you the story about that eye. You'd find it quite enlightening. But enough of that for now. I have to say sorry, because I may not have been entirely truthful with you. Salman doesn't work for me, but for my friend here.'

Peake stared at the man who was standing at the back of the room, looking cautious and a little bit disturbed.

'It's true that we always take security measures for people meeting the sheikh for the first time. Threat detection, for his benefit, but... doing so also has a dual purpose. Seeking out people... of interest. In this case, I'd say we got extremely lucky. Lucky for us, unlucky for you, that is.'

The man at the back of the room stepped forward and crouched down in front of Peake.

'Do you know who I am?' he asked.

Peake thought he probably did, but he didn't confirm it.

'My name is Omar. Omar Al-Qarni.'

Peake kept his mouth shut.

'You knew my brother, Hassan. I think you and your friends called him "Alpha". Am I right?'

Peake stared at the man but still said nothing.

'You killed my brother. In fact, you tortured my brother. I saw what you did to him. So did his wife, his son.' He shook his head as if in despair.

'If you don't open your mouth and respond, perhaps you don't need that tongue. I'll come over there and cut it out for you right now,' Salman said, his voice unusually husky.

Peake glared at him but still remained silent.

Salman stormed to the side of the room, picked up a pair of scissors from the table of instruments and marched to Peake's side. Hands from behind held Peake in place as Salman prized Peake's mouth open. He resisted for only a second before resorting to an alternative defense. He opened his jaw...

Chomp.

He bit down as hard as he could on Salman's fingers. Two of them, caught between his teeth. He ground down and Salman roared in pain and thumped Peake in the gut. Hit him again and again then, when it made no difference, thrust the scissors down into Peake's thigh.

He released his hold and grimaced in pain.

'Leave it!' Khalid shouted. 'He'll get what's coming.'

Salman grumbled, nursed his bleeding fingers as he stood straight and backstepped behind Omar. The guy hadn't moved a muscle. Remained on his haunches in front of Peake, still staring.

'You're an animal,' he said.

'Only when provoked,' Peake added.

'So he does have a voice,' Khalid said, smiling for some reason.

'You tortured my brother,' Omar said.

Peake swallowed hard on the building regret inside him.

'I was trying to stop a war,' he said.

'You didn't succeed.'

Peake closed his eyes, not wanting to think about any of it.

'My brother had nothing to do with those bombs.'

'I know that now. But... Ask me why I didn't run.'

'What?'

'Ask me. I'm not stupid. Bad luck? Yeah. But when it was clear Khalid had taken an interest in me, when he brought Salman along to scope me out... Ask me why I didn't run.'

'Why?' Omar asked.

'Because I knew this moment would come, one day. I've been waiting. And... I deserve it. Whatever you're about to do to me... I deserve it.'

Omar didn't respond to that, but he glared at Peake who saw just the smallest doubt in the man's eyes.

'You tortured an innocent man,' Khalid said. 'And a whole nation suffered because of your mistake.'

'I tried to stop the suffering,' Peake said. 'Perhaps you need to look at the real culprits.'

'And that would be?'

'You know. The Saudis,' Peake said. 'The same people you've been working for, who you're sucking up to now.'

Omar's face remained as passive as ever, but Khalid looked offended.

'It's called a long play,' Khalid said.

'Keep your enemies close,' Omar added.

'A long play?' Peake said. 'What play?'

'What were you doing in our country?' Khalid asked.

'I already told you.'

'No, not you – your people. Why do you think your government had an interest there?'

Peake didn't answer.

'Money, yes? That's all any Western country ever wants from our region. Exploitation. Peace, stability, on their terms, for their gain. If they can't have that? War, until they get what they want again.'

Which was exactly what Peake had always feared about the intentions behind Operation Zeus, the Chief and those above him.

'So what? Now you want to punish the UK? The US?' Peake said. 'Not very original.'

He laughed and saw the anger ramp up on both Khalid's and Salman's faces. Not Omar's though.

'The Saudis funded those attacks,' Khalid said. 'The Saudis wanted a war back then, and they got one. That came at a time when your government supposedly wanted the opposite. Yet did the UK, the US, anyone ever reprimand Saudi Arabia, the sheikhs who benefitted from those bombs and the war that followed?'

Peake knew the answer, but didn't bother to say.

'Of course not,' Khalid said. 'Why?'

'Money,' Omar answered for him.

'Saudi Arabia has one of the worst human rights records in the world, is responsible for wars in multiple countries, but who helps to prop them up? Who keeps their economy turning, the billions rolling in, who supplies them with endless arms?'

'Wait,' Peake said, looking up as though thinking. 'Is it... the penguins in Antarctica?'

'America. The UK,' Khalid said, his face emotionless and his tone blunt.

'Blah, blah,' Peake said. 'Same old.'

'No,' Khalid said. 'Not same old. Yes, we're going to attack our enemies – the UK, the US, anyone else who knowingly turned a blind eye. But the attacks won't be in our name. We want to benefit. The world will see Saudi Arabia for what it really is. Do you think it'll be enough to get the people of your country to wake up?'

'So get on with it,' Peake said. 'You didn't come here for Tiffany's but to kill some infidels and blame it on the Saudis. What do you want from me?'

'In my brother's home,' Omar said, 'you chose to torture one man to try to save hundreds. Today, it's the reverse.'

Khalid smiled and moved to the table. He picked up a tablet and took it over to Peake.

'Pier 17,' he said. 'One delivery truck, one bomb. Hundreds of people out to eat and drink, not knowing this will be their last night on earth.'

Khalid tapped on the screen then pushed his thumb onto it, then held it up to his face – retina scan? A beep from the machine and he turned the screen to Peake. A countdown. Thirty minutes.

'The bomb can only be disarmed from this device,' he said.

He let the statement hang, as though he expected Peake to say something.

'Ask him,' Omar said. 'Ask how you can stop it.'

'Who says I want to stop it?' Peake said. 'This is on you, not me.'

'But Peake... you can stop it,' Khalid said. 'But not yet. Salman?'

Omar stepped away as Salman came back toward Peake. In his hand... a scalpel. The arms from behind pinned Peake in place once more. Salman crouched down to Peake's feet.

'Tell me what you did to my brother,' Omar said.

Peake braced himself but said nothing.

'Tell me what you did,' Omar said, so calm still. 'That's what you'll get. Or... much worse if you like.'

Peake shook his head...

Then gritted his teeth and tried his hardest not to roar in agony as the scalpel dug into the skin on his big toe. He couldn't see, he didn't need to. Slice, slice, tug, tug. Then Salman yanked and Peake opened his mouth and yelled as loudly as he could, so hard that he thought his chest would burst.

Salman straightened up holding the dripping skin in his hands.

'You know what that's called?' Khalid asked. Peake couldn't find any words even if he'd wanted to. 'De-gloving.' He quivered theatrically. 'Just the word alone makes me squeamish.'

'Were you squeamish when you tore my brother's skin off?' Omar asked, finally showing emotion: anger.

'Yes!' Peake screamed. 'But... I had to.'

'De-gloving,' Khalid said. 'Salman is quite skilled. Do you know who trained him?'

Peake didn't answer.

'The Saudis, of course. They really are butchers.'

'One toe down,' Salman said. 'Lots more to go.'

He tossed the bloody tissue away and came back toward

Peake who writhed in the chair but could do nothing. This time Salman disappeared out of sight behind, and a moment later Peake felt the stinging pain in his thumb.

He bucked and squealed and squirmed and when Salman eventually yanked the torn skin free, for a moment the pain became so intense that everything in front of Peake went white – like the piercing strobe of light from a nuclear blast.

'Tell me,' Khalid said. 'Was that better or worse than the toe?'

Peake shook his head but said nothing as dribble trickled from his lip, down his chin, onto his chest.

'Time is ticking,' Khalid said. 'So here's your choice.' He played with the tablet some more before turning the screen back to Peake. His already ramped heart rate ratcheted up further as he stared.

Katie... Tied to a chair, just like Peake. Two hooded men stood behind her.

'Please...'

'Pleading? OK, we'll get to that. You care for her?'

Peake nodded. At least he thought he did.

'She's in this very building,' Khalid said. 'And she'll suffer the exact same fate as you. Unless you intervene.'

42

'This isn't the time to be silent, Peake,' Khalid said. 'Time is running out.'

But Peake didn't know what to say and his mind was drifting – a subconscious attempt to escape from the pain.

'OK. Salman?'

'No, wait!' Peake shouted out, somehow finding the strength.

Khalid looked pleased with himself for the intervention.

'You know who she is?' Peake slurred.

Khalid didn't respond.

'Harry's niece.'

Khalid laughed. 'What are you trying to say?'

'You're... working with Harry.'

'And?'

'You had... Harry hand me over to you. Now you're going to hurt... his niece?'

Khalid looked offended. 'You really think I give a crap about Harry Lafferty or what he thinks of me?'

'No... but if you hurt her—'

'Salman, get on with it.'

'No, wait!' Peake shouted. 'Tell me... what I need to do.'

'But Omar already did,' Khalid said. 'Like before, when you tortured his brother, but reversed. You're in the hot seat today. You're the one with a choice.'

Peake closed his eyes and shook his head and tried to make sense of it all.

'In twenty-two minutes, hundreds will die,' Khalid said. 'Or, only she dies.'

'Twenty-two minutes of hell for you,' Salman said. 'Whichever you choose.'

'Please,' Peake said, though he wasn't even sure what he was asking for.

'You can do better than that,' Khalid said. 'You need to beg. Grovel. I want to see your desperation.'

Peake shook his head and tried to speak but only a jumbled mess came out.

'Choose wisely,' Khalid said. 'You only get to make the choice once. Beg for her life. Or beg for me to disarm this bomb.'

'Tick, tock,' Omar said.

Salman went behind Peake again, who grimaced even before he felt the stab of the scalpel. Within seconds he was roaring in pain once more, frothing at the mouth.

'Beg me,' Khalid said, coming close, crouching down. 'Come on, beg.'

But Peake didn't. He couldn't. How could he make that choice?

'If you don't, you're all dead,' Khalid said. 'You, her, those innocent diners. Be a hero. Save at least one life tonight.'

'I... was never... a... h-hero.'

'Probably not. So here's your chance. Redemption.'

'It's... too late... for redemption.'

'But it's not. This is your chance. Pick one. Her, or those strangers. Who do you want to save?'

Did Peake even trust that Khalid would stick to his word?

'Less than twenty minutes to go,' Khalid said.

Minutes that would feel like a lifetime as Salman performed his grotesque work. And Peake would become weaker and weaker by the minute.

'I'll beg,' Peake said.

The room went silent. Salman slipped back into view, wiping clean the blade, his blood-soaked hands too.

'Please,' Peake said. 'Please don't hurt her. Let Katie go.'

Khalid looked shocked. He glanced at Omar then Salman then back at Peake.

'You picked the woman. One person. You'd kill hundreds for the sake of one?'

Peake didn't answer.

'You really haven't changed at all, have you? Salman, carry on.'

'No, please!' Peake said.

But Salman took no notice. He came forward again.

Peake knew he only had one chance.

Crack.

His left hand already had two mangled fingers, so it wasn't a difficult choice to make. As best he could with the ties, he grasped the knuckles of his left hand with his right and crushed. The thumb dislocated and he whipped the hand out of the tie. He reached around and sent a spear-hand strike into Salman's throat who collapsed to his knees gargling for breath with a broken windpipe. The hands from behind grabbed him. Peake pushed his knees together then in a swift motion yanked his legs apart, the raw power of his body's biggest muscles and momentum enough to snap the ties on his ankles. He planted his feet and pushed back, toppling the chair. An arm grabbed him around his neck. He sank his teeth into flesh. Searched with his hand... found it. He grasped the man's testicles and squeezed until he felt them pop. The arm came loose. Peake jumped to his feet and smashed his foot onto the man's jaw which shattered.

The other meaty guard... racing for Peake to tackle him to the ground. Peake launched himself into the air, right above the onrushing hulk, and slammed back down, flattening him into the ground. He picked up a broken wooden slat from the chair and drove it through the back of the man's neck.

'Don't move,' Khalid said.

Gun in his hand.

Peake picked up another piece of wood and bounced to his feet and hurled the makeshift weapon. Khalid fired as Peake closed the distance. A bullet hit his upper arm. Not enough to stop him now. He clattered into Khalid and the gun came free. Omar went for it.

Peake swiveled on the floor and took his legs from him. Omar's head cracked off the wall as he fell and he lay unmoving.

The door to the room burst open. Peake reached for the gun. Five shots. Five hits. Both of the hooded men who'd rushed in went down.

Peake heaved a sigh as he collapsed to the floor. His body ached, his grievous wounds wept, the agony as unbearable as he could imagine.

He pulled himself along the floor to Khalid. Grabbed the tablet.

'She's... dead,' Khalid said, finding a sickly smile. 'You killed her.'

Peake said nothing. He grabbed Khalid's hand, his thumb.

Crack.

Khalid screamed as Peake pushed the twisted digit to the screen.

'Eye-scan needed,' Peake said, looking at Khalid's creased face. 'Can I borrow yours?'

Khalid looked like he was about to beg but Peake hammered his elbow into his face to keep him subdued then grabbed the scalpel from the floor and jammed it underneath Khalid's eye socket.

That woke him up some.

Peake dug deeper and twisted the eyeball out. With a quick snip he pulled it free, and Khalid's body crumpled. Peake held the retina up to the screen.

Seven minutes, twenty-three seconds... The timer stopped.

Peake dropped the eyeball, dropped the tablet, and fell back onto the floor.

43

His brain had given up. His body too. If he'd closed his eyes there and then, he wasn't sure if he'd have woken again. So he pushed all the pain and the torment aside and reached within for something else to get him to his feet. To the door...

He looked back into the blood-soaked room. Omar stirred...

Peake couldn't explain why, but he left him there, left him breathing.

He moved along the corridor. Two rooms along. The door there had been left wide open as the hooded men had raced out to assist their friends.

Peake closed his eyes a moment as he looked at the slumped figure in the chair. He didn't need to go inside to check her. Katie was dead. It didn't look like she'd suffered, but he'd failed. Again.

Which would he have preferred for himself? A quick death, no pain, like her, or to be alive and in his own position now?

He went back to the room of death and found a set of keys on Salman, a phone on Khalid. He took the clothes and shoes from one of the dead men – the shoes thankfully two sizes too big which kind of helped his damaged foot. He found the black

Cadillac outside the factory building. New Jersey. He could see the twinkling lights of Manhattan in the distance across the water.

He set off, driving one-handed, one-footed, his body spent. What even fueled him? He didn't know. His eyelids were heavy, his brain mush.

He made a slurred call to 911. Kept it brief. Pier 17. Bomb on a truck. He tossed the phone.

Somehow, he made it to Manhattan. To Soho. Lights on in the apartment. Shadows moved about beyond the glass. Jelena wasn't alone.

Peake dragged himself out and to the door. He knocked and waited.

Chops opened up.

'Fuck.'

Peake lifted the gun up and pushed the barrel into Chops's eyeball. The guy backtracked into the apartment. Movement to Peake's right. Dolan, gun in hand, to Peake's temple.

Across the room, Harry sat on the sofa. Joey hovered behind him. Gun in his hand too.

Jelena... sitting on a dining chair in the middle of the room. Not tied up, but hurting.

'Drop the gun,' Dolan said.

Peake lifted his hand and let the gun dangle from his finger. He dropped it to the floor. Jelena jolted at the sound. Chops ducked down for the weapon. He didn't bother to point it at Peake but took a step away.

'Are you OK?' Peake asked Jelena.

'Hey, asshole, talk to me, not her,' Harry said.

'You set me up,' Peake said.

Peake slowly lifted his mangled hand.

Chops looked repulsed. Joey shocked. Harry... nothing.

'You should see what I did to them,' Peake said.

Chops gulped.

'My son is dead because of you.'

'Your niece too,' Peake said. 'They killed her to punish me.'

The look of shock on Harry's face showed he hadn't known about Katie.

But seconds later rage took over. Rage directed at Peake.

'You really shouldn't have trusted them,' Peake added.

Harry said nothing but was seething.

'Did you find Chan?' Peake asked.

'Chan's gone. We'll find him. Tonight we deal with you.'

'Someone else already tried that,' Peake said.

'But I'm not someone else.'

Joey now decided to join the party, lifting his weapon to point it at Peake as he moved around the old man and closer to the door.

'If you leave now...' Peake said. 'This can be over.'

'This is over,' Harry said, 'for you.'

Peake twisted and ducked and grabbed Dolan's arm, turning it upward in an arc as quickly and as abruptly as he could. The wrist snapped as his hand turned back toward him, at about the same time as the dumb bastard pulled on the trigger – or maybe it was involuntary. The bullet hit Dolan in the neck and Peake let go and dove for Chops as Joey opened fire. He scythed Chops to the ground and darted behind the kitchen island and grabbed the knife block from the top.

Harry hurled abuse his way, but Peake didn't even register the words. He jumped up and tossed the paring knife which spun through the air and hit Joey in the chest – subdued, but not dead.

Chops was just pulling himself up, trying to aim his gun...

Peake turned that way and tossed the big, long, thick chef's knife. Chops saw it coming and managed to edge out of the way, but he couldn't get out of the way of Peake's knee as he flew through the air toward him. The solid joint made solid contact with Chops's cheek and eye socket, and he collapsed back to the ground. Unconscious. Until Peake grabbed the knife and plunged it into his heart.

Joey fired. The bullet hit Peake's hand and the knife clattered away. Another shot hit him in the back. He rose to his feet. Turned to face the youngster, who pointed the gun directly at Peake's chest. Peake who was now unarmed. But it was Joey who looked petrified.

He took a step back...

Jelena reached out a foot and sent him stumbling.

Peake grabbed the knife from Chops's chest and lunged for Harry. The old man cowered, no fight in him. Joey shot again but soon couldn't without hurting his uncle.

Peake slashed the knife across Harry's gut before turning a full three-sixty and slamming the blade upward into Joey's chin. An uppercut, but with a seven-inch blade. Joey's body lifted off the ground, hanging from the knife as he convulsed. Peake tossed him and turned and—

Bang, bang.

Two shots from Harry. One to Peake's chest. One to his gut.

He didn't stop moving forward. He stumbled into Harry, blooding oozing from all over, dribbling from his mouth. The two of them fell backward in a heap and Peake found the gun in his hand.

'You said you don't like guns,' Peake said, pushing the barrel toward Harry's mouth. 'You said you and your boys never use them.'

Harry tried to clamp his jaw, but Peake thumped him in the kidney and Harry cried out – a muffled cry once Peake had shoved the barrel into his mouth and toward his throat.

'You should have stuck to your principles.'

Peake pulled the trigger. Blood and teeth and bone and sinew splattered all over him.

He dropped the gun and went to get up but stumbled and found himself on the floor, staring up at the ceiling.

'Peake!' Jelena shouted.

He couldn't move. Couldn't even move his eyes to find her.

No, there she was, bottom-right of his picture. The world in front of him like a cinema screen, slowly moving further and further away from him as he drifted.

'Peake, stay with me!' she said.

'No.'

'You have to stay with me!'

He tried to shake his head and wasn't sure if he managed it or not.

'You did it,' she said.

'What?'

Did he actually say that or not?

'You said the people you care for always die. But not this time. You saved me.'

And those innocent people at Pier 17? Did they even know what might have been?

It didn't even matter. It wasn't about the people he'd saved... the problem was all the people he'd hurt.

Katie...

'You did it, Peake. Please... don't leave me now.'

But he knew he didn't have a choice. This ending was nothing more than he deserved.

Life flashing before him? No, not exactly. But one memory in particular burned in his mind. In the car, chatting to Sean. Heaven.

'I'll... see you... one day,' Peake said. 'But... not for a long time... Stay... safe.'

Then the cinema screen in front of him became smaller, smaller, smaller, until it was nothing but a pinprick of light in a sea of black.

I will.

An echoey voice from the blackness.

I will you see you again... Hades. On the other side.

Was he smiling? He thought so.

I owe you my life. Thank you.

The distant echo of her voice dissipated. The pinprick of light disappeared.

And then there was nothing at all.

EPILOGUE

She finished off her coffee and looked out of the window to the street three stories below. Traffic rumbled along. People walked about, on the way to work, or just roaming like so many people in this gargantuan city did. Busy down there, but totally normal.

'What time are you finishing tonight?' Anna asked.

Jelena turned to her friend. Her roommate, now. The two of them had only met a few weeks ago – a chance encounter really as both of them stood at a clunky coffee machine trying to figure out why it wasn't working. They'd hit it off. Had a lot in common. Mostly their struggles making it in a city like this as single, young women.

Anna worked at a bookstore in Greenwich but had dreams of becoming an author. Jelena had taken a job at a bar not far from Anna's apartment. The hours were erratic, no guarantees, but the pay – once topped up with tips – was decent enough. At least, decent enough for the heavily subsidized stay at Anna's place.

'Probably not until after midnight.'

'You want me to come get you?'

Jelena kind of did. But she also knew Anna would be up and

out early in the morning and she was already starting to feel like she was becoming too much of a burden on her new friend.

'No. I'm sure everything'll be fine.'

Anna looked like she didn't quite believe that. And Jelena didn't really feel it either – a position exemplified by the fact that she was constantly on alert, both inside and out, had to check the street about ten times before she ever even left this place.

She headed out and paused at the head of the stairs only a moment, looking down. Feeling foolish for doing so. But even if the last few weeks had in reality been about the quietest of her entire life she could well imagine the bubble suddenly bursting and for Chan to have tracked her down and to jump into view ready to throttle her or worse...

Nothing. She was soon outside on the street where everyone was out minding their own business.

She didn't need to be at the bar for another two hours so she took the subway up toward midtown and to the hospital which had been a second home to her recently.

She carried on through the main entrance, up to the third floor. Along the corridor. She passed the waiting area and that coffee machine that was still clunky and forever seemed to have confused people standing around it scratching their heads, wondering why it had taken their money if it wasn't working. Although it did work. If you only selected black coffee.

The two women at the reception desk were deep in conversation so Jelena simply headed on past and onto the ward. Four doors down until she stopped. To start with a police officer had been stationed outside night and day. Jelena didn't even know why that had stopped but she hadn't seen anyone else here for nearly two weeks now.

She knocked and opened the door a little, stuck her head in...

opened the door fully and paused as confusion, sadness, something else took over.

The bed was empty. Made up, but empty. The room was empty. No sign anyone had been here at all recently, but it was less than twenty-four hours since she'd been here. Peake too.

'Hey, Sweetie,' came the voice from behind her and Jelena turned to see Claire, a middle-aged nurse who Jelena saw as a kind of motherly figure to the other workers here. And to many of the visitors too. 'What'd he forget?'

The smile fell from Claire's face. Likely because she noticed the distress on Jelena's.

'Oh. He—'

'He's gone?' Jelena asked.

'Yeah. He...'

'He could barely get out of bed. He couldn't even walk!'

'He... left this morning. I thought...'

Claire didn't finish the sentence. And Jelena didn't say anything in response. The awkward silence said everything, and Jelena felt like such a fool.

'I'm sorry,' Claire said.

'Yeah.'

Jelena spun around as her eyes welled. She headed off back toward the elevator.

'Jelena!' shouted out one of the receptionists.

She turned back to see the folded paper being thrust out toward her.

'He said to give this to you.'

The pained look on her face suggested she already knew what the note said.

Jelena took the paper and unfolded it and stared at the few scrawled words.

I hope you can forgive me. Be safe.

They provided little comfort really.

But they also made perfect sense. There was nothing left for Simon Peake in this city.

And she did forgive him – she owed her life to him after all – even if the manner of his leaving hurt like hell.

She scrunched up the note and tossed it into the trash, then carried on out, an uncertain future ahead of both of them she felt. But a life at least.

* * *

MORE FROM ROB SINCLAIR

Another book from Rob Sinclair, *Dance with the Enemy*, is available to order now here:

www.mybook.to/Dance_EnemyBackAd

ABOUT THE AUTHOR

Rob Sinclair is the million copy bestseller of over twenty thrillers, including the James Ryker series. Rob previously studied Biochemistry at Nottingham University. He also worked for a global accounting firm for 13 years, specialising in global fraud investigations.

Sign up to Rob Sinclair's mailing list for news, competitions and updates on future books.

Visit Rob's website: www.robsinclairauthor.com

Follow Rob on social media here:

- facebook.com/robsinclairauthor
- x.com/rsinclairauthor
- bookbub.com/authors/rob-sinclair
- goodreads.com/robsinclair

ALSO BY ROB SINCLAIR

The James Ryker Series

The Red Cobra

The Black Hornet

The Silver Wolf

The Green Viper

The White Scorpion

The Renegade

The Assassins

The Outsider

The Vigilante

The Protector

The Deception

Angel of Death

The Enemy Within

The Enemy Series

Dance with the Enemy

Rise of the Enemy

Hunt for the Enemy

The Simon Peake Thrillers

Dead Reckoning

Standalone Novels

Rogue Hero

THE *Murder* LIST

THE MURDER LIST IS A NEWSLETTER DEDICATED TO SPINE-CHILLING FICTION AND GRIPPING PAGE-TURNERS!

SIGN UP TO MAKE SURE YOU'RE ON OUR HIT LIST FOR EXCLUSIVE DEALS, AUTHOR CONTENT, AND COMPETITIONS.

SIGN UP TO OUR NEWSLETTER

BIT.LY/THEMURDERLISTNEWS

Boldwood

Boldwood Books is an award-winning fiction publishing company seeking out the best stories from around the world.

Find out more at www.boldwoodbooks.com

Join our reader community for brilliant books, competitions and offers!

Follow us
@BoldwoodBooks
@TheBoldBookClub

Sign up to our weekly deals newsletter

https://bit.ly/BoldwoodBNewsletter

Printed in Dunstable, United Kingdom